BLACK LIGHT: FEARLESS

MAREN SMITH

BLACK COLLAR PRESS

☙ Created with Vellum

BLACK LIGHT: FEARLESS

He was the last thing she thought she needed, but she was everything he wanted.

Abused and alone, Kitty had no idea how far she'd have to flee after she finally got the courage to run. She never would have guessed she'd end up halfway around the world, or in the home — much less the arms — of dominant Australian whip-master, Noah Carver.

He knows she's damaged, that she needs safety and time to heal, but the way her submission calls to him has Noah thinking more about what could be between them than her history.

The only question now is what she fears more: standing up to her abusive ex-dom, or staying with a man she's afraid to love?

A NOTE FROM BLACK COLLAR PRESS

Dear Reader,

Kitty and Noah first appeared in Maren Smith's novella *Shameless* in *Black Light: Roulette Redux*, released in February 2018. In this powerful story, we followed Hadlee's return to BDSM after surviving Ethen's torment. During the Roulette Redux event, she found her strength with the very sexy help of Garreth and Noah. While Kitty's part was small, Maren left us *all* hanging by a thread with the brief mention of her at the end of *Shameless*, which led to the incredible novel you are about to read — *Black Light: Fearless*.

If you haven't read *Shameless* yet, that's okay. *Fearless* reads beautifully as a standalone, but we promise you will love it even more if you take the time to read the novella in Roulette Redux before you dive in. Check out the blurb below, and grab a copy if you'd like to know the story of Hadlee, Garreth, and Noah as well.

Shameless by Maren Smith

He called her Piggy-girl, and for six months now Hadlee has struggled to leave that part of her in the past. Then Black Light sends out its second annual invite. For Hadlee, making it through the night means more than a month's free membership. It means a return of dignity, courage, respect — and just maybe, the one thing Hadlee isn't looking for... love.

Available on Amazon + in Kindle Unlimited
Black Light: Roulette Redux

Without further ado, enjoy *Black Light: Fearless!*

Thank you all for wanting to hear Kitty's story as much as I wanted to write it.

- Maren Smith

CHAPTER 1

*E*then O'Dowell had been her contracted dom for more than a year now and she'd never been more terrified of him than she was right now. Of course, she was such a mousy thing, Kitty-girl couldn't remember when last she *hadn't* been afraid. Like when traffic made her late coming home at nights, or when she stepped on the scale for morning weigh-ins to find she'd gained a few ounces—at five and a half feet tall, 115.2 was the weight he'd assigned her, that was her magic number—but this... this was different.

This fear was colder, sharper. It cut in through her fingers, tightly clasped as they were in her lap, because this was the proper way for Kitty-girls to ride in the car. Straight and tall, and not shaking, because showing one's fear only invited punishment. Only the guilty need be afraid of anything, as Ethen so often liked to say, but Kitty couldn't help it. She shook, and shook, and couldn't make herself stop. Every breath was a struggle; a shuddering inhale that her too-tight chest strangled back out on the exhale. The drumbeat pounding of her heart was so loud she was sure even *he* could hear it. Maybe that was why he kept glancing back at her as he drove them home. His eyes in the rearview mirror were every bit as cold as she was and, unless they happened to pass beneath an amber-lit streetlamp, they were black as the shadows that covered his lean, chiseled face.

Pony-girl wasn't shaking. As regal as ever, she sat on the front passenger seat, naked but for her harness and pony boots, and the tan trench coat they were allowed to cover themselves with only when they were out in public. Not that play nights at Black Light counted as 'public,' but the brief walk from the secret entrance through the psychic shop and down the street to the parking garage where Ethen had left his car, did. Usually they were allowed to take their headgear off for those walks, but not tonight. Tonight, Pony-girl sat with her white-blonde hair still pulled up tight in its ponytail mane and her black leather bridle and blinders still on. Her high pointed ears touched the cloth roof of the car. She knew something was wrong, but she didn't show it. She knew better.

Behind Pony-girl on the seat to Kitty's right, Puppy-girl was practicing slow, deep breathing behind the stifling black leather of her puppy mask. Her hands still encased in glove paws were on her knees, palms turned obediently upwards. Not once did she glance in Kitty's direction, because to look anywhere but straight ahead was forbidden. Talking was forbidden, fidgeting was forbidden. The rule was eyes forward, attention fixed on the only one in this car whose comfort mattered: that was Ethen.

Taking the highway out of D.C., they passed under another streetlamp. Again, Ethen's cold stare found her in the mirror. What parts of his face that she could see were a mask of absolute calm, but she wasn't fooled. No one in this car was. The silence was suffocating. The metallic bitter taste of bile kept creeping up the back of her throat. Her knee refused to stop jiggling up and down, despite the no fidgeting rule, and her hands squeezed at her own fingers, wringing and pulling at them in her nervousness. Her nipple rings under her trench coat were jingling. Could he hear that traitorous vibration over the hum of the engine and the rush of heated air blowing through the dash vents? God, she hoped not. She was in enough trouble as it was, and this wasn't even her fault.

How could it be? It wasn't like Piggy-girl had told Kitty she was going to run away. Kitty hadn't known, no one had. And for sure, she hadn't kept Piggy hidden out of Ethen's reach these last six months, either. She'd been as surprised as anyone else that Piggy-girl—Hadlee now, since she'd taken back her birth name—had shown up at Black Light to play in tonight's Valentine Roulette challenge. From the moment Piggy—Hadlee—had ascended the stage to accept the dom who had spun her name on that wheel of chance, Kitty had known someone was going to pay for Hadlee's new-found freedom. She'd known Ethen's temper would be pricked by the time they left. She'd *known* he would choose a victim.

She'd known then that, unless Hadlee took this same long and terrifying ride home with them, that the victim would be her. Because she had once dared to be Hadlee's friend.

Tapping the turn signal, Ethen took the next highway exit onto a rural backroad that would eventually wind them to the remote farmstead that he called home, and she called hell. As the car slowed enough to turn, he looked at her again. There were no lights here, just the neon glow of the driver's dashboard illuminating the hard lines of his face. She didn't need anything brighter to read the dark promise etched in the chiseled tightness of his jaw. He was going hurt her tonight, and it was going to be bad.

The drive took twenty of the longest minutes of her life and yet was over way too soon when Ethen finally turned off the main road onto his unpaved driveway, sheltered on both sides by the naked branches of the Yoshino Cherry trees that led all the way to the farmhouse yard. He pulled into a graveled circular area and parked the car not far from the front porch steps.

Both knees were jiggling now. Kitty was sure she shook the

car. Her breathing was too loud inside the kitty mask that clung to her face, damp from her breath and the cold sweat beading her skin. She had to get a grip on this. She had to stop, because if he didn't intend to hurt her before this, he absolutely would the second he saw her. Hands on her knees, she pushed down, willing the shaking to stop. *Please, stop.*

He shut off the engine, the click as he unlatched his seatbelt in the stifling silence of the car almost as loud as her breathing. Like a good little Menagerie should, none of his pets moved—except for Kitty, who couldn't stop shaking or jiggling, no matter how hard she pushed at her knees.

Without looking at her again, Ethen got out of his car. He walked around the front to open Pony-girl's door, offering her a steadying hand.

"Step out," he commanded, granting her permission to unfasten her seatbelt.

The horse-shoes on her black pony boots ground against the gravel as she carefully stood before him, straight and almost as tall as he was, waiting while he divested her of her trench coat.

"Tea," he said. "With cream and honey. You know how I like it." Giving her bottom a pat, he sent her into the house ahead of him.

Stepping carefully on the rocks, Pony-girl obeyed.

Ethen took the time to fold her coat before dropping it back on the front passenger seat. Shutting that door, he continued on to Puppy-girl, offering her a hand out, taking her coat, sending her into the house with a pat upon her bottom and the coveted words, "You did well tonight. Go on, I'll be in momentarily."

Puppy-girl scampered into the house while he took the time to fold her coat, left it resting on Puppy's assigned seat, and shut that door too. In measured steps, Ethen rounded the back of the car.

She couldn't breathe, she couldn't breathe. And yet if she didn't control her breathing right now, she would be hyperventilating before he reached her side.

Too late. With a soft click, the door yawned open and a rush of icy cold that had nothing to do with the frozen temperatures outside swept in over her. Kitty stared in dread at the hand Ethen offered.

"Step out," he said, as calm as could be.

She had the most absurd urge to bolt, but inside the back of his car, surrounded by woods and the remoteness of his farm, in the middle of the night, in the dead of winter, dressed in only a harness and the thin cover of her trench coat—honestly, where could she go?

Trembling, Kitty took the hand he offered. She felt sick. Her legs barely held her as she stepped from the car. Was it her imagination or did he really stand there for a few seconds too long, staring at her with that cold, unreadable stare of his before stripping her out of her coat? He said nothing as he bared her to the merciless February cold. It wasn't snowing anymore, but two inches of icy drift covered the ground. Her nipples pebbled around the rapidly chilling rings that pierced her. The studs and attachment rings that linked the thin black-leather straps of her uniform harness over her shoulders, around her ribs and her breasts, turned to ice against her skin. She was already shivering, but that didn't help.

Rather than releasing her as he had done with the others, Ethen took his time folding her coat, laying it back in the car, and finally, drawing her aside far enough for him to close the door. Thin ice and snow crunched dryly under her bare feet. Her knees all but knocking, Kitty stood where he put her, staring up at him in dread. This man who had once promised to guide her with love and care through the labyrinthine world of BDSM.

Taking a moment to adjust his coat, at last he clasped his hands before him and said, "You seem quite frightened, my little pussycat. And that confuses me, you see, because only the guilty have reason to fear anything from me."

It was going to be bad. Hot stinging tears rushed her eyes, slipping through her lashes and turning cold halfway down her cheeks. She didn't dare take her eyes from him, not even to blink them back.

"I've often wondered these last few months what role you might have played in our dear Piggy-girl's premeditated leaving, but I wanted to believe the best of you. Now, however..." He dropped his gaze, letting it travel slowly back up her and noting every twitch and quiver with growing disdain. "Now, I begin to think I may have put my faith in the wrong place. Did I do that, little pussy?"

"No," Kitty whispered, but he was a dragon—too big, too strong, his teeth too white and his breath steaming the air. Her throat choked her, killing all sound before it could reach her trembling lips.

Only the guilty need fear him and his stare did not warm. Nor did he react at first, although when at last his smile did come, it came gently. The smile of a lover.

Cupping her face, Ethen stroked her cheek with his thumb, then tsked. "Liar," he lovingly decided, then he punched her.

He moved so fast, Kitty had no time to react. One moment, his hand was on her cheek. In the next, his other fist slammed into her gut and she buckled over, a marionette with strings abruptly cut, collapsing to hands and knees as she sucked, then retched, then sucked for air again. The pain was almost a belated thing, eking in around the shock, because of all the things he'd ever done to her, he'd never punched her before.

And then she heard it, the telltale clank of a buckle working open and the slithering hiss of a belt yanking free of trouser loops. Kitty looked up as Ethen drew back his arm. He didn't wind the buckle around his hand or fold the length in half. He simply whipped her.

Kitty flattened to the ground. She covered her face with her arms, but each lash bit at her in white-hot bursts of agony that she could not lay still for. She tried to crawl under the car. Grabbing her ankle, Ethen hauled her out on her belly and whipped her harder. She had no air to scream, but the agony retched out of her as he spared nothing—not the backs of her shins, the bottoms of her scrambling feet, or even her head.

It was brutal, but it was brief and he was not even winded by the time he dropped the belt in the snow, grabbed her by the hair and dragged her to her knees.

"Get up," he ordered.

No part of her was free from pain when he flung her facedown over the trunk of his car.

Kitty knew better than to scream, but she was dry when he forced his cock into her. She bit her lip, the taste of blood filling her mouth but she managed not to cry out. Not until he yanked from that hole and switched to a different one. Knowing better did nothing to ease the savagery with which he shoved back into her. Kitty did scream then, over and over again until he yanked her back off his car, dropping her to her knees and forced his cock into her mouth.

When he finished, he left her there. Lying in the scuffle of snow, ice and gravel, in so much shock and pain that she could not move.

"When you're ready to apologize, you know where to find me." Once more as calm as could be, he walked away from her. His heavy shoes climbed the porch steps, and then the front door opened and closed.

Somewhere between gasping and panting, Kitty broke down. She covered her mouth with both hands, her sobs ripping out of her in wracking, jerky coughs that made her harness studs jingle. But that would only get her punished again, so she quickly got herself back under control. Rolling over was nothing short of sheer hell. Her back was ablaze with growing welts. There was no part of her that didn't hurt. Even her kneecaps were red and scuffed where she'd fallen on them, first when he'd punched her and then again when he'd... he'd...

Cold as it was, she lay on her belly, staring aimless under the

7

car. She didn't know for how long, but eventually the lights in the house winked out.

He never once came outside to check on her. Not one time. But then, why would he? She couldn't go anywhere. Dressed like she was, no shoes? She'd freeze.

She was freezing now. Every shiver that wracked her, from the cold now instead of fear, made the welts all over her body pull tight, burning and hurting that much more. She didn't want to get up. Getting up was going to hurt and she was too much of a coward to want to face it.

She was too much of a coward to simply lie here and die too, and it was getting colder. Or maybe now that the attack was over, her body was ready to deal with the next most immediate threat to her survival. Her shivers grew worse. As much as she didn't want to get up, she had to. Get up, go inside, go to bed. Maybe when she awoke in the morning, she'd find all of this had been merely a very bad dream.

A bad dream that wasn't over yet. She had welts on the bottoms of her feet and her two littlest toes were already bruising, which made every limping step she took sheer torture. She dragged herself up the stairs by the railing, but when she at last reached the door and pushed her way inside, she found a note waiting for her on the whiteboard by the fridge. None of the lights in the house were on, apart from two Coleman lantern-style nightlights. One by the stove, lighting up the countertop, and the other by the whiteboard. It was bright enough for her to read the stark missive he'd written her.

You are restricted to the kitchen until further notice. You will use your litterbox and you will sleep on the floor. When you are ready to apologize, you will bring me the Punishment Paddle. Until then, you will not speak and you will not be spoken to. For every day you delay, a penalty will be added to your sentence.

Sure enough, he'd pulled the litterbox out. It was tucked up against the wall on the far side of the island, where everyone would see her use it. He'd left no blankets, no pillow. Nothing between herself and the red kitchen tiles. He hadn't even granted permission for her to take her harness off. In the morning, she would be chafed. But then, she was wet and dirty now, welted and bruised, so really... what did a little chafing matter? What did any of it matter? She was trapped in a nightmare where the worst was far from over and from which there was no escape.

Except, Hadlee had escaped. On a night very much like this one, she had got up out of the muddy mire in which Ethen had forced her to kneel and simply walked away. So... it could be done. But could *she* do it?

Not dressed like this, she'd freeze to death. She needed clothes, but those were all in Ethen's room, in his closet with a lock on the door.

Maybe if she had some way to call someone, so she didn't have to be outside for so very long...?

Frozen where she stood, terrified her slightest movement might give her traitorous thoughts away, Kitty did not even look to the kitchen counter where their cellphones lay charging in a neat row, according to each user's rank. Ethen's was always first, then hers, Pony's, and finally Puppy's. Hadlee's used to be last, back when she was Piggy and lived here. The girls in his Menagerie were forbidden to touch their cellphones at the farmhouse. Use was only allowed during the workweek and only when Ethen needed to get a hold of them.

Kitty hugged herself. Every wound on her body pulsed in dread thinking about it, but if she were going to pull a Piggy and walk away from here, then how much worse could it get if she took her cellphone with her? She'd bought the silly thing, with her own money. It wasn't like she was stealing it; Ethen, of course, would disagree.

The man with the paddle makes the rules. Ethen was fond of saying that.

Everything you own became mine the day you signed my contract. He liked to say that too. He also had tracking apps on each of their phones, as well as apps that logged their usage. He could pull it up on his computer, and he did. Every single day, just to check on them. Kitty could take her phone and run, but if she did, he would find her. If she made a phone call, he would know when, where, and to whom. Her phone, Pony's, and Puppy's, they were all extensions of Ethen's prison.

Piggy's phone, however, sat in the kitchen's catchall drawer where Ethen had thrown it the morning he'd found her gone. That had been six months ago. By now that phone would be dead as hell. He might even have shut off service to it, and it absolutely would have all the same tracking apps that hers did. But he might not check it the way he did theirs. And it was a phone, the only one she had access to that he might not think of right away when it came time to hunt her down.

Her heart in her throat, slowly, Kitty glanced at the kitchen catchall drawer. Hugging herself tighter, she looked to Ethen's bedroom next. Was he asleep, or was he lying there listening for any sounds her movements might make? What about Pony? Pony was a light sleeper and she liked to tattle, but she was also the only one of the Menagerie allowed to sleep in a bedroom. It was decorated to look like a horse stall, complete with hay on the floor. Right now, the door to it was closed.

Puppy, on the other hand, slept in her kennel in the living room. If she heard anything, she'd start barking and then Ethen really would come out of his bedroom.

The whiteboard expressly forbade her from leaving the kitchen. As much as it itched at the back of her head to creep down the dining room wall far enough to steal a peek at Puppy in her kennel, she didn't dare. The floor there creaked. The floor in the kitchen creaked too, but she could always say she was getting a glass of water. Except that Ethen hadn't given her permission to drink anything. He hadn't even set out her food and water bowl. She wouldn't see those until the morning. Depending on how angry he was with her, she might not see them for days.

Why was she even thinking about this? She ought to lay down, shut off her mind, and go to sleep. What was she doing, acting like this was as bad as it could get? It wasn't, not by a longshot. So what, if she didn't have a pillow or a blanket to comfort her? So what, if she had to spend tomorrow or the next day or even the next few weeks, embarrassed because she had to squat over a litterbox? And yes, maybe he wouldn't feed her for a few meals, to reinforce the message he was sending now. But at least he'd let her sleep in the kitchen. What right did she have to complain when he *could* have put her in the Box?

Shuddering, Kitty's grip on her own shoulders tightened. She tucked her chin, burying the lower half of her face in the vee of her crisscrossing arms.

Simply because he hadn't done it yet, didn't mean he wouldn't. He might do that tomorrow. The last time—her knees almost buckled—the last time, he'd left her in there for two full days.

Kitty began to shake all over again and, for a moment, the darkness in the kitchen seemed to close in tight around her.

She couldn't do that again. She couldn't go back in the Box. Ethen could do anything he wanted to her so long as he didn't—

Kitty froze all over again, every muscle in her body locking as tight as a cramp when her gaze fell on the line of cellphones. Ethen's blinked an angry red while it charged; the other three showed solid green. Her cellphone had been moved. No longer did she hold that coveted position of preferential rank right next to Ethen's. Pony had that position now, and Kitty's had been shifted all the way to the end of the line, in absolute last place. Where Puppy's had been up until tonight. Where Piggy's had been right up until she ran away. *Because shit rolls downhill,* Ethen would say when the mood for cruelty overtook him.

Oh God...

Beating or not, Box or not, Kitty dropped to her knees and crawled around the cooking island to the catchall drawer. Her heart in her throat, hearing nothing but her own frightened breathing, she pulled it open. She expected barking, sirens, for Ethen to come stalking out of his back bedroom, alerted by some hidden alarm and his belt in his hand. But apart from her own panicky gasps as she struggled to keep from throwing up, the house stayed quiet.

Rising on her knees high enough to see into the drawer, she dug past the new phonebook, a loose accumulation of whiteboard markers, and finally found it: Piggy's abandoned phone and charger.

The alarms really would go off now. Scuttling across the floor to the nearest wall socket, she plugged it in. Flattening herself between the wall and pantry closet, she smashed the phone to her chest so no charging light would be seen. It took almost a full minute before it charged enough even to acknowledge it was plugged in. Kitty jumped as, somewhere in the house, something popped and creaked. A moment later, she all but wet herself when the heater clicked on, circulating warm air through the vents.

Any minute now, she was going to get caught. Any minute now, someone was going to wake up. They would walk in here, take one look at her, and *know. Oh Jesus... Oh Jesus...* Her leg started jiggling, bouncing rapidly up and down as she fought herself for control.

She looked at the phone display, three percent power. Not good enough yet, but, she noted, it still had service. Not only that, but when her fumbling fingers accidentally tapped the wrong button, the text screen came up. She was shocked to find a message there from someone other than Ethen. It was undistinguished, a number without a name and made up of only a few words: *If you need me, call.*

Had Hadlee read this message? Was this what had given her

the unbelievable courage to run in the first place? Had she called this number to get the help she needed? If Kitty called it, would Hadlee pick up on the other end of the line?

Nine percent.

This was it. The point of no return. Stay or go, go or stay. She would be punished either way.

Kitty closed her eyes, she fought herself for calm. It helped to be pressed this hard up to the wall, the pain across her welted back grounded her.

Twelve percent. Close enough.

She yanked the cord off the phone, clutching it one-handed to her chest while she crawled on one arm and her knees through the dining room (and right over that squeaky floorboard), past the living room (with Puppy still sound asleep in her crate by the cold hearth) and to the front door.

This was it. She reached for the door knob with a badly shaking hand.

This was a bridge-burning event, the kind a girl didn't come back from. The cold enveloped her as she slipped outside, shutting the door as silently as she could behind her.

She barely had a plan—run until she was safe and then call Hadlee —and she was still every bit as scared now as she had ever been, but she knew what she had to look forward to if she stayed. And still it took the snap of some ice-laden tree branch scaring the hell out of her before Kitty could make herself bolt. But once she did, she put everything her wounded body had into it. The gravel hurt her feet. The ice and snow hurt them more after that, and it was such a crock of shit that cold numbed. It didn't numb. It prickled and it burned, and anyone who saw her like this likely would not have recognized her as a human being running down the road. She was hunched and crying and probably looked like Quasimodo running for the safety of his bell tower. She fell multiple times. Sometimes she crawled. She cut her feet, her hands and her knees, and she sobbed pathetically every step of the way. Though she followed the road, not once did she ever see the lights of an approaching car. She didn't know if she would have hidden from one if she had, but eventually, she found that half-thought-out thing she was looking for. Safety.

It came in the form of an archaic phonebooth on the outskirts of an abandoned gas station parking lot. Had she gone all the way to town? Jesus. Her hands were purple and barely obeyed her as she pushed and shoved to get the rusty door open far enough for her to crawl inside. It wasn't any warmer than outside had been, but it did shelter her against the breeze that periodically cut across her skin as if with actual razors.

Collapsing in a chattering, shaking heap in the bottom, cradling her wet and stolen cellphone to her chest, Kitty gave in to her exhaustion. She closed her eyes, resting her head against the frosty plastic-glass wall while she caught her breath. Cold as she was, she could almost have gone to sleep right there. Through sheer force of will, she dragged her head back up off the wall and looked at the phone. Five percent power.

Her fingers refused to work. It took three attempts and she had to blow on them before she could get the phone on and the screen to swipe. It was nothing short of a miracle that she hit the right number to call, instead of Ethen's. And still her heart leapt right into the back of her throat when she heard the click as it was answered, almost immediately a male voice, gruff with sleep, mumbled, "I'm up. Be there in five."

That wasn't Ethen, although her ears tried hard to convince her otherwise. It wasn't Hadlee either. What was she going to do if Hadlee wasn't even there? What if he said 'Wrong number' and hung up on her? Where was she going to go? What could she do?

Her breath caught in the back of her throat, and here came a whole new rush of tears, burning her eyes with the kind of warmth no other part of her currently felt. How many tears did one woman have to cry before she ran out? Kitty would have thought she'd hit her limit two damn miles ago.

She was so pathetic.

"Is Hadlee there?" she finally begged, only no sound came out, just a rasp of breath broken by the relentless chattering of her teeth and the movement of her lips.

Panic hit her. *Oh God... Oh noNoNO!*

"D-d-don't hang up," she cried, but still without sound. Just a harsh cough of air where the 'h' should have been and a squeak of helpless frustration when that was all.

From the other end of the phone, she thought she heard a familiar female voice sleepily ask, "Who is it?"

Hadlee! It was Hadlee!

Grabbing her throat, Kitty swallowed, bringing moisture back to a mouth and throat gone dry from panting the cold winter air. Still, her voice was more like a squeaky gate hinge when she at last managed a real sound, "H-Hadlee?" *It's me,* she tried to add, but again, her voice winked out.

The response on the other end, however, was as instantaneous as it was brusque. "Hang on."

Kitty did. To the cellphone. With both hands.

"Who is it?" she heard Hadlee say again, but clearer now.

"Hadlee?" she croaked again, her voice squeaking in and out, but it was coming back. She almost started crying all over again.

"Kitty?" The shock in her old friend's voice was as clear as the night was freezing cold.

"I've left him." Her eyes burned even harder and though she gritted her teeth to keep back the uselessness of another round of sobs. *Please,* she mouthed. *Help me.* She had to cough before her voice warbled back into an audible range. "I don't have anything"—she squeaked in and out of sound—"not even my shoes. Please, can you come get me?"

"Where are you?"

"At a payphone." Kitty looked through the frosted plastic-glass, taking stock of her surroundings. "I think I'm at a gas station, but

I don't think it's open anymore. The pumps are gone. It looks abandoned."

"I know exactly where you are," the male voice broke in, startling Kitty once more. He'd been so quiet up until then. He must have her on speaker phone. "Hang tight. We're on our way."

The sound of rustling clothes and jostling as the phone moved about nearly drowned out everything else.

Almost afraid to ask, Kitty whispered, "W-who is that?"

"Garreth from Black Light. It's okay," her old friend assured her. "You can trust him. We'll be there as fast as we can."

"Hurry," Kitty begged, swiping her numb hands to brush to cooling tears from her face. "He'll be up any minute and when he finds me gone…"

The phone beeped. Pulling it back, Kitty looked at the display. Two-percent.

"What is that?"

"Your phone," Kitty said dully. "I barely had time to put a charge on it. It's almost out of power."

"Hang up," the man ordered. "Save what battery power you have left. If Ethen finds you before we do, use it to call 9-1-1, do you understand?"

"Yes," Kitty said, but she also knew that wouldn't happen. She couldn't afford to call the police, and if Ethen found her first, she wouldn't have time to call anyone much less emergency services. Huddling in on herself, Kitty hugged her knees to her chest and tried to stay warm. If Ethen did find her, with any luck it wouldn't be until after she froze to death.

At least that gave her something to hope for.

CHAPTER 2

"*Y*ou zonked out yet?" Noah Carver asked, leaning over the side of his boat. He peered into the dark, calm water of the Endeavour River and promptly set off the sixteen-foot salty snagged on his bait line. Two tons of angry crocodile splashed and thrashed, its massive tail slamming into the side of the small boat, rocking it wildly. Quickly sitting before he ended up in the water on top of the beast, Noah waited until the thrashing subsided and, with a low growl, the massive crocodile fell still once more.

"Sadly, mate"—Noah tsked with a sympathetic shake of his head—"this is what happens when you go eating people's cats and sleeping in their kiddy pools. Sooner or later, I get a phone call."

As if on cue, the Bluetooth hooked to his ear chirped.

"See?" Noah pointed out. "It's always busy in the wet season." He tapped the headset. "Hello, hello," he said cheerfully. "When wildlife invades, I can make 'em behave. How can I help you?"

"Hey, Noah. How's business?"

"Blokey!" Noah brightened, a grin splitting his sun-bronzed face as he recognized the voice. "Never better, never better. On the job right now, as a matter of fact. How the hell are you? It's been a couple of weeks."

"Yeah, it's been busy." Garreth sighed heavily, which caught Noah's immediate attention.

"You say that like you'd rather say 'it's been hell.'" Standing up, Noah moved to the far end of his small boat and away from the low, rumbling hiss of the angry crocodile. Propping his foot up by the resting motor, he looked out over the night-blackened water. "What's the trouble? It's not the ol' ladyluv, is it?"

"No, Hadlee's fine."

"The roommate, then?" The stars were out, the moon was full, and there were no houses along this stretch of the river. Something that suited his immediate needs just fine. "Are both girls still living with you? I thought you once said Hadlee has her own place."

Garreth snorted. "She does, but with Ethen stalking their shadows like some psychotic serial killer? I'm not letting either one of them out of my sight."

Noah couldn't argue. He could see himself doing the same thing. "What was her name again?"

"Kitty's all she claims," his American friend said, but Noah detected notes of bitterness. From Garreth, that was saying something.

Garreth was a dungeon monitor he'd met in D.C. almost two months ago, while he'd been touring the United States. At the time, Noah had been bouncing from one BDSM club to another, teaching others not only how to crack a bullwhip, but how best to use it without flaying the flesh from their submissive's back. Black Light had been the last club on his tour, and never had he met a dom more silently tortured by the pangs of love as Garreth. He didn't know Hadlee's story, but he'd gotten to scene that night with her and halfway through the first session, he knew there was some trauma in there somewhere. Still, Garreth had been ass over teakettles in love with her, and Noah never could resist a chance to play cupid. Privately, he was sure he'd never visit another playspace that was half as much fun—or half as much drama—as that one.

Plus, he'd come away from the experience with one good friend and a special lady he wouldn't mind kissing on the cheek if ever he saw them again.

"So what's the issue now?" Noah asked, settling in to be a good agony aunt, if nothing else. "That feller you were telling me about, he hasn't found her, has he?"

"Oh, I'm pretty sure he knows exactly where she is," Garreth growled. "He wouldn't dare come anywhere around here. So instead, he's made his displeasure known in other ways."

"Yeah?"

"You remember how I told you she left with nothing, right? No clothes, no shoes, no wallet, nothing. Right?"

"Right." Noah nodded, though no one but the croc was there to see it.

"Okay, so she has a car. But when she signed a contract with Ethen, he made her put his name as co-owner on the title. First thing I did was drive out to his property to get the car, only to find out he'd sold it months ago. Did she get any of the money for it? No. Will police do anything about it? Of course not, because he was on the title and it only takes one owner's signature to sell a car."

Noah tsked.

"She's got her own house, used to be her grandfather's, been in the family for years. All this time, she's been working and putting money in her bank account to keep up the insurance and maintenance fees on it, but guess what? She signed the house over to Ethen too and I'm pretty sure you can guess what that bastard did with it not two months after they got together."

Noah was pretty sure he knew too.

"He sold it!" Garreth snarled. "We walked up to her front door only to find another family living there, and there's nothing we can do about it. Ethen was registered as the legal owner! And that bank account she's been putting all her money into?"

"The asshole had his name put on it," Noah guessed grimly.

"And closed it out! She had thousands in there, by her estimate. Thousands! And that jackass... that... what is that sound?" Garreth asked, anger audibly diminishing, before in a startled tone, the American suddenly accused, "Dude! Are you peeing while we're on the phone?"

"Nah," Noah said, shaking off before stuffing himself back into his pants. "I'm on the river. That's just the gentle sound of waves lapping at the boat, mate."

He could hear Garreth's frown in his voice. "Like I haven't stood in front of a urinal every single day, multiple times a day, to the point that I don't recognize that particular sound?" Garreth let it go. "It doesn't matter. What matters is that we had to order her birth certificate from the state so we could get her a new driver's license. I paid the fees so she could get copies of her teaching license and certificates, and college degrees. We put her up in my spare room while she tries to rebuild her life and for the last five weeks, I have spared nothing in the attempt to make at least this one small corner of the world feel safe to her. What does that son of a bitch do?"

Returning to sit on his perch by the croc, Noah was almost afraid to guess.

"Monday, she went into work. She's a teacher at Deal Middle School, been there since she graduated. Ethen hasn't let her have friends, but she knows these people and they know her. And yet she gets met at the front doors by security, taken directly to the principal, who starts to show her all the private videos that Ethen anonymously messaged the school system during the night. Everything he's forced her to do, including a bukkake party with half a dozen men coming on her face and the words 'dirty cum slut' written on her body. There is no more intimate way of attacking a woman in public than that."

Garreth spat.

Noah agreed. He'd never met this Kitty woman, but his heart went out to her.

"She was fired on the spot for behavior unbecoming."

Swearing under his breath, Noah bowed his head. He stared at his hands, loosely clasped between his knees.

"She's done nothing for the last three days but sit in her closet and cry. That son of a bitch has her convinced that, one way or another, he'll get her no matter where she goes. And I still can't get her to go to the police. And I can't get her to understand that while the contract she signed to Ethen might hold meaning in certain BDSM circles, it's the next best thing to useless out in the real world, especially considering the abuse she's suffered at his hands. She's convinced she earned it, that she deserves it, and she's even starting to say things like, if he's going to get her anyway, she might as well go back. I'm halfway tempted to go to the police myself, except it would piss Hadlee off, Kitty would lose what little trust in me that she has, and Ethen is one of the best God-damn civil lawyers in his God-damn field. He'd happily ruin me, Kitty, Hadlee, our families and friends, and even Black Light. If he finds something he can't do himself, then he's got plenty of friends in high places to guarantee it happens anyway."

His friend's frustration was so palpable, Noah could feel it hanging in the air around him from all the way from America.

"I don't know what to do," Garreth finally said, and for the first time his tone was completely void of anger, aggravation, and even hope. He sounded defeated. "I... I don't know."

"Send her to me," Noah said.

Garreth laughed, but it wasn't really a happy sound. Even that sounded hopeless. "Yeah, right."

"Nah, blokey, I'm serious." He was too, which somewhat surprised even him. "Send her to me. She thinks he can get her anywhere she goes in the States? Well, he's not king of shit out here. I got me a nice house on eighty-some acres of land, not far from a town of less than three thousand people, every one of whom'll be happy to treat him like a tourist. Your friend can stay with me until she's ready to start over."

The other end of the phone fell silent. All Noah could hear was the gentle lapping of the river water against his boat, the chirping of night insects, and the low, seething growl of the crocodile no longer thrashing or even pulling at the bait line that held it trapped.

"Are you serious?" Garreth finally asked, in a tone that suggested he didn't know which of them was crazier: Noah for making the suggestion, or himself for considering it.

"Yeah, sure." Noah sat back, smiling once more now that the problem was decided. "I'm not royalty, but I'll move some of me shoes out of the spare room and be on me best behavior."

Garreth was quiet again. "If we do it on the downlow and I take her the next town over, we might be able to get her a replacement passport before Ethen can do anything to stop it."

"You might even get her all the way out of the country," Noah put in cheerfully. "Once she's over here, it's no worries. I'll take care of everything. This'll be a good place for her. Nothing but wide-open spaces. Nature, peace, and solitude everywhere you look. How can a person not heal out here? Plus"—he added, when Garreth remained silent—"I'll be right beside her every step o' the way, looking out for her."

After a long moment, punctuated only by the chirping night sounds and low reptilian growls, Garreth finally said, "I'll talk to Hadlee and it'll take at least a month to get the passport. But frankly, I think that's the best option we've got at this point."

Noah grinned. "Of course, it is. I thought of it."

"Arrogant ass," Garreth snorted, a trickle of real amusement leeching back into his voice. That was reward enough for Noah.

"Best mates, blokey," he said fondly. "Best mates."

When Garreth hung up the phone, Noah tapped his headset and indulged in a contented sigh. Good though it might be for this Kitty whoever, Noah was a little surprised at himself for offering. He liked his life. He liked living alone. Occasionally, a mate or two might wander out of town as far as his place for a beer and a chitchat, but honestly, he wasn't one for indulging company for long. He couldn't remember the last time he'd had someone stay over. His sister, probably, maybe eight or ten years ago. When it came to visiting with the ladies, well... he did all that at the clubs he toured while on vacation or in Cairns on party nights.

"A little change is good for the soul," Noah decided, because the offer was already extended and Noah was nothing if not a man of his word. He could adjust himself to the idea of a houseguest, for at least a couple of weeks.

And really, where else in the world could a person find this kind of beauty and peace in which to heal a battered soul? He tipped his smile first to the multitude of stars that speckled a near-cloudless sky, and then down to the salt-water croc still hooked on his bait line.

"Are you zonked?" he asked it. All he could see of the animal was a six-inch length of snout above the waterline about two feet from his boat. When all he got was a low, seething hiss, Noah swiveled on his seat, took hold of the reel handle and put his back into drawing the crocodile in closer. He reeled until the massive, craggy head was all the way out of the water. It hissed again, the moonlit water all around it rippling. "I know," Noah soothed, and not without some sympathy. Standing up, he picked up his rifle from the bottom of the boat and put a shot in the chamber. "I know it's not much o' a consolation for you, but I'll make sure your meat don't go to waste and your hide'll be treated with respect. Next reincarnation, mate, try to steer clear of the pets and kiddies, all right?"

His aim was dead-on. It only took one bullet, a mechanical

hoist and some under his breath swearing to haul the animal up into the bottom of his boat. Patting it on the hide, he flopped down on the rear bench by the motor to catch his breath. Disturbed by first the rifle report and then by the ruckus that followed, all the nighttime insects that had fallen silent cautiously returned to singing again. Noah closed his eyes, listening. He'd vacationed all over the world, touring from one dungeon to the next, letting his skill with the bullwhip lead the way, but there truly was no place on earth better than home. He was going to do his best by Kitty Whoever, but there was no doubt in his mind that, by the time she was ready to go home again, she would be rested in both body and mind, and braced to tackle whatever she had to as she attempted to re-start her life.

Australia was irresistible that way.

Who knew, she'd probably never want to leave.

Six weeks later...

Kitty hadn't been in Queensland for more than ten minutes before Australia tried to kill her, and that was only the first time.

She stepped off the plane with nothing but the carryon that held all her worldly belongings. Which only meant, that that was all she had. Nothing in that bag was actually hers. Hadlee had given her a nightshirt, a dress that was almost too short for her, some t-shirts, and a pair of jeans that they'd found at the Goodwill. The jeans were bought with Hadlee's money because Ethen had stolen all of Kitty's. Not even the bag was hers, or the toiletries, or even the hair ties. Kitty had nothing, was nothing, except a burden that had grown too heavy for her old friend and her new man to carry, and which now had to be shuttled off onto someone else. Someone she didn't even know.

That wasn't exactly fair or true, and the minute it crossed Kitty's ungrateful mind, she was heartily ashamed of herself.

Making this move had been a group decision. Sort of. Hadlee and Garreth had sat her down over a pizza dinner and presented this as a plan. While Kitty forced herself to choke down half a slice (every bite tasting like ash because she still could barely make herself eat without Ethen there to grant permission), Garreth laid out all the pros and cons of traveling to Australia.

First, she wouldn't be staying with a stranger. She knew this Noah Carver, he had said. She might not have met the man properly, but she had seen him that night at Black Light when he'd scened with Hadlee. Kitty didn't tell him that all she remembered of that night was the horrible ride home and what Ethen had done to her once they got there.

Ethen couldn't touch her in Australia, Hadlee had pointed out. But probably only because she'd been away from him for so long now that she'd forgotten Ethen could touch them from anywhere. He had connections. When those connections weren't enough, he had friends with even longer connections. Oh yes, Ethen could touch her in Australia. Kitty knew that all the way down to her bones.

In Australia, Garreth had said, she wouldn't have to be afraid that she might run into Ethen every time she left the house. Or see him when she looked out the window, just sitting in his car and staring at the apartment — like he'd done almost daily during the first few weeks after she'd run away, because even though she'd left Hadlee's cellphone in the ice and snow outside that archaic phonebooth, he'd still known exactly where she'd gone. Or wake up in the night in a cold sweat because he'd snuck into her bedroom to stand over her, with his belt or the Punishment Paddle in his hand — which he hadn't done ever, but which happened in her nightmares every time she dozed off.

On the surface of it, their arguments all made sense. Underneath, however, Kitty knew it didn't matter what she did. She could fly to the moon; Ethen would still find her, punish her, and drag her back home again. She knew that, but she agreed to go so they'd stop talking about it, and then excused herself to the bathroom and promptly threw up. In the last five weeks, she'd lost eleven pounds she didn't have to lose. She was starting to look bony and her eyes hollowed, especially with the bruise-like circles that lack of sleep had painted beneath them.

Four hours at a passport agency and two weeks later, she had her passport in her hand and Garreth had gone online to buy the plane ticket. Four days after that, she was on a plane, with a fantastic view of the right-side wing and the sickening fear that behind each new passenger, she was going to see Ethen stepping onboard. He never did, but that didn't stop her from expecting it to be him each time someone passed by her. It was a twenty-seven-hour flight with two stops, first in Los Angeles and then in Sydney, and not only did Kitty not sleep, but her leg never stopped jiggling once.

And then Australia tried to kill her.

Unsure where to go or even what this Noah Carver might look like, she stepped out of the airport into the full blanket of the Australian sun and a gigantic wasp flew straight into her hair. Kitty dropped her luggage right there in front of the revolving doors. Screaming and leaping around, she tried to disassociate herself from her hair. She could feel it crawling in the long strands. That the angry buzzing she could hear would eventually precede a sting, she knew without doubt, and she was so terrified of the coming pain that she didn't even react when a strange man grabbed her around the waist, bending her straight forward with all her hair hanging to the pavement.

"Hang on, love. I've got you," the man said, tugging and plucking at her hair in a ginger attempt to get the wasp out without getting stung himself. She could not have cared less that he accidentally pulled a couple strands out. All she cared about was that blessed moment when the buzzing ceased to be right by her ear and he flung it away. He jerked her upright, jumping back as it dive-bombed them with a single pass and then flew off somewhere where people weren't half so crazy.

Hugging herself, Kitty stood frozen in that strange man's steadying embrace, shaking, panting, and struggling to swallow her pattering heart back down into her chest.

"You're all right now, love," he said, low and comforting, his hand petting down the length of her dark hair from the top of her head to the middle of her shoulder blades. "You're a good girl, and you're all right."

Her whole body shuddered, but not in an unpleasant way. Rather, it was the first small measure of relief that she'd felt in almost eight weeks, and it came from the hand of a stranger, caressing the back of her head.

The relief lasted only a heartbeat or two. As the fear dissipated, suddenly Kitty became aware of the squeeze of masculine arms. It was a very odd thing, to know with such certainty that Ethen had not caught up with her and yet to also know it was him. Her panicking body chose the irrational over the logical, and with a violent twist, she shoved against the stranger's chest, knocking them both back a step.

Her fists came up, which was laughable. She'd never taken a defense course or been in a fight in her life. Also, she was shaking. If she hadn't visited the ladies' room on her way out of the airport, she'd have wet herself before taking a swing.

"Get away from me!" she gasped through a throat grown hoarse and tight.

His hands were already up in the air. Although smiling, he also backed away. It was the smile that stopped her first. She tried to see it as ugly at first, mocking. But the more she blinked and the further he backed away, the more that smile turned open and friendly. His had to be the whitest teeth she'd ever seen, but maybe it was because his skin was so bronzed from the sun.

She was tall, but he was taller, by at least five inches. His shoulders were broad and his forearms muscular, which made the rest of him—dressed as he quite casually was in loose-fitting tan khaki trousers and a white button-down business shirt, with the sleeves rolled up to his elbows—look chiseled, lean, and completely relaxed. He was handsome too, in a rugged, outdoorsy kind of way. His hair beneath the cover of the cream-colored cowboy hat he wore was short and more blond than brown. Like his mouth, his bright blue eyes were friendly and smiling.

"Sorry about that," he said gamefully. "Wasn't my intent to give you such a fright." Tipping his head, he edged closer and lowered his voice, as if they were playful conspirators. "Truth be told, you looked to be in a bit of trouble. Me manliness overcame me. I couldn't help myself." Dropping his arms, he stuck out his hand. "Name's Noah Carver. I believe I've been sent to fetch you."

Kitty didn't lower her hands an inch and she certainly didn't shake his. His accent was thick and she was having trouble processing what he was saying. "Wh-what?"

Smile fixed firmly in place, he held up a finger and reached into the square leather holster on his belt. It was a crocodile belt, shiny and mottled in colors that ranged from brown to yellowish-green, and it had more than one holster clipped to it. They dotted all the way around his waist—some for pocket knives, sheathes for longer knives, a hook for his keyring and, of course, his cellphone, which was what he pulled out of its square holster once he unclipped it.

"Here." He turned it on, tapping the touch screen. As if it were the most natural thing in the world, he edged even closer, turning his big body until he was standing beside her, showing her a picture of herself on the screen.

She looked traumatized. That was her first thought. That Garreth must have taken it was her second, because she was dressed in a pair of Hadlee's hand-me-down shorts and t-shirt, sitting on the window bench in his apartment living room and hugging her knees to her chest. She didn't know what day that was, but she was pretty sure what she was staring at outside that window had to be Ethen.

"You've lost weight," Noah said, still cheerful, without a hint of censure in his tone. Reaching down, he picked up her dropped duffel bag and shouldered it. "Come on. We'll grab some burgers before we head for home."

Glancing back once, encouraging her with a smile and a wink to follow, he started across the airport parking lot. Presumably towards his car.

Feeling stupid, Kitty lowered her fists. Belly and legs both quivering, she chanced a quick look around. This was an international airport. From wasp-induced panic all the way to now, there were people around her and some were openly staring. They'd probably been staring the whole time.

Heat, that had nothing to do with the 80° sun, burned her face and chest.

This Noah Carver person was leaving with her stuff. Cheerfully leaving, in fact. He was whistling, as if picking up unwanted burdens at the airport and hauling them around Australia were the most natural thing in the world. His grin was wide and friendly and he waved her on to follow with a laughing, "Come on, love. Can't rightly stand here all day. The boys in blue'll shove us off."

Kitty didn't know what that meant, but she did know Noah was right about one thing. She couldn't keep standing here, an object of pity and curiosity for heaven only knew how many strangers to gawk at as they hurried on about their lives.

She also knew that thing people liked to say about first steps being the hardest... well, it was true. She didn't know where she was going, and she didn't know what she was going to. That made cutting the roots her feet had sprouted, anchoring her to the airport sidewalk, one of the hardest things she'd yet done in her life.

What people didn't say was how every step that came after did not magically get any easier. She followed Noah to his pickup. Candy-apple red, extended cab, it wasn't anywhere near as beat-up looking as she imagined vehicles belonging to a man as rugged as Noah should be.

He put her bag in the backseat, then held the front door for her. "Up we go."

He smiled, but he didn't help her. He simply waited for her to make the choice. For almost one perfect second, Kitty lost track of where she was. The warmth of the sunshine vanished. Australia and Noah vanished. Instead of standing in the parking lot looking into his truck, she was standing on Ethen's front porch, enveloped by cold, knowing if she took that first step nothing would ever be the same again.

Reaching up to grip the interior handle, Kitty climbed into the front passenger seat. She barely noticed it was on the wrong side of the car from what she was used to. He waited beside her, door open and silent, for what she didn't know. Not until, slowly and gently, he took hold of the seatbelt strap, stretched it down and around her, and clicked it into place.

He'd done his best not to touch her; Kitty swallowed hard and did her best not to flinch the entire time he was close by.

"Good girl," he said again as he withdrew from the car.

Nothing could have been further from the truth, but she didn't correct him. She stared out the front window, her posture as straight as she could make it and her hands clasped tight in her lap. Now and then she pushed on her knee but it never stopped jiggling. Not once.

CHAPTER 3

*I*t was a four-hour drive from Cairns airport to his
home on the outskirts of Cooktown. With Kitty in the
car, it took six.

On the way out of town, he stopped at a café for two of the
biggest burgers they had to offer. He even indulged in a milkshake
because, frankly, the more she ate the better, in his opinion. The
pictures Garreth had sent hadn't done the situation justice, and
not in a good way. She was thinner than in the photos, with her
stress showing openly on her too-pale face. It was in the
hollowness of her eyes and in the tiny, premature frown lines
etched around her mouth. She probably hadn't smiled in at least
as long as she hadn't eaten.

And yet, in the time it took him to scarf his burger down, she
only managed four small bites, not even a fourth of the burger,
and maybe as many sips of the shake. Less than ten minutes later,
he yanked the truck over to the side of the road while she hung
her head out, vomiting. It happened so fast and without any
warning from her, right up until she vaulted out of her seatbelt to
roll the window down.

The wrong question entirely was out of his mouth before he could censure himself. "Are you preggo, love?"

She didn't answer. Accepting the burger napkins he handed her once she'd eased back in through the open window, she gave him a withering frown and wiped her mouth.

Okay, then. Well, stress was certainly known to have this kind of effect on people, and obviously she was under a fair amount of that. So did a touch of the stomach flu. So did travel sickness, for that matter, and she had just got off a plane and promptly into his truck.

Pulling back out into traffic, Noah continued on his way, comfortable once again in his mind that, while this was going to be a big change for him, it was also the best possible thing for someone in Kitty's position. "Give your gut time to settle, then sip your shake," he said with a nod, because while he couldn't do much about travel sickness, once he got her home and into bed, time and rest would sort out the other two.

Kitty didn't answer but ten or so minutes later, she did take another sip of her shake. Then putting it back in the cup holder, she didn't touch it again. She didn't touch her burger either, not until they were a good hour underway. And then, she only touched it long enough to roll her window down and chuck it, wrapper and all, out into the wood brush.

"The smell," she said by way of explanation as she rolled her window back up again. Gathering every other remnant of their meal, she stuffed it all back in the sack and tossed it into the backseat as far from her as she could get it. Hugging her stomach, she curled against the side of the door, turned her face to the window and closed her eyes.

Noah let her pretend to sleep. With any luck, the real thing would creep up on her while she was doing it and she'd get some much-needed rest. If it did, however, she didn't snore and, every now and then, when he happened to glance over at her, more often than not he could tell by her lashes that her eyes were open.

He had to look carefully, though, because she was listening for his movements. If he turned his head or shifted, or even dropped a hand from the steering wheel into his lap, she heard it and closed her eyes. No, all of his cautious spying had to be done via the rearview mirror if he wanted to catch her. He wasn't offended. If he'd been through half of what Garreth reported that she had, he'd have been a cot case too.

The sun was almost gone by the time he pulled off the road to Cooktown. He went slow, but the single-lane road to his house wasn't paved and the truck bounced in and out of the well-worn ruts and runnels so badly that even one as stubborn as Kitty gave up on 'sleeping.' She sat up.

"Home sweet home," Noah said, somewhat proudly, as he pulled up to the front porch of his one-story ranch house. Once upon a time, it had been his grandfather's house, built by the Carver patriarch's own work-rough hands and to the aesthetic tastes of most 1930s farmspreads in the Outback. Not that being located on the outskirts of Cooktown qualified as the Outback, but the house didn't know that and Noah was always proud to show it off.

It was red brick with an upgraded grey metal roof and white shutters, window awnings, porch posts and railings, and an extra wide, screen-enclosed veranda that kept the bugs out all the way around the house. The windows were huge and many, and although his property did not butt up to the ocean as so many did in Cooktown, he was close enough to it that opening all the windows north to south still worked as the best summertime air conditioning by catching that saltwater breeze that swept in off the Pacific. Shade cast over the house by the towering mango and eucalyptus trees did the rest, at least until it got too hot and muggy. At that point, Noah figured God made indoor air conditioning for a reason.

In the seat beside him, Kitty scrunched down low enough to stare, wide-eyed and open-mouthed at the leafy awnings of the sheltering trees and—in particular—at the koala lazily climbing from one grazing spot to another higher up in the canopy.

"What—" she breathed, but stopped herself and looked at him instead.

"Koala," he told her. "Which, by the way, are nowhere near as cute as the movies like to portray. They mostly stay up in the trees; sometimes they come down to the porch, especially when the weather gets bad. I've a watering trough and a screen left open for them out back."

"I thought koalas didn't drink," Kitty said hesitantly.

"Used to be I thought that too. But, I suppose climate change'll catch up with all of us eventually. Most of the year, they get what they need from the leaves. The rest of the time, they know where the watering trough is. The point is, cute they may be, but they're also wild animals; they can and do bite. If you see one on the porch, give it a wide berth and leave it be. That's Rule Number One." He flashed her a smile as he snagged her bag from the backseat and got out of the truck. "Come on. I'll give you the tour."

He was all the way to the porch steps before she, reluctantly, unclipped her seatbelt. He used a smile to encourage her to follow, though he couldn't help but note the supreme reluctance with which she stole glimpses of the field around his house and then the surrounding woods beyond them. He loved the natural seclusion his home offered and, especially, he was fond of the fact that nothing could be seen of any of his neighbors. Not so much as a porchlight at night. Judging by the shuttered absence of expression on her unsmiling face, Kitty did not feel the same. She did follow him, but only to the bottom of the porch steps. Then she stopped again.

Kitty wasn't a short woman. Slightly taller than the average female he knew, nevertheless, she wasn't as tall as he was and it didn't help that he was standing one step shy of the top of his porch. So, Noah made himself smaller, lowering himself to his haunches and gentling his smile. Yet another that she would not return. She was a skittish one, he'd give her that.

"If your friends didn't trust me," he reminded her. "You wouldn't be here. Right?"

Breathing in, she swept the remoteness of their surroundings before her gaze grudgingly returned to him. She nodded once.

"All right, then." He straightened again, pointing west. "Cooktown lies three kilometers that way. Nearest neighbor is a bloke named Harris, almost a kilometer past those trees." He directed her gaze back behind her, southeast past his truck. "If you feel like exploring, there's no place on my property that you cannot go so long as I'm with you. If I'm not with you, you need to be within a quick sprint of this house. That's Rule Number Two." He waved her up the steps. "Come on inside."

He put his car keys into his pocket. The door was never locked; he just went in.

"Welcome to my home." Her bag still clutched in one hand, his smile morphing into a grin, he gestured broadly from living to dining room. "Come in, come in. Don't let the A/C out, love. That's Rule Number Three."

A hand to the small of her back as soon as she crossed the threshold helped to hustle her far enough inside for him to close the door. Dropping her bag on the end of the couch, he crossed the room to the hallway that divided the two front rooms. "Living room," he said, quite obviously to the pleasant sitting area to her left. A beige couch for company, an overstuffed easy chair for him, the blue curtains his mother had given him to help block out the sun, several dozen sporting trophies and winner plaques, plus a television that he almost never turned on made up the whole of its contents.

He pointed the other way. "Dining." Four chairs were currently tucked up to the oversized table his grandfather had hand carved and which could easily have seated twelve when the three leaves were put back in. "Kitchen's through that door."

She obediently glanced to the open archway to the dining room's far right.

"And here right behind me—"

Her eyes followed when he pointed to the other archway directly behind him.

"Toilet's across from it. Only one, sad to say. We're going to have to be nice roommates." He winked, then beckoned her to keep following as he strolled down the long hallway. He flicked on the lights as he went, in case she had problems with the dark. His office with its backyard exit was next to the bathroom. "This door's always open." His bedroom dotted the end of the hall. "This one not so much. I like my privacy," he said as he touched the closed door. He then touched the closed door to the right of it. "This one's yours. Now, I reckon you like your privacy too. Sad to say, there's no lock. But, my mum raised herself two of the finest gentlemen this town has ever known. I promise always to knock first and never to enter without your say so. Privacy and trust are very important, to about everyone I suppose. We'll make that Rule Number Four."

"Is that all of them?"

He swung his gaze back to hers, both startled and a little pleased that she was at least speaking to him. Her voice was pretty too, soft, not too high-pitched and not too low. She wasn't smiling, but at least she wasn't mute.

"That's it," he replied. "It's a small house, but seeing as it's just me, it fits right fine."

"No, I mean the rules. Is that all of them?"

Her tone was as guarded as her expression, but he could have sworn his dominant's ear had picked up a hint of sullen defiance. He kept his smile. "Nah, not even close. Rule Five: Shoes on at all times and check 'em in the mornings before you put them on. Rule Six: I forgot to pay the maid service, so pick up after yourself, yeah? The rest of them I figure we can plot out as we go along. How's that sound to you?"

She was here, maybe by her own agreement but not necessarily of her own free will. Still, when he locked his eyes with her, his persistent smile doing little to soften his commands, she only kept his stare for a moment before dropping hers to the floor.

"Fine," she said, no trace of that momentary sullenness. Something told him it might still be there, but she was good at hiding her feelings. Her refusal to hold his gaze made it harder for him to get a good read on her, and that bothered him. He'd seen this kind of defense mechanism before. It wasn't the sort born out of pleasant past experiences.

"Are you hungry?" he asked, softening his tone.

She shook her head.

It had been hours since she'd thrown up what few bites she'd attempted, and heaven only knew if she'd eaten anything during her travels. The poor girl was little more than a skeleton as it was.

"I'll make a sandwich," he decided. "Thirsty? We're on well water here and it's the best you'll ever taste coming from a tap, but I've also a pitcher of tea in the fridge. So long as you bring your glass back out every morning for a scrub up, feel free to take some in to bed with you at night."

"Rule Seven?" Her face was a careful mask, pale American porcelain without a trace of disobedience. But again, he could have sworn he detected a hint of it in her voice, and the dominant half of him was definitely taking notice. That tickled him. Noah liked a little spunk in his submissives. Not that Kitty was his. In fact, up until this point, he hadn't wanted to think of her even as a submissive. More, she was like the koalas in the trees above his house. A wild thing, something that needed a little help from him to get by, but definitely not a thing for him to hold or keep.

"We'll chalk that one up under cleaning up after ourselves, eh?"

She said nothing.

"I'll get your bag, shall I?"

Funny, how he'd never before noticed how close the hallway

was. But, from the moment he made that suggestion, suddenly he found himself eyeing what little space there was between her and the wall. If she didn't turn sideways, they were going to touch. A curious pang thumped once in his chest as he envisioned his hand contacting her shoulder as he squeezed past her, his back brushing full up against the wall, maybe even bumping some of the family pictures that still hung there from his grandparents' day. And yet it was the incredibly physical brush of the back of her arm against his that exploded that imaginary tingling into the realm of the very real all throughout his skin.

"I'll get it," Kitty said, turning on her heel and retreating in long, quick steps all the way back to the living room.

Just like that, the spell was broken.

What the hell, mate, he thought to himself. No, he didn't invite a lot of company back to his house, but he wasn't a hermit. Now and then, he did have guests. Some were even women. He couldn't count the number he'd slipped past coming in and out of the kitchen or the bathroom, but none had made his skin break out in tingling chills.

It was because she was submissive, he decided as he watched her grab her duffel bag off the end of the couch. He usually did well with submissives, but it wasn't often that he brought one home for... close encounters.

Not that she was that. He watched as she hugged her bag close for comfort before turning back to him. He was a man who could touch a woman, study her, know without words whether she wanted more, softer, harder, or enough. Right now Noah couldn't read a single one of Kitty's thoughts, but the way her arms tightened around her luggage gave him the distinct impression that the same could not be said for her.

Who was reading whom, he found himself wondering, and did she like what she was seeing in him?

Like that made a difference either way. *Don't forget what you're doing here, mate,* he told himself.

Embarrassed at his own wayward thoughts, he pointed to the kitchen's hall entry. "I'll get those sandwiches."

Slipping into the other room and out of her immediate sight, Noah stood for a moment in front of the fridge. Every inch of him was aware of the woman standing frozen in the other room, listening intently back at him.

A creak from a squeaky floorboard in the hallway was his only warning, and thank goodness he heard it otherwise when she slipped past the open doorway, glancing awkwardly in at him on her way to her new bedroom, instead of busily gathering sandwich material, she'd have seen him standing there like an idiot. Only when he heard the hinges on her door squeak open and then the soft bump as it swung shut behind her did Noah dump his minor armload of supper components on the counter.

Hands braced to either side of the cutting board, he hung his head in absolute amazement at the lingering tingles of that accidental touch still swimming through his flesh and his chest.

What. The. Hell?

Kitty sat on the edge of the narrow bed in her new room and tried not to see all this as being every bit a prison as Ethen's remote farmhouse had been. She was just as isolated, but no. This was worse. Living with Ethen, at least she'd been in America where—if necessary—she could run out the front door, four miles down the road and call someone to come and get her. Who could she call to come get her now? Three months ago, when standing in front of Ethen's open front door staring out into the cold, for all that she hadn't been able to see them clearly at the time, at least she'd had options. What were her options here? Now, she really did have no place to go. Now, she really was trapped.

Hers was a corner bedroom with a window in each of the outward facing walls and a narrow twin-sized bed tucked up beneath them. For all that a layer of boxes completely lined one wall from floor practically to ceiling, an obvious attempt had been made to make it cozy. Although the mattress seemed newer, the bed itself with its white wrought-iron frame had to have been at least fifty years old. The box springs squeaked when she sat down, but a few experimental bounces told her it might not be uncomfortable to sleep on. White pillowcases adorned two goose-down pillows and the light patchwork quilt made up with military perfection looked old and worn, but clean.

White, lace-trimmed curtains were drawn across both narrow windows. They were new. Not only did they still have their folding creases, but the torn wrappers they had come in were crumpled into balls and discarded in the trash bin, tucked up between her bed and the antique nightstand set directly beneath the north window. That one offered a view of the back porch and koala trees, and wasn't locked. An experimental push opened it fairly easily, letting in a gust of hot air. She closed it again.

Through the east window, she saw the front of the screened-in veranda with its front porch swing and smoking chairs, Noah's long driveway, his truck and the wide-open pasture leading off to the surrounding woods.

She opened that window too. It stuck a little, but again, wasn't locked. The insects here were horribly loud and for all that the sun was gone, taking most of the daylight with it, the night air was warmer than she was used to. She closed it again, but left the drapes parted.

What was she doing here? Why had she ever agreed to this?

Ethen would never find her here, a part of her brain supplied.

Neither would anyone else. She'd seen 'Wolf Creek.' She gave herself three days before she ended up buried under a koala tree.

"Knock it off," she whispered. She didn't know Garreth well, but she knew Hadlee. For all that she'd run away and left Kitty behind to bear Ethen's wrath alone, Hadlee was her friend. Not for a second did Kitty think she would trap her in the middle of nowhere with someone who would hurt her.

Not knowingly, anyway.

"Stop it," she hissed, hands clenching so hard that her nails bit red crescents into her palms. She squeezed harder, deliberately welcoming the pain. It was calming, grounding, and the very least of what she deserved for letting her uncharitable thoughts run in such terrifying directions. It was as if her brain wanted to keep her as frightened as it could, for as long as possible.

She was tired of being scared. And yet, being scared had become so familiar to her that it was almost... comforting. How fucked up was that? She buried her face in her hands, willing herself to get angry. At least then, she'd have a good excuse for how badly she was shaking.

Maybe she ought to eat something. The nausea that had overcome her in the car had passed; she was hungry now. Thirsty, too. The sweet tea he had mentioned sounded good, but this was a small house and she could hear the clatter of dishes, the muted hiss of water turning on and off and his footsteps as he moved back and forth from fridge to counter to sink and back again. She didn't want to go out there until he was gone. If she sat here long enough, eventually he would go to bed, right?

How late was it? She didn't have a watch and, jetlagged as she was, she didn't trust the time her body was trying to convince her it was. The sun was down, so it might be late enough for him to crave sleep.

Maybe even above other things.

Yeah. Right. Said no man in the history of Ever.

That wasn't true. Kitty didn't know about other men. She could barely remember her life and relationships... before, but she knew Ethen. She knew about him so well that when at long last those heavy footsteps clumped across the kitchen floor and started down the hallway, her heart erupted all the way up into the back of her throat and her stomach fell cringing to her toes.

It was coming now. She knew it with such certainty that every inch of her braced for it. That moment when he came up against the unlocked barrier of her prison door and, instead of knocking as he promised, his hand took hold of the knob and turned it. She could already see that door pushing open and the shadow of him filling up the threshold a half step before he came inside. She could see him, Ethen-tall and Ethen-thin, pulling his belt from his pant loops and letting the folded leather hang from his ready hand until she decided how obedient she wanted to be.

Her fingernails bit deeper into her palms, because she could already see herself standing up, turning around, peeling out of her pants before getting down in her kitty-position—head down, ass up, legs together in the hope that might protect her pussy and anus from the whipping bite of the belt if he decided to use it anyway.

And of course, he would; obviously she needed it. Just look where she was. Look what she'd done. If anyone deserved whipping, wasn't it her?

Her whole body jumped at the soft single-knuckle knock that rapped twice at her closed bedroom door.

"Dinner's ready," Noah called, snapping Kitty sharply back to herself. Her heart still thundered in the back of her throat. Her stomach still cowered, sunk so far into herself she felt sick all over again.

He wasn't Ethen, she told herself. He'd obeyed his own rule, at least for now. But, one thing living with Ethen had taught her: He who made the rules, could and would change them at whim. Sooner or later, she was going to be even more defenseless than she was right now— but Hadlee would never deliberately put her in such a situation. Except, Kitty didn't know that. Nobody ever really *knew* that about someone else, right? And Noah was right here. Right outside her door. *His* door. *His* house. His *prison*, with all the bars of his rules firmly locking her into place. All he had to do was wait. Eventually, he would catch her sitting on the toilet or taking a shower—

Noah knocked on the door again. "Kitty, are you awake, love?"

Or lying in bed late at night, when she at last fell so exhausted that she couldn't keep her eyes open not one second longer—

Her panicking heart missed a beat.

"Yes," she quavered, her voice weirdly hoarse and shaking. She cleared her throat, trying hard to quell the fearful trembling. "I-I'll be right there."

He hesitated a moment, but then his footsteps retreated back down the hall. She heard him go back into the kitchen, but there was no relief in this newfound distance. Only the awful sinking dread that accompanied knowing he had all the power, and all the time in the world. All he had to do was wait. It was coming. Eventually, he would decide when the moment was right to strike, but until he did, she was stuck… waiting right along with him.

CHAPTER 4

*S*o she waited. All through dinner.

She managed almost half the sandwich, which was cheese, avocado and lettuce with a smear of greenish-brown stuff unlike anything she'd ever tasted before. She got a blob on her thumb and licked it off. As far as she was concerned, that right there was Australia's second attempt at killing her. She choked. That she didn't immediately throw it up again was a wonder.

"Vegemite," Noah supplied. "It's good for you. Puts hair on your chest."

Just what she'd always wanted, but when he deliberately took a big bite of his sandwich, unspoken pressure not to be wasteful or rude induced her to keep eating too. So long as there was other stuff in each bite and not the vegemite alone, she found the strong yeasty flavor tolerable.

"No worries about that, love," Noah said after they'd both finished eating and she started to pick up the dishes. "They'll keep until morning. You go on and get your rest."

He took his empty plate and her mostly empty one away from the table, carting both into the kitchen and laying them in the sink.

"If you want to use the toilet, now's the time. Unless you want one too, I'm going to get my things for a shower."

The last thing Kitty wanted was to make herself vulnerable in a room that didn't lock while he... what? Waited for her to drop her pants and get trapped in the middle of it before he finally made his move? If it was going to happen eventually, she might as well get it over with. Besides, it had been a long time since the plane and she had to pee.

Kitty waited until he vanished into his bedroom to get his things and then she quickly ducked into the bathroom. She spent the entire time perched on the toilet, staring at the door in dread and waiting for it to come flying open. It didn't, but it was still the fastest she'd ever used a toilet in her life.

Quick as she'd been, Noah was still standing right outside the bathroom door, leaned up against the wall while he waited his turn. Ducking past him, head down, she fled straight to her room.

"G'night," he called before she could close the door. His tone said they were the best of friends. Her chest was so tight it hurt. Sinking down on the edge of her narrow bed, she braced herself to wait all over again.

The walls in this house were thin. She could hear the pattering rain of water pouring into the bottom of the shower, even through the door. She could hear the splashing of his movements as he soaped up and rinsed off. She heard the squeak of the faucet as it was twisted to off and the shower ended. She waited, barely breathing, through the bumping of cupboards and rustling of cloth. Eventually the bathroom door opened. Her hands became fists on her knees. Hard and unblinking, wanting to see it coming, she stared at the door until her eyes burned. But all she heard was the click of the light in the hallway turning off, the padding of his bare feet, softer now without his shoes on, pass right by her door.

"G'night," he called again, before shutting himself in his room.

It seemed a small forever before the creak of his bedsprings told her he'd laid down. The quiet and the darkness went on for a small forever more, before, suddenly, Kitty found she could breathe again. She gasped in, filling lungs that ached, forcing her too-tight chest to expand enough to allow it.

He wasn't coming into her room. He really, honestly wasn't. She was safe, at least for tonight.

Safe.

She didn't even know what that word meant anymore, but she knew what it felt like. And frankly, if this was how it would always be, then what in the world had she run away for in the first place? What was better? What was different? She was every bit as afraid now as she had been with Ethen, only now without all those little moments of comfort that came with having a set routine. Of knowing what that routine was. Of knowing she was favored first among the Menagerie, with all the added bonuses that came with it.

There was no routine now. There was no comfort and no certainties, and certainly no bonuses. Everything she had was either borrowed from Hadlee, purchased through someone else, or a giant unknown.

What was she *doing* here?

Getting up, painfully aware of how thin the walls here were, Kitty unzipped her bag and took out the sleeping shirt Hadlee had given her. She hated the feel of it. With Ethen, the Menagerie were never allowed to wear anything to bed. They were never allowed to wear anything at home at all. They were to be open and available to him at all times. For all that he'd done terrible things to her, she missed the comfort of that. Every moment she spent in clothes now made her skin itch and her heart beat anxiously. Most days, it was all she could do not to think of herself as a traitor. Like now, right now, as she turned out the light in her new prison and crawled beneath the light patchwork quilt to lay her head awkwardly upon the pillow. The thin glow of light spilled in under the door, providing only the most shadowy illumination across the hardwood floor of a room she should never have been in.

He must have left the bathroom light on for her.

She closed her eyes, but they wouldn't stay closed. She thought she heard breathing from the room next door. Her skin kept crawling, kept waiting. And yet, in the back of her exhaustedly wide-awake mind, instead of imminent rape, all she could see was the minor stack of dirty dishes that Ethen never would have tolerated in the kitchen sink, no matter how late it was or how few needed to be washed.

The bed was too comfortable and too squeaky, although she knew that part was only an excuse since the only time it made any sound was when she tossed from her side to her back, casting her wide-eyed stare to the ceiling. She couldn't sleep, though God knew it wasn't because she wasn't tired. She was exhausted and had been for days, even before she'd set foot on that plane.

Unable to stand the itching any more, she sat up long enough to peel out of her nightshirt, throwing it onto the floor before flopping back down and pulling the soft quilt up to her chin. Now she couldn't sleep because there was a castoff piece of clothing on the floor of her room, something Ethen had tolerated even less than he did dirty dishes.

The box springs squeaked in symphony as she scrambled out of bed, grabbed the nightshirt and folded it neatly. She put it back in her duffel bag and then got back into bed. She rolled from her back to her other side, putting her back to the soft sliver of light creeping beneath her bedroom door and locking her stare on the wall beneath the window.

She was going to be here for a while. She ought to put her clothes away. It was silly to live out of a duffel bag for heaven only knew how long. Plus, duffel bags did not belong on bedroom floors any more than dirty clothes did. A place for everything; everything in its place. She'd been here an hour now at least; there was no excuse for not having put what few things she had into the closet.

Getting up again, she turned on the light and, as quietly as she could, unpacked her things. Her bare feet made only a whisper of sound as she crossed to the closet and opened the old-fashioned door. She leapt back, dropping everything as she clapped her hands across her mouth. She barely muffled her inadvertent scream. An effort had been made to empty the closet enough to provide space for her. Indeed, there were no other clothes hanging there, just seven empty wire hangers and a minor mountain of more boxes stacked almost waist-high inside, as many as could be made to fit. And in the very back, like brown snakes on wall hooks, were a series of belts and leather straps, all of varying lengths and widths and thicknesses. Only two of the three belts had buckles. The widest of the straps had a worn wooden handle. All were supple, and well taken care of despite their age—every one of them the sort capable of delivering the most agonizing bite of a kiss if ever they were to be put to such a purpose.

Kitty gasped once, the only breath she was aware she had taken since opening the closet door. No longer in danger of screaming, still she kept her hands over her mouth.

Noah was a dom.

Well, of course, he was. He'd been at Black Light, hadn't he? Snapping that whip of his against Hadlee's naked back and buttocks while Ethen stewed in the audience, silently furious that anyone would dare touch what was his. For her part, Kitty remembered the sound of that scene more than she remembered watching it. The sound had been crisp and loud. Almost as loud as Hadlee's gasp as she broke under the cracking snap.

Of course, Noah would have his own toys. It only made sense that he would keep them in his spare room. This wasn't some unspoken threat. He wasn't Ethen, leaving such things as a silent promise that her behaviors had not gone unnoticed any more than they would go uncorrected.

Shivers danced up her back as, with equal parts trepidation and helpless fascination, Kitty reached far enough into the closet to touch the nearest strap. The aged leather was deceptively soft. Snatching her hand back again, she tucked both beneath her chin, trying to banish how her fingertips tingled and now so too did the backs of both her thighs and her naked, cringing bottom.

She was being silly. Tearing her eyes from the collection of belts and straps, she picked up her fallen clothes and hung them up, some two to a hanger. Laying her duffel on the stack of boxes, she quickly shut the closet door and hurried back to bed. Clicking off the lamp, she tossed onto her side again to face the wall, hands clasped tight against her lips and burrowed so far under the quilt that it practically covered her head. Sleeplessly, she lay there, still feeling every bit the traitor as before, only now it was different. Better somehow, the way misbehaviors always felt both dreadful and better while she lay caught in that purgatory of waiting for correction.

This was how it used to feel, back before Ethen. Back when BDSM was all fun and games, and she still went by the name her parents had given her. She remembered a moment almost like this with the very first dom she'd ever had. He'd liked roleplaying games. In particular, he'd liked disapproving Daddy-themed games and his favorite was when he got letters sent 'home from school.'

She'd loved getting spanked back then. She'd loved the fun, exciting playfulness of it. But then, none of those 'punishments' had been real. Oh the spankings had been, but the offenses were nothing but make-believe. There was a big difference between being sent to her room to await 'Daddy's' displeasure and the icy terror that twisted in her guts every time Ethen locked her in one of his death stares. Like he would do if she was more than three minutes late getting home from work or she failed to get dinner on the table in time, or if he found a cobweb during a house inspection or like when the belt on the vacuum broke and Puppy could only vacuum half the carpets. They'd all grabbed brooms—Puppy, Kitty even Pony had swept until her arms hurt—but the floors had not passed Ethen's standards of cleanliness and they'd all been punished.

But that had happened around Christmas time. It had been months since last Kitty had been punished for anything. Months since she'd been rewarded, too. Simply months, without the thing that once upon a time she'd thought her world could never have revolved without. Not impact play, per se, although once upon a time she used to love it. Crave it. So hungrily that she used to write those silly letters from 'school' at least once or twice a week to help provide Daddy with fun reasons to spank her.

Yes, she missed impact, but more than that, she missed being allowed to submit. She missed being bent to another's will. Not forced so much as seduced into it. And God, could she be seduced. She'd fallen for Ethen's seduction so completely that here she was, even after all he'd done, pining for him.

No, not him. *It*. The routines and rituals. Showing her respect and appreciation for another by keeping his house, cooking his meals, bending her body to his desires... warming his bed. Being the canvas upon which he exorcised his sadistic impulses because in turn it sated all of her own masochistic hungers.

She couldn't stop thinking about the belts. Closing her eyes, Kitty saw them, hanging in the closet, ready for use when and if required, and a low thump of heated arousal pulsed between her legs. Heady and unexpected, something she hadn't felt in a long, long time.

Trying to ignore it, she rolled onto her stomach, but from there it was such a short and seductive impulse to rise up onto her knees. Head down, ass up, hands clasped above her head to keep her from reaching under and between her splayed thighs to touch where she knew she shouldn't. She couldn't even pretend this was a come-to-Jesus moment. A real punishment would never be initiated with her hiding under a blanket.

Cool whole-house air conditioning moved over her as she slipped the patchwork quilt off her. Hoping the squeak of the hinges weren't as loud as they seemed with her head lying on the mattress, she adjusted herself to the center of the bed. Spreading her knees wider apart, she bowed her back and arched her hips, making herself properly submissive... to no one.

This was ridiculous. Burying her face in the sheet, she bit the inside of her cheek until the stinging rush of tears was forced back. She shouldn't want this. No person who'd truly, legitimately gone through the hell Ethen had put her through would want any part of this again; she could already hear people saying that, whispering it behind her back. It was why she hadn't gone to the police when Garreth had tried to convince her to, because no one who didn't want this to happen would have put themselves in the position she had. And they wouldn't cry themselves to sleep at night because they were so empty without it, so desperate to run right back into it all over again.

Pushing herself up onto her knees, Kitty stared at the darkness of her shadowy bed. She needed punishment. She wanted it; at least then she might be able to sleep afterward. A real punishment wouldn't have been given like this, though. Not with her in this position and not with a sink full of dirty dishes.

The muffled rumble of a man's steady breathing told her Noah was probably asleep, but that was almost a secondary concern. She crawled out of bed on all fours and crept to the door. Her heart was in her throat; her stomach was nothing but knots, but though she paused at the closet, she could not make herself open it. Couldn't make herself face those straps, not even long enough to snag a nightshirt that would only itch at her for putting it on.

The rules here were different than the ones Ethen enforced, but still clothing shouldn't be allowed. Not for traitorous submissives who, above all, needed reminding of their place.

Knowing she risked being seen, she left her bedroom. Any inadvertent sound could bring Noah out into the hall. She was terrified of that, but the hunger was awake in her now. Her flesh vibrated with every hand and knee step she crawled down the hall to the kitchen.

She hadn't been Kitty-girl since she left Ethen. Living with Hadlee and Garreth had made that impossible, not when any sight or sign of Kitty-girl might reopen Piggy-girl's wounds. She didn't even have her mask anymore. Hadlee had snatched it from her hands and thrown it as far as it would go. She hadn't even allowed it in the car the night she and Garreth had rescued her, and Kitty never told her how it had made her feel to watch that mask go flying off into the snowy dark. It had hurt. Like seeing a piece of her unloved self being cast away, it had physically hurt like hell.

That was okay. She told herself she didn't need the mask. She had been Kitty before Ethen; she could be Kitty without that mask.

One could tell one's self that all day long, but standing in front of Noah's sink on two legs instead of four, without the mask it was harder to keep her Kitty-self in mind. It took all of two minutes to wash the dishes, dry them thoroughly, and search the cupboards for (hopefully) each item's proper place. She wiped down all the surfaces and when she was done, the whole house was silent and she could almost pretend that she was the only person here. Or that she was back in Ethen's house, going about her daily chores—her normal routine—and that once more she was back in her place as the most favored of his Menagerie.

She hadn't felt the security of this in so long, she didn't even try to fight the urge. She got down on her hands and knees and crawled back to her bedroom.

She hesitated—bad Kitty—but in the end, she left the door open, because her body was not hers and never had been. She had no need for privacy. She was to be open and available to her owner in all places and at all times, even when she did not want to be—even when the consequences might include Noah wandering out of his room, something that truly, deeply terrified her. Still, she left the door open and continued on hands and knees all the way to the foot of the bed.

She knelt there, a position of penance with her knees wide apart, hands behind her head, waiting for someone who would not come. Aching for the discipline she didn't deserve and hadn't earned, but which she wanted so desperately that, when her time of reflection was done, she rose up to bend over the foot rail. Feet spread apart, she put herself into position for either whipping or fucking, the choice was not and should not ever be hers.

Except this wasn't right. This wasn't realistic. Bad kitties were always sent to await their punishment with an implement, even if one might not be used.

She didn't want to, but then it shouldn't ever be about the things *she* wanted. Sometimes, it should only be about following what she knew was expected of her. She got back down on the floor and crawled to the closet. With her bedroom door now open and the dull light of the mostly closed bathroom door seeping into her room, the straps in the back of her closet looked less like snakes and yet far more formidable than before. She selected the first one she touched, her hand erupting into the same prickles of dread now dancing across her flanks. Carrying it in her mouth, she crawled back to bed.

Back into position she went, this time careful to balance the strap so it lay across her back, above her hips. The weight of it there was both heaven and hell, familiar and comforting and painful because no matter what, she had lost all right to have this. She'd run away from the one dom who had understood her. And yes, he'd been an ass, but wasn't everybody at some point? And yes, that last night he had hurt her terribly, but it wasn't really all his fault. Didn't she deserve some of the blame? Had he really been so bad that she needed to run away?

The important thing here was, she had lost all access to the discipline she loved the most because of *her* actions, not his. It was gone and she would never get it back again. Because everyone who knew her also knew Garreth, so eventually, sooner or later everyone was going to know what had happened between her and Ethen. They were going to know she was a submissive who couldn't be trusted. That she had failed and betrayed her dom in the most subversive way. Betrayed his trust by revealing to both Hadlee and Garreth how she'd gotten all those welts the night they'd rescued her from that freezing cold telephone booth.

Nobody needed to know about the other thing, the rape. If rape it could even be called, because really, if it *had* been rape, then why was she doing this—bending over in naked remembrance of all the things Ethen would do to her if she were with him right now? Why was her heart hurting, her legs spreading wider and her hips pushing back to make her even more available for nobody's use?

It had been so long since last she'd been used in that way she so deeply craved. Broken with need, her hand moved down, covering her achingly empty pussy. Such touches were forbidden; a submissive's pleasure was never for herself. She tried to make her hand feel like someone else's as she pressed. She didn't dare rub, no matter how much she wished just once to feel the caress of fingertips circling her waking clit. But she held, knowing even this much would have been enough to bring the strap laying across her back into extensive and painful use.

Kitty buried her face in the mattress. She tried to remember. When she'd been a little girl, everyone used to say she had a great imagination, but she must have lost that skill. Try as she might, she couldn't summon a single lashing memory sufficient enough to bring those echoing lines of real pain snapping and stinging and burning across her ass and thighs. She felt only pulsing, the slow, languid throb of her own needs coming to life beneath her hand.

Just one rub. Who would know, or care?

Covering her eyes with her other hand, Kitty gave in to temptation, but it felt awful. A pale mockery of what it could have been with a strong man standing behind her, one fist tangled in a leash of her own hair, breathing those intoxicating words of censure into her ear. Things like, *'Is this what you think bad girls deserve? Is this how you think I'll treat you? Ah, love, you haven't earned a pet on the kitty from me.'*

Pussy molten and throbbing, Kitty opened her eyes. That wasn't Ethen's voice. That was Noah's, his thick Australian accent making those words echo in her head.

Her chest was tight, but for the first time in days, it was tight because it was lust (not fear) making it hard for her to breathe.

She took her fingers off her swollen clit, pulling her hand back to take the belt off her back so it wouldn't fall when she stood. She should have put it back in the closet. She should have closed her bedroom door. At the very least, she should have put her clothes back on, but Kitty didn't do any of that. As quiet as she could, she crawled into bed alone.

Pulling the quilt up over her head, she buried her face in the pillow so as to muffle the sound and hugged the strap to her chest while she cried.

CHAPTER 5

*N*oah stood frozen in his own doorway, knowing if he moved any further out into the hallway he risked the bathroom light casting his shadow into her room. But then, he didn't need to lean out any further. From here, he could see the metal rail that made up the foot of her bed. And, up until a minute ago, he'd seen what she was doing to herself as she bent over it, hips thrust back for punishment, strap laid across her back as if waiting for someone to take it up. God help him if his own hand didn't itch to do exactly that. When she'd slipped a hand down to touch between her thighs, it had itched even harder... but not for the strap.

The thing about having thin walls, it was easy to hear how restless she was. When he'd heard her leave her room, for a moment he'd wondered if she was planning to run. He'd actually gotten dressed, in case he needed to chase out after her into the night. But she'd only gone to the kitchen. He'd heard the water run, heard her washing and putting away the dishes he'd left in the sink. He'd then heard her make her way back down the hall, past his closed bedroom door and into her room again. The sound of her passing had been a singular sound, not the padding of two feet, but the crawling of all fours. He knew that sound. Hell, his cock had recognized it before his perking ears did. The whispering brush of bare hands and the slightly louder thump of bare knees on wooden floorboards. Oh yes, she was crawling.

Before he could stop himself, he too was down on hands and knees, cheek to floor as he peeked under the door and caught that first intoxicating glimpse of confirmation before she neared too close. The tip of a naked breast. The shadowy curve of a mons shaved naked and smooth. He'd never been as frustrated with an inanimate door as he became a half-second later, when she closed the distance and all he could then see was her hands and lower legs as she crawled into her room.

She didn't close her door.

She was absolutely naked, in his house, and she did not close her door.

She did not go to sleep, either. Instead, kneeling at his own door but staring incredulously at the shadow-blackened wall that separated his room from hers, Noah listened as her whispered movements continued restlessly for some time. From her bed to her closet—the door scraped open and bumped closed once more —and then back to her bed again.

He should stay hidden. Hell, when it came to 'should' he *should* go back to bed and give her her privacy. He didn't. Instead, knowing if he got caught he'd have a lot of hard explaining to do, he opened the door far enough to lean out. No more than an inch, maybe three. Just far enough to glimpse around the span of wall that separated their two doorways and into the darkness of her bedroom.

The bathroom light was on, but the door was only cracked. That left enough light to illuminate her bent-over position. The slope of her long legs; the curve of her hips as she arched her back to offer her ass. The minute wiggle as she pushed her hand down under her, between herself and the railing, and touched herself.

She was beautiful, and yet she covered her face with her hand

and buried both against the mattress as if she were ashamed. The strap across her back—one he'd patterned after his grandfather's razor strap; one of the first Noah had ever made when he was first learning how to leathercraft—spoke volumes as to her desires.

Was she aching for impact play for the sake of release alone, or was her need for something more? Something disciplinary. Offenses could be real or imagined, with some submissives the two were often the same, but he didn't think it mattered. If she were his, he would not have left her waiting long. He'd have given her what she needed—not the punishment she was offering herself for, but the peace of mind that would follow.

How long had she been doing this, trapped, her submissive needs going unrelieved? If she was his—

But she wasn't his, the sensible part of his brain replied. That's what the problem was, she wasn't anybody's.

Her soft breath hitched. A moment later, Kitty carried his strap into bed with her. Though she kept it quiet, he knew when she started crying.

Noah stood in the doorway, every inch of him straining to lock back the urge to go to her. It wasn't a creepy moment. For all that he'd wanted her body beneath his hands a raw second ago, what was in him now was nothing more than one human being's selfless ache to comfort another in her misery. He would have stroked her hair, rubbed her back, lain behind her on top of the blanket so he could wrap her tightly in his arms and whisper that, believe it or not, things really would be okay. For all that she might feel lost in the middle of nowhere right now, she was in the middle of *his nowhere* and he would keep her safe. Whatever or whoever was out to hurt her in the States, they couldn't get at her here.

Comfort might be his only motivation at the moment, but deep inside, Noah knew if he went into her room right now, she would neither welcome nor accept his touch, his sympathy or his whispered words of anything. She had completely cocooned herself within the folds of her blanket, but beneath that thin barrier she was naked and they were strangers. No, she wouldn't welcome him at all and, frankly, if he'd heard of another dom doing what was right now burning through his brain, under these very same circumstances with a traumatized submissive, he'd have called the man an idiot for not thinking it through.

Police got involved over less.

Closing his bedroom door did little to muffle the plaintive sounds of her weeping, but Noah forced himself to go back to bed. He lay down, but after what he'd witnessed, sleep did not come for him until long after Kitty had cried herself out. And when it did come, it was fitful at best. He tossed, he turned. He had questions, and every time he startled awake in the night after dozing off, it was to find his questions had multiplied and he didn't have the answers for any of them. But he knew who would.

The pre-dawn sky was little more than a blanket of grey, dotted only by the brightest stars and the thinnest line of golden amber along the tree-studded horizon when Noah gave up on sleep. Pulling his jeans on, he grabbed his cellphone and padded barefoot out on his front porch. Sneaking around the side of the house to make sure her windows weren't open, he followed the screened-in veranda all the way around, putting the entirety of his house between her and this conversation.

"Hello," Garreth said around a mouthful of something. The upbeat jingle of a McDonald's commercial was singing in the background before it cut abruptly to a much more obnoxious car commercial.

"Get you in your tucker?" Noah asked.

"Just sat down to dinner," his American friend confirmed, "but that's all right. Wish you could be here. Hadlee makes a mean spaghetti sauce. Homemade meatballs, too. I'm going to have to step up my exercise routine or I won't be able to fit in my leathers before the year is out. What's up? How's she doing?"

"Sleeping still," Noah deflected, making the effort to sound far more cheerful than he felt.

"That's good. She barely slept the whole time she was here. The last couple days or so, I don't think she slept at all."

"I could tell. If you've got a moment, though, I've got some questions."

"Shoot," Garreth said between bites.

"This bloke she ran away from..."

"Ethen."

"Right. This bloke, is he the same fellow what was harassing your lady the night I attended your club?"

"Black Light, yeah. He's been banned now, thank God."

"She was his submissive too?"

"He had four at one time. He'd make them come to the club naked, except for the halters they wore and these black leather animal masks. Called them his 'Menagerie.' Each was a different creature." Garreth wasn't eating any more, and the sound of a tv commercial in the background grew abruptly fainter as, presumably, Garreth relocated himself to somewhere quieter to talk. Perhaps somewhere out of Hadlee's earshot, although Noah only knew that because he would have done the same. "He had a pony, a puppy, and then Kitty."

Leaning against a porch post, Noah stared into the growing amber and pale pink of the distant horizon. "And Hadlee?"

Garreth cleared his throat, but it wasn't enough to hide the tight anger when he finally answered. "He called her his pig, and yes, we're still working on that. The man's a son of a bitch. I can almost guarantee, whatever you are imagining happened between her and Ethen, it's not dark enough. Literally every inch of her body was a bruise or a welt the night we picked her up, damn near naked, in eighteen-degree weather. It's a good thing he's been banned. I don't think I could stop myself from killing him if we ever met face-to-face again."

The only clear image Noah had of Ethen's face was that

moment he'd stepped in to stop the man who had grabbed Hadlee and shoved her into a wall. The more he thought about it, the more he seemed to remember the man harassing them here and there throughout that evening. At the time, he'd thought it little more than an annoyance. The scale of the abuse, however, was clearly greater and deeper than he'd known.

"Did you ever take Kitty under your protection?"

"Yes, of course. That's why I brought her into my ho... wait a minute." Noah heard the arch of incredulous eyebrows in Garreth's voice as he said, "Do you mean as my submissive? No. Hell no. I would have thought that the last thing she'd either want or need."

After what he'd seen last night, every gut instinct Noah had was screaming the opposite. Or was that simply wishful thinking? He rubbed his eyes, scrubbing a restless hand down his face. His palm rasped across last night's beard growth, seeming obscenely loud in the quiet of a morning only otherwise broken by the waking of local insects and the birds that would soon be hunting them.

"All right," he said, more for Garreth's benefit than anything else. "In any case, she's here. She's doing well." He paused a moment, but even before he finished his own inner debate on the wisdom of not keeping his next comment to himself, his mouth was open and moving. "How long has she been sick for, do you know?"

"Sick?" Garreth didn't sound so much startled as he did carefully neutral.

"Yeah." Noah decided to specify. "Could be motion sickness, I suppose, but she spent most of yesterday unable to hold anything down until tucker time. Thin as she is, I reckon it's been going on at least a while."

Garreth was quiet for so long, Noah pulled his cellphone back far enough to check that they were still connected. "Jesus, you don't think she's pregnant, do you?"

"Nah," Noah said, with far more certainty than he currently felt. "Like I said, could be motion sickness. She had just got off a plane after more than a day's travel, layovers included. Could be a summer-flu or stress, or any half a dozen other things. Give her a couple days to relax and no worries. She'll be right, mate. Have a g'night, you and your lady love."

"Keep us updated," Garreth replied, not at all sounding comforted.

"You know me, blokey." Noah let his tone grin, but all hint of it was gone when he ended the call.

Watching the sun creep over the horizon, he thought for a long time on what he wanted to do, on what a responsible bloke would do, and longest of all, he thought on what he probably would do. Maybe it was a good thing Garreth really didn't know him well. Oh, they were friends, the way two mates got to be after playing with the same submissive for a night, followed by months' worth of affable conversation on the cello. But how well did one bloke really know another after that sort of subtle socialization?

Maybe that was for the best. Because if Garreth had any inkling the plans now taking root in the back of Noah's head, he had a feeling his American friend would be on the first plane to Oz and he'd be coming to punch Noah square in the nose.

Before this day was out, Noah suspected he might actually earn every cartilage-crunching ounce of force behind that up-and-coming blow.

AUSTRALIA MADE ITS THIRD ATTEMPT ON KITTY'S LIFE BEFORE SHE even had a chance to get out of bed. The morning sun was high, shining squarely in through the crack in her bedroom curtains and across her closed eyelids. Her hands, still clutching the strap she'd stolen from the closet last night were cramped from the grip she'd held on it all night long. But as the brightness across her eyelids began to pry her from her sleep, and the ache in her knuckles filtered in beneath the retreating hazy of her dreams, it was that seductive scent of old leather as she breathed in and started to stretch that, for the first time in months, lent her comfort. She'd always loved the smell of leather.

She rolled sleepily onto her back and at last opened her eyes. She felt peaceful. Relaxed. Right up until her blinking, slow-to-focus eyes fixed on the large black thing crawling slowly across the ceiling directly above her. It had eight legs. Widening, her eyes locked on it. A spider! The biggest spider she had ever seen!

Whether it was by accident or by evil fucking design, the spider lost its grip. Kitty didn't even have time to sit up before it landed with a plop directly on her chest.

Kitty exploded out of bed, throwing spider, blankets, strap and pillows everywhere. She first fell on the floor and then crab-scrambled to get as much distance from her and the wildly fleeing spider as she could. She lost sight of it under the bed. She didn't care. She bolted from the room. The bathroom was open. So was Noah's door. Not seeing or hearing any hint of him, she ducked through the open door and slammed it shut behind her.

Hands pressed over the battering ram that her heart had become, she backed all the way to the tub. Her eyes cast nervous glances all over the room, but nothing in here was big, black or crawling. Everything was brightly lit. Morning sunshine poured in through the high and narrow window above the toilet. Everything was clean and peaceful, and slightly dated. Like her grandmother's house, back when G-ma had been alive. Blue stripes on white floral wallpaper reminded her strongly of the 1950s. So did the matching peach-pink tub, toilet, and sink.

But, at least there were no spiders.

There were also no clothes. There was, however, a tan bath towel and, confronted with the choice of wrapping that around her and going back to her now uninhabitable, arachnid-infested bedroom, she opted for the towel.

Her heart was still pounding harder than normal and her palms were sweating. She rubbed them against her towel as she cautiously ventured out again. She listened, but everything in the house was silence. Outside of it, however, she could make out the muffled strains of Dire Straits *So Far Away* playing on a distant radio, the beats of which were steadily punctuated by an unusual popping sound.

Noah's bedroom door was a-jar. What must he have thought when he got up this morning to find her bedroom door standing open? Hopefully she'd been covered enough that he hadn't known she'd been naked. For the life of her, she could not remember what parts of her might have been exposed or not before the spider landed on her chest.

Kitty shuddered, her whole body undulating with revulsion. Backing from both bedrooms, she retreated down the hall, only to spy something that paused her at the kitchen's side entrance. The coffee maker was sitting on the counter. Beside it, was a grinder with a serving of fresh coffee beans in it, and a carafe filled with water but not yet emptied into the dispensary. Cream, sugar, and two cups had been placed beside the coffee maker. It was as if Noah had started the process, only to become distracted and walk away.

Should she finish it? Back in her other life, it was Pony who made the morning coffee. Kitty had only ever done it twice, both times only because Pony had been so sick she couldn't stand and Ethen had restricted her to her room so she wouldn't infect the rest of them.

Outside, both the music and the popping continued unabated. Kitty looked to the coffee maker again. Most people didn't get mad if house guests helped out a little here or there, and really, she wasn't a house guest so much as a roommate. Who knew how long she'd be here? She ought to help whenever and wherever she could.

Except he hadn't asked her to.

In fact, last night he'd told her not to and she'd done it anyway. Was he upset that she'd disobeyed? Nothing in the kitchen let her know either way.

Ethen would have been upset. Well... Ethen would have been upset by the dirty dishes too, but he would have been far more upset at her for disobeying a direct order.

Noah wasn't Ethen. Something that could not have been more clearly contrasted simply by the fact that she had been awakened by a spider instead of by him, grabbing a fistful of her hair and dragging her on her knees to the kitchen, scolding and whipping her every step of the way to make sure his reprimand struck home.

He hadn't asked her to do anything. She should keep her hands to herself and stay out of his kitchen.

But the coffee was only half made, and something about that stuck like a thorn inside her far deeper than all the reasons she could think of not to tiptoe up to the coffeemaker, pour the water into it, grind the beans and start the machine brewing. After all, if he was mad about something she did, he would say something, wouldn't he? It was okay to help out where she could. It wasn't like she was rearranging his furniture. All she'd done was wash a few dishes and finish what he'd started with the coffee. No big deal.

She backed away from the coffeemaker once she'd got it started, rubbing her sweating palms against her towel-wrapped stomach, feeling both nervous and yet... helpful. Which was more than she had felt with Hadlee or Garreth. Ashamed as she was of that uncharitable thought, the truth remained no matter what she'd tried to do, one or both of them had stopped her. 'Oh no, don't worry about the dishes. I'll get those later.' 'No, no. You're our guest, not our maid. You don't have to pick up after us.' Hadlee was her friend. Garreth was her boyfriend and seemed perfectly nice in a lot of ways, but every day in their company made her feel more and more like an outsider. More and more useless.

Well, she wasn't useless now, was she?

It was just coffee, she told herself and turned from the counter. Facing the stove and refrigerator now, she paused all over again when she saw the frying pan and spatula sitting on the forward right burner and the short stack of two plates, knives and forks stacked on the left. On the counter was a silver toaster, a loaf of bread, butter tin and tube that read, 'Vegemite.' There was also a bowl of eggs and package of thick bacon pieces that were more like slabs than the American-cut slices she was used to. And it was all sitting there. Set out. Waiting.

For her to make breakfast? He hadn't told her to make breakfast. There was no note, either. He could have set it all out while waiting for her to wake up or for himself to get done doing whatever he was doing...

- What was he doing?

Hugging her towel, Kitty crept through the second kitchen archway, edging between the massive dining table and built-in china hutch, to peek out through the half-open drapes into the yard. She saw the radio first, sitting on the white-painted front porch rail, blaring its '80s music out into the yard where Noah was standing—no, not standing, dancing—step dancing, in form-fitting jeans, crocodile boots and worn tan hat, and a white t-shirt that fit him in a way that was at once loose and yet a second skin. She could see the ripple of muscle playing across his shoulders and back, bunching and flexing in his biceps as his arms moved to the beat, rising and falling, snapping out the rhythm with each of the whips he held, one in each hand. That was the source of the popping. Not one crack at a time, but two and three snaps to each fluid movement as he turned and stepped, and tapped his way through to the end of that Dire Straits song.

When it was over, the music paused long enough for him to reset himself. Head slightly bowed, he rolled his muscular shoulders, shook the whips out like long snakes in the dust around his feet, and then AC/DC started up. *Thunderstruck.* His foot started tapping. He found the beat, and then he began all over again. Fluid, graceful, line-dancing motions that he so effortlessly filled with a whole new accompaniment of tempo-keeping cracks from his whips.

She caught her breath, suddenly aware that her stomach was tightening and quivering right along with his punctuating music.

Abruptly retreating from the window, Kitty stood for a moment at the table, hands clutching and tightening and adjusting at her towel, feeling at once hot and flustered and confused and scared, and then stupid because she didn't know why. Two tiny steps forward could have carried her back to the window for a second peek, but she made herself turn away.

The heavenly aroma of coffee drifted from the kitchen.

She hugged herself, knowing she ought to get dressed, but also knowing there was no way she was going back into her bedroom. Not now, possibly not ever.

She wandered as far as the living room, stopping again between the dark yawning maw of the hallway leading back to spider-infested doom — and the front door, with its multi-paneled glass windows that provided another peak at Noah out in the yard.

A sparkle of gold drew her eye into the living room. There wasn't a lot of furniture to stumble around or useless decorations, but there were a lot of display boxes hanging on the walls. In each one, attached to a green-felt backcloth, was a coiled brown-plaited whip with a golden plaque the size of a business card. Noah's name was engraved on each one, with the division of whip cracking that he'd won—most of which read simply 'Mens' Champion'—and the year. There were fifteen of them total, and they spanned nine years' worth of achievements.

Scattered among them and along the fireplace mantel were pictures. Some of Noah at various ages; some of other people.

Everybody had whips, and one was a newspaper clipping taken from the local paper in which the headline included both Noah's name and the 2000 Sydney Olympics, where apparently he and others from the Australian Whipcrackers & Plaiters Association had put on the Opening Ceremony and, as the paper put it, opened the eyes of the world to the competitive sport of Australian whip cracking.

She was looking over his framed collection of Guinness World Record titles when the front door suddenly opened and Noah walked in. How she had missed hearing the music shut off, she didn't know. It wasn't as if he were trying to sneak up on her. The heavy tromp of his boots when he crossed the threshold, took one look at her in nothing but a towel, and abruptly stopped, was damn near deafening.

To his credit, he didn't ogle her. He kept his eyes locked with hers and any hint of discernible expression locked tight behind a mask she could not read. It was probably disapproval. It had to be disapproval, though there wasn't so much as a single censuring note in the way he finally said, "Rule Number Five, love. Admittedly, I did only specify shoes, but in my defense, I assumed you would know to put your clobbers on and not to go nuddy about."

Both whips were in his hand, coiled and tied. But every experience she had in regards to whips had taught her how easy it was to make them ready for use again. It would have been so easy, especially with that thought running wild in her head, to be afraid of him. And yet, with his face void of expression, and his tone careful not to be too scolding, he made no move to come at her.

He smelled like sunshine, too, her brain supplied.

Like that should make a difference, she wanted the rest of her to argue, but in some weird way... it did make a difference. It was all she could smell, the sunshine, the dust and leather of his boots, the faint spice of his deodorant or soap, and the warm coffee spreading through the house. It made such a difference that, standing there, staring at him with those whips in his hand, her nipples budded into tight little peaks and a single thump of warm neglect pulsed between her tensing legs. She clutched her towel, tightening her thighs in an effort to kill the sensation, but like ripples on a still pond, that thump spread up through her belly, becoming a series of smaller pulses that she could feel steadily throbbing out through her sex and into her womb.

He was waiting. Expecting her to say something, but her throat was too tight. She thrust out her arm, pointing toward her bedroom.

He tipped his head.

"Th-there's death in my room," she finally managed.

He didn't exactly smile, but his eyebrows arched. "Death?"

"It went under the bed."

"I see. All right." Faintly bemused, he dropped his whips on the end of the dining table and headed down the hall.

Her feet rooted her to the floor, but the farther he went, the stronger the pull became for her to follow. Helplessly, she gave in. He was pushing open her bedroom door before she found the courage to slip into the hallway behind him. By the time she reached her temporary bedroom door, he was cautiously picking through her fallen bedding.

Oh God, she'd forgotten about the strap. She clutched her towel tighter, praying he wouldn't notice, but he did. Picking it up, he said nothing, he simply put it on the bed next to her wadded up quilt. Getting down on his knees, he looked underneath.

"Well, hello there," he said and reached into the shadows beneath.

"Oh my God." Her body erupted in a whole new wave of spasmatic shivers. She ran back to the bathroom, quickly shutting the door so she wouldn't have to see him climbing to his feet with that spider in his hand.

The heavy clump of his boots travelled past the bathroom door and down the hall.

"Get your clobbers on," he called from the front door. And in a softer voice, no doubt to the spider, he crooned, "Sheilas, yeah? They just don't understand. When the mating call hits, sometimes a bloke has to go walk-about. Go on with you. Betcha there's a girlfriend under the porch."

She heard the unmistakable open and closing of the front door again.

Prickling tingles danced all the way up her back and down into the hardened points that her nipples had become. She was stranded in Australia, in the middle of nowhere, with the Spider Whisperer.

And why in the hell was her pussy throbbing to that?

CHAPTER 6

*B*y the time Kitty got her act together and her clothes on, all the spider-induced fear she had felt earlier had morphed into a deep sense of embarrassment. On the other hand, she had never in her life checked the inside of her shoes quite as thoroughly as she did before she slipped her feet into them. And when she walked back down the hall to see where Noah had gone, what she found was the coffee completely made, but untouched. The breakfast preparations were still sitting on the stove. Noah was also sitting, but at the table, reading a newspaper.

"They're saying record highs today," he mentioned, as if it were the most casual thing in the world that she be left standing in the middle of his kitchen, at a complete loss for what to do. Everything in here felt like a silent directive and yet, it wasn't one she was familiar with.

Out in the dining room, Noah had positioned himself at the head of the table, legs crossed and comfortable in his chair. The closest to him, however, had been pulled out. Again, another silent directive, complete with the brightly-colored cover of a magazine and another newspaper neatly folded on top of it. He never said one word, but it felt like a choice. She could either go out there and sit down, or... she looked from the hot coffeemaker to the items on the stove.

A current of absolute electrified nervousness shot from the back of her head all the way down her spine, jolting into her hands and her legs. Her fingers buzzed from the scariness. Was this a test to see if she'd do the obedient thing? What was the obedient thing, making him breakfast or joining him at the table until he told her what he wanted her to do?

A second electrifying jolt hit her—part terror, part... was this excitement? She couldn't tell, she hadn't felt such a thing in so long—but maybe, what he was waiting for her to do was serve him.

Hands shaking, she hesitantly picked up one of the two waiting coffee mugs.

"Two creams, love," Noah said, turning the folded paper over to continue reading. "One sugar, if you please."

It felt surreal, but she fixed him a cup and would have brought it to him, but he stopped her when he said, "Make yourself one too, if you like. I prefer we have our coffee together."

She hesitated. Ethen had preferred to be served first. Always. It felt very odd to pause and make herself a cup of coffee with Noah still waiting for his. Then what was she going to do, sit at the table and drink it with him?

An ocean of anxiety pricked by the unknown swelling inside her, Kitty carried both mugs out to the table. It felt surprisingly good when she finally set his cup in front of him. It felt like the tiniest, most insignificant return to normal.

Conversely, it felt awkward as hell to sit on the chair he'd so obviously pulled out for her, but that didn't last long. The second her butt made contact with the hard wood of the seat, Noah set his newspaper aside, scooted back his chair and, with a smile that seemed perfectly genuine and completely lacking any ominous foreboding of punishments to come, announced, "I'll make the tucker."

And leave her sitting here, with coffee in her hands while *he* served *her?*

Erupting out of her chair, Kitty ran back to the kitchen. She ducked behind the stove, shaking her hands as though they were covered in ants as she fitfully paced in tight, tiny, silent circles. From refrigerator to wall, she was careful to stay well back from the open doorway so he wouldn't see it. He was testing her. This felt like a test. It had to be a test, and she'd failed it somehow, she was sure of it. Dropping to a squat, she hugged her instantly roiling stomach, squeezing tight until the queasiness subsided, then covered her eyes with a shaky hand and pulled her stupid self together.

Standing, she rolled her shoulders and then she made the breakfast.

She didn't know how he liked anything and she was too afraid she'd be censured for asking. Pony made the breakfasts and she always made everything the same way: toast lightly toasted, eggs over medium, bacon crispy but not burnt. Hadlee had done breakfasts when Kitty had been staying with them. Breakfasts at Garreth's house had been toast and cereal with milk. Sometimes fruit. Sometimes donuts. Sometimes oatmeal, because Hadlee did everything she could to avoid the old comfort of routine.

Uncertainty making her sick to her stomach, Kitty copied Pony's routine to the best of her ability. Unfortunately, the bacon was too thick and didn't quite cook up the same. She overcooked the yolks and, having no idea what to do with the Vegemite, she put a dollop on top of each egg. She had another mini panic attack before she brought his plate and set it in front of him. Heading back into the kitchen, she quietly panicked in another round of tight, tiny, hand-shaking circles, wondering if she'd done anything to his preference.

He wasn't eating. Out in the dining room, she heard him turn the page of his newspaper and refold it before continuing to read.

He was waiting for her to come back to the table. It was the only preference he had made clear. If he wanted her to sit and drink with him, he probably wanted her to eat with him too. Had she forgotten anything? Had she brought him everything he might need? Because if he jumped up the minute she sat down again, the stress alone was going to kill her.

Unable to stand the tension, she peeked around the wall far enough to check. But no, he still wasn't eating. His plate remained untouched in front of him, his eggs getting cold.

Her throat was so tight it was choking her. "Did I do it wrong?"

"Not at all." He paused his reading long enough to cast a smile at his plate, and then directed it at her. "I'm waiting for you, love. We'll eat together."

He winked, then went back to his paper, content to wait her out.

She couldn't tell if that made the tangling knots in her stomach better or worse. She did, however, know the more she fretted, the more unsettled her stomach became. She rubbed it while she considered what out of anything she'd cooked that she might actually eat and keep down. Toast. She could probably handle toast.

She made a single slice and took it out to the table dry. When she sat down, he promptly stood up, fulfilling her worst-case scenario. She tried to jump up too, but his hand on her shoulder stopped her. Taking her plate, he went back into the kitchen, leaving her to sit at the table. Shoulders slumping, she listened with growing guilt to the calm clatter of a man making another breakfast. The pop of the toaster added another slice to her plate; the crackle of a hot pan and the scrape of a spatula added an egg. She felt scolded and so far, Noah hadn't said a word.

Ethen would have been annoyed and he'd have banged things so everyone would know it. But then, annoyed or not, Kitty couldn't quite picture him making her breakfast. He was far more apt to take her plate, throw the contents to the hogs and banish her from the table. He barely made food for himself; she had never known him to fix anything for someone else.

But, Noah didn't do that. He didn't bang anything. Once or twice, as she listened to the soft scrap of a spatula in the bottom of the frying pan, she thought she heard him humming. He had a nice hum. It dipped into the low side of tenor. She had no idea what melody it was.

A few minutes later, out he came again and set her plate once more before her. The toast was thoroughly buttered and he'd spread a thin cover of greenish-brown Vegemite all over it.

She stared from her plate to his as he sat down.

Savoring a swallow of coffee, he picked up his fork. "Let's eat."

Kitty picked up her fork, but by now his breakfast was cold and she was painfully aware of what she'd done wrong. She'd put the green stuff on his eggs instead of his toast.

"Good job," he said anyway, savoring his first bite of bacon.

It couldn't have been that good. It was cold. She picked at her toast, which was still warm, and shredded the crusty edges, too uncomfortable to eat. "I didn't know the vege-whatever was supposed to go on the bread," she said. It was all she could do not to cringe because she hadn't meant for that to come out sounding so pathetically self-criticizing.

"No harm in trying something new." Cutting into his egg, he plopped a bite onto his toast and bit into it. "Mm." He chewed, nodded and then looked at her.

Expectantly.

Her stomach knotted again. "What?"

"I'm wondering," he said, as if that should answer all for her.

Kitty waited for him to elaborate, but he only took another bite. He offered zero complaints and frankly, there was nothing worse than cold eggs. Or lukewarm coffee, for that matter. This was so alien to anything she was familiar with. She was so sure any minute his temper would erupt, it was all she could do to keep up with the conversation. "Wondering what?"

"Whether or not you realize you had choices this morning." Pushing the newspaper away from his plate, he leaned back in his chair. "There were no wrong answers, you know. If you'd come sat at the table, I'd have gone and made the coffee and the brekkie. You didn't. In fact, it actually made you uncomfortable when I fixed your plate. Why is that, do you think?"

He may as well ask why the sky was blue. Kitty didn't know that answer, either. She blinked at him, the silence stretching on into what Ethen would have viewed as defiance, but she couldn't think what to say.

She shredded her toast too, but she didn't realize she'd picked it all to pieces until he pointed at her plate.

"Sorry, love. I do want you to eat that. Every single bite. I don't care how small you make the crumbs first. Nobody starves themselves in my house, at my table. Rule Number Seven."

She stared at her shaking hands, then tucked them into her lap, clenching them tight because she didn't understand why she couldn't make herself stop trembling. "I-I don't think I can eat."

"Why not?"

"I... I'm not... n-not hungry."

"Are you pregnant?" he asked pointblank.

Kitty snapped her eyes to his. She couldn't open her mouth; she was terrified she'd throw up right then and there. She shook her head.

"Are you running a fever, do you think? Should I take your temperature? Via your mouth," he specified after a brief pause. "I'll save the bum for when the situation deserves it."

Exactly what kind of situation would deserve it, she almost asked, but stopped herself in time. Her face felt hot. Her breathing had quickened, though she tried to slow it down. There was nothing about the way he was looking at her, his body language or the tone of his voice that should make what he was saying sound threatening, and yet her brain kept trying to twist it that way.

"I-I'm fine." She shivered.

"Going without eating for prolonged periods can make a body feel sick to their stomach. So can stress and anxiety, and heaven knows you've had reason enough for both. But it's time to stop now." For the first time, a measure of steel wove itself into his voice. "Your body needs to heal, love, and to do that, you need to eat. In this matter, I will not be argued with."

The temptation to do just that—argue—leapt into the back of her throat so fast she had to lock her teeth to keep it from bursting free. She could hear it, the unspoken, 'or what' that reverberated on the back of her tongue, an ill-thought out challenge she never, no matter what the provocation, would have spewed at Ethen.

But Noah wasn't Ethen. Noah wasn't anything but a friend of a friend. The guy putting her up in his spare bedroom for a while.

The guy who had made her breakfast.

And cleared her room of spiders.

The one who was right now, sitting to the side of her, one hand in his lap, the other resting lightly beside his plate, idly rubbing his thumb against one finger while he waited for her to either obey or work up the nerve to go ahead and issue that challenge he obviously expected. Maybe he could hear it in the silence now stretching out again between them. Or maybe, he could see it, lurking in the back of her guilt-laden eyes.

She picked up the biggest shred of toast and put it in her mouth. It was still faintly warm, soft from the butter he'd put on it. Ethen considered butter an extravagance and something to be enjoyed only by him, not his Menagerie. Kitty didn't realize how much she'd missed it until the creamy taste touched her tongue. Her eyes closed of their own accord. Then the Vegemite hit her taste buds and Kitty's face screwed into a grimace.

"Good, isn't it?" All of that prior severity melted into his next grin.

She covered her mouth, not sure what to make of the strong,

grassy flavor. If she'd had a napkin, she would have discretely spit it out. She didn't. Reluctantly, she made herself chew.

"Let's go back to what we were talking about." Scooping more egg onto his toast, Noah said, "I'm going to do something I don't like to do and make an assumption, so correct me if I'm wrong: Are you a service submissive?" He gestured to her plate. "Try some of the egg on the toast."

He'd smeared that Vegemite crap with sadistic evenness over both toast slices. It was on every piece she'd picked apart and the last thing she wanted was to put more of that against her tongue. And yet, she obediently dipped a small shred of crust in her egg and put it in her mouth. Surprisingly, the yolkiness did make the green stuff more palatable.

"Yeah?" Noah said, smiling as if to say, *It's good, right?*

She wasn't quite willing to go that far, but she did manage to swallow.

"So," he said, getting back to the main topic, seemingly without noticing she hadn't answered his last question. "Most service submissives that I know personally—admittedly, it's only been the one. But I did live with her for a couple years and, believe me, that was long enough to know there was no faster way to plummet her into the depths of absolute depression than by stripping her of everything she did to serve."

The knots in Kitty's chest were so tight, her heart felt strangled by them. It hurt, but she dared not reveal that. He was seeing too much as it was and it scared her. Frozen in her chair, she chewed her next bite until it lost all its flavor.

"Conversely," he added, "there was no faster way to bring her back into her element than by allowing her to perform those things she considered to be her set tasks. Your egg is almost gone. You're doing good. Take another bite, please."

She wasn't even tasting the egg anymore. "What are you telling me?"

"I'm saying I have a job here. My job is to work for a living, keep a roof over our heads, put food on the table and make sure you're safe for as long as it takes you to learn how to trust it. But, what does that leave you right? It's not like you can walk into Cooktown and find a job. You're not from here. Legally, you can't work, but that doesn't mean we can't find you something to do."

He was going to demand sex from her now. Kitty waited, frozen in dread.

"I figure, I can treat you one of two ways," Noah smiled at her. It was such a handsome smile too. Not that handsome things couldn't hide monsters. God knew she'd learned that lesson thoroughly. "Either I can treat you like a guest, meaning you won't be required to do anything but lounge about, relaxing, resting, and recuperating. Or I can treat you like you live here, in which case certain things will be expected of you."

And here it was. Under the table, her leg started jiggling and wouldn't stop.

"Like what?" Her lips, numb, hardly moved.

"Coffee," he said decisively. "We both drink coffee, so that can be one of them. First thing every morning, a fresh pot of coffee needs to be made. Second, meals. Brekkie by eight, lunch between noon and one, and dinner at seven. I don't mind a spot of tea about four-ish. But if I get called out to work, then that can be iffy, so I'll take care of me own on that. Your last job, total care of the kitchen. I relinquish all control of it. That means you can do anything you want—rearrange the cupboards, paint the cupboards. So long as you take care of it and treat everything in there with the respect it deserves, then that is your domain. Which doesn't mean I expect you to pick up after me. I don't. I'm a grown-ass man; I can pick up after me self. It doesn't mean you'll be a sheila stuck in the kitchen all day if you hate it, either. It means, for the next couple of days you've got a job. After that, if you want to stick with it, you can keep your job as long as you like. If you want to switch to something else, then all you have to do is say so and we'll see what we can arrange. What do you think?"

She'd been braced for so much worse, for so long now, that her nerves no longer knew how to settle for anything less than absolute panic. She almost got up and walked away from the table before the full meaning—and sexual lack thereof—of his words finally permeated all that baseless certainty that her brain had built up.

"The kitchen?" she echoed, a startled pang bursting in the pit of her stomach.

"For a start." He took the last bite of his breakfast before pushing his plate aside in favor of nursing his coffee mug. He watched her, that incredibly relaxed and super personable smile on his face. The one that said he was nothing but trustworthy and would never hurt anyone, including her. She trembled, knowing better than to believe it.

And yet, where was the threat? She rubbed her hands against her hips. There was a trap waiting for her somewhere, but she couldn't see it. What she could see was how unbearable it would be if she didn't have something to do with her time. Like at Hadlee and Garreth's house, where they'd all but jumped to assure her she didn't have to help them every time she tried. As if she were too fragile to cook a meal or wash a load of clothes, or sweep a damn floor. After that first week, she couldn't even lose herself in her job; Ethen had stolen that from her too. He'd left her with nothing to do but stand in front of a window all day, staring out… sometimes at him.

She shuddered.

"I can do that," she finally agreed.

"Good." His smile widened, even as he hid it behind another sip of his coffee. "Finish your breakfast, please, and we'll move on to the next issue."

She still had half an egg left and a lot of shredded toast on her plate. Shifting in her seat, she picked up her fork and tried to sop up loose breadcrumbs with her egg. "What other issue?"

"Rule Number Eight," he said, taking another swig of coffee before lowering his cup to the table. His fingers remained hooked in the handle. He looked so relaxed, so calm, and yet the bomb he dropped was brutal enough to shake her. "In this house, submissives are allowed neither to discipline themselves, nor to pleasure themselves."

He'd seen. Somehow last night, without her hearing him or knowing it, he'd seen her doing... oh God! Kitty shoved back from the table, vaulting up from her chair before she knew she was going to move.

"Sit down," Noah ordered, the quiet thunder of his suddenly steely voice as sharp as the crack of his whip had been earlier. That sharpness snapped beneath her panic and the submissive in her reacted. As fast as she'd shot to her feet, Kitty was back in her chair.

"You're not my submissive," he said, that note of steel that had so completely bound her to his will melting once more into softness. "Sadly, right now you're not anybody's submissive and I think that might be a huge part of the problem."

Now, here it came. The seedy order thinly disguised as an offer. A choice that wasn't really one at all. Jesus, how stupid could she be?

He tipped his head, the corners of his mouth curling even as his eyes narrowed. "Do you think I'm going to offer you my dominance?"

Something on her face must have given away the direction her wildly churning thoughts had shot in. Despite that curl, he wasn't smiling anymore. Although he hadn't moved, he didn't look quite as relaxed either.

"Aren't you?" She locked her hands in her lap to quell their shaking, but it didn't work.

"There is no way for me to do that right now without violating your consent."

Tiny shivers danced through her, up the backs of her legs, across the flesh of her belly and her back, all the way up into her breasts. Her nipples peaked, at instant odds with nearly all the rest of her, including her mouth. "Why would you want to do that?"

She could have bit her own tongue off. Why would she say that? Why *that* of all things? Not, what makes you think I would give you consent? Or even, what makes you think I would welcome that? She didn't know Noah. She wasn't comfortable around him. He scared her, but then everything scared her. So really, that hardly ranked as an argument.

"I don't believe you are in the right place mentally for me to do that," he said bluntly. "I'm not comfortable at this point in entering into anything binding, not even as simple play partners. But that is what you need. Isn't it?"

Her shivers grew shivers.

His thumb lightly tapped the table as he studied her. "It's the reason you crawled into bed last night, clinging to my old strap, and cried yourself to sleep."

Her heart fluttered, the vibrations of which she felt echoed all the way down through her stomach and in between her thighs. She squeezed her legs together. Hidden in her lap, her hands became fists. She fought to keep her breathing even and her expression properly masked, but inside, all she could think was: What else? Had he seen her touch herself? Had he seen her being Kitty-girl? Oh God, had he seen that?

"It's the reason you crawled through the house in the middle of the night," he said, sinking both her stomach and her arousal and, for a fraction of a second, making it impossible for her to breathe. "I think you washed the dishes I said could wait, because you couldn't bear the thought of them sitting in the sink. What else can't you bear, love?"

She couldn't hold his unwavering stare and yet, she couldn't make herself look away.

"Do you even know?" he wondered out loud.

Her chest felt so tight, it was strangling her heart. Her stomach was a nest of serpentine knots all flexing and tightening, and yet her nipples felt hard, swollen, aching to be touched. Pinched. Rolled, between the thumb and fingers he rested on the table when he could just as easily have reached out and caught her. Hurting her the way bad Kittys deserved to be hurt... needed to be hurt.

Her shallow breaths shook. Her pussy heated and throbbed. Unable to stop herself from asking, instead of a question, it came out a plea: "Do you know?"

He tipped his head, a single nod that made the shivers inside her go wild.

"What?" She was almost afraid of the answer.

"I know how to give you exactly what you need, and I will," he promised. "But if you want it, you're going to have to do one thing first."

She struggled to swallow. "What?"

"You're going to have to ask."

CHAPTER 7

The moment he said 'ask,' Kitty froze in a mix of anxiety, disbelief, and despair. She pulled away from both the table and him, every inch of her verged on running. Yet, she didn't. Something stronger kept her rooted while he said, "I'm offering you scenes, love. Nothing deeper or more lasting than that. But if you need it, and if you can work up the courage to come to me, I promise I will give you exactly what you crave each and every time."

She shoved her plate away from her, as if it were a physical representation of his offer. She still had half a breakfast left to finish before he intended to let her leave his table, but he knew when and where to pick his battles. His current engagement was far more important.

"Y-you..." Kitty tried to laugh, but her shivery breaths wouldn't let her. It came out too high-pitched and shuddery, and on the side of her neck, her pulse danced a frantic beat that he could see. "Y-you can't possibly..."

"I know," he assured her. Only a very new dominant—or an unobservant one—could take more than a glance at her in this condition and not know what she needed more than anything was relief. Her shoulders were hunched under a burden she didn't know how to bear. She stared at the table, looking small and lost and far too thin for a woman of her height. She needed to eat. She needed to put roundness back into her face, the slight bumps of her breasts and the boniness of her hips. She needed rest and, if nothing else, to ease the bruise-like half-moons beneath eyes that would have been lovely if they weren't so damned haunted. "I know."

Had he blinked, he might have missed the way her chin lifted, the tiniest hint of 'prove it' creeping into her eyes. She wasn't quite brave enough to say it out loud, however. Someone had beat that out of her. He couldn't help wondering if it were too late to coax it back in.

"Would you like a sample of what you can expect?" he softly challenged her. His hand itched for an immediate follow through —seize her by the hair, drag her out of her chair and straight to the floor. He could almost feel the back of her head under his boot. He could almost see the lines of her body relaxing as she gave herself up to total subjugation.

The look in her haunted eyes said she already regretted her minute, unspoken defiance, and yet he thought he glimpsed a flicker of... what, hope? Wistfulness?

Oh yes, she might be hesitating, but she was curious. Wry humor pulled at the corners of his mouth, but he suppressed it, not wanting her to think he was laughing at her. "You know what you have to do to get it."

Her knee beneath the table was jiggling again, bouncing fitfully up and down. It made all the rest of her tremble, though he suspected she might have trembled anyway. Her lips certainly were. The tip of her tongue darted out far enough to wet them. Her eyes were a battlefield of longing and doubt, and as the seconds ticked on into minutes with no answer coming from her, he began to think that might, in fact, be his answer. He was about to stand, lay his hand on her shoulder—if she actually allowed him to touch her at this point—and tell her his offer would stand for as long as she might need it, but she broke first.

"Please," she haltingly whispered. Proving once and for all, it truly was the magic word. It was also as close to asking as he was in the mood to require.

"Go to your bedroom. I want you standing at the foot of your bed, the strap in your hand. Be ready when I get there. Go on," he said gently, when she made no move to obey. Her trembling had intensified. If he did nothing else today, he hoped he might help banish some of that fear. "What's my name, Kitty?"

She blinked twice. He hadn't realized how unfocused her eyes had become until suddenly she locked them on him again. She'd been staring right at him, but it wasn't him that she'd been seeing; he was sure of it.

"Noah," she quavered.

"Go on, then."

She got up from the table, leaving her half-finished plate. Her soft footsteps retreated down the hall. He listened as she paused at the bathroom, then slipped inside. He listened carefully, but there was no sound of vomiting, which he took as a positive sign. The water did run, though, but only briefly. Then the door opened and she continued on to the bedroom.

He heard the rustle of the closet door open and wire clothes hangers knock together. He heard her take up her position at the foot of the bed. Were this any other time and were she any other submissive, standing in her penitent pose to contemplate what had sent her there and what was yet to come, he'd have left her there to think a while. Ten minutes, maybe more. But she was frightened enough as it was, and that wasn't the point of this.

Draining all that was left of his coffee, Noah got up to follow her. With every step, he checked himself. He found his center of calm, but the Dom inside him was already perking. He had tremors of his own as he approached her open bedroom door. She hadn't turned on the light, creating echoes of last night's illicit view into what he seriously hoped had not been her bedtime ritual for long. If so, that ritual was about to be permanently interrupted.

He turned on the light. No one else was in the house, but he still closed the door behind him. Not because he thought she might run, but because it enclosed them in that tiny backroom together. Increasing the intimacy between them. Could she feel the vibrancy of his authority as clearly as he could feel the warring emotions inside her? Her fear was palpable and that was what he attacked first.

Standing exactly where he'd ordered her to, her hands moved on the strap's handle, clutching and re-clutching with spastic nervousness. He could see the trembling of her knees even through her pants. That trembling did not ease the closer he came. He took the strap from her, moving it to his right hand out of her sight and her reach. He took her by the throat with his left.

That was a risky move. She might have panicked, especially if what he was doing now in any way echoed abuse inflicted by her last dom. But she didn't and he was careful to keep his touch firm, but light. He didn't apply pressure, but he did hold her, his fingers resting lightly on her pulse. It jumped erratically beneath his fingertips, especially when he shifted close enough to bring his mouth to her ear. She shook, all of her, a thoroughly battered leaf still lost in the storms of her past.

"This isn't a punishment," he murmured, letting his thumb stroke the curve of her neck. "I want you to remember that. You haven't done anything wrong; you aren't in trouble; I am not angry. This is a cleansing. This is just you and me, lighting a fire hot enough to burn away the ghosts. We can do this as often as you need, whenever you need, even if you must wake me in the middle of the night. Your safeword is red, and you will use it if for any reason you want me to stop. Is that clear?"

She swallowed hard, her tense throat moving against his palm. Her nod was barely a quiver, but it was assent and he accepted it.

"You may not keep your pants on. I need to see the damage I'm doing. Take them down."

Her hands were shaking so badly now she barely managed it, but he didn't help her. She needed to do this on her own and he had all the time in the world. His hand kept its hold on her throat, even when she bent to push her jeans down over her hips. Gravity dropped them as far as her knees.

"Repeat after me," he said, shifting his grip from the front of her throat to the nape of her neck. When he applied gentle pressure, she haltingly bent over the metal footrail. "I'm a good girl."

Her hands fisted against the patchwork quilt as her cheek came to rest upon it. Her eyes were huge, her face pale. Her lips barely moved and there was little sound to it when she whispered, "I'm a good girl."

"I'm safe." He stroked her back between her shoulders, every inch of her feeling as tense and tight as a drum.

"I'm s-safe." Her teeth chattered.

From shoulders to hip, he did his best to soothe her with both his touch and the calm of his voice. "I am loved."

"I'm loved."

"I don't need to be afraid of anything."

Her eyebrows quirked. She opened her mouth, but nothing came out. He waited while she struggled to give voice to the lie, and that was okay. It might be a lie right now, but it wasn't always going to be. He would make sure of that.

"Good girl," he said, once she'd repeated the phrase. Patting her hip, he raised the hem of her shirt well off the target area. She had a small bottom, clad in a thin pair of white daisy-print panties. Her spine was too prominent for his taste. So were her hips.

Eventually, he would take care of that, too.

He gave her bottom a readying caress. An experienced dom, he'd taken many play partners. Every year, he took mini touring vacations to show off his whip skills, teaching it to others in exchange for a little traveling cash and places to stay along the way. It was a great way to see the world without emptying the wallet. In the process, he saw a lot of sights, made a lot of friends, and couldn't count the number of submissives he'd topped—place after place, year after year. Some he'd whipped, some he'd spanked, most he'd fondled—little rubs like this, the tactical pleasure of a dominant man making physical contact with the submissive in his care. It was both deeply sexual and not at all sexual, and God knew, while he hadn't fucked all—or hell, even half of them—he was not a monk. But this touch, this first contact of his bare hand to what wasn't even her naked ass, was instantly the most seductive he'd felt in a very long time.

Ethen, the asshole, had obviously taught her well. Her head was down, her ass up. Hips thrust back to offer her bottom with her legs widely spread. Without needing direction, she'd made herself open to him. Even with her panties still up and all the feminine parts of her still covered, she was available to him. He wouldn't at all have minded peeling that cotton cloth down and letting it fall on top of her divested jeans. He wouldn't have minded filling his palm with the curve of first one buttock and then the other, squeezing and molding her flesh with his grip. He wouldn't even have minded giving her a few roving smacks, just flesh to flesh, in a way that would have warmed her up for what was yet to come and yet, this was a test. Kitty was grading him now, and soft gentle pats or even warmups was not what she wanted.

She wanted relief. She wanted absolution from the horde of sins—real or imagined—clawing at her back. If he ever met Ethen a second time, he was going to feed the man his own teeth, but for now Noah put his mind where it needed to be. Taking his hand off Kitty's trembling backside, he stepped back into position.

"Say it for me again," he told her, shifting his grip on the strap, letting it become an extension of his ready arm. She'd chosen the

89

widest one, the same one she'd taken to bed with her last night. Two strokes would cover the whole of her small bottom. Every stroke after that would ignite a painful fire, building on it lash after lash, without mercy or pause until the movements of her writhing body let him know she was done. That wasn't going to happen any time soon. He could tell by looking at her, she'd been haunted for so long she didn't know how to let go of it. He was going to have to show her. "I want you to repeat each phrase after every stroke I give you."

She hesitated, her brow furrowing further.

"I am a good girl," Noah supplied, helping her remember how it started.

"I-I'm a good girl," she whispered, and he struck.

It wasn't his hardest blow, but it wasn't gentle. And yet, the only sign she showed as her flesh absorbed the impact was the catch in her breath and the tightening of her knuckles against the multicolored quilt. Her bottom barely flinched, though he knew it had to hurt.

Oh yeah, Ethen had 'taught' her all right.

"I am safe," he prodded her.

All the pain he hadn't seen in her reaction was right there, trembling in the whimper of her voice as she repeated, "I am safe."

The crack of the strap wrapped the base of her buttocks, hugging them in its painful embrace.

Her breath caught again, but she didn't so much as arch onto her toes. Anyone else would have been squirming. Noah frowned, not at all liking what he saw.

"I am loved." Her voice broke.

There was no help for it, but to whip where he'd already struck.

Her hands spasmed—her fingers snapping open, then clawing up tight again. She made no sound apart from a shaky exhale.

What was it with doms who robbed their submissives of the cathartic freedom of expressing their pain in movement. Bucking, writing, crying—there was beauty to be seen in the full wallow of the hurt as it engulfed them.

"I-I-I d-don't ha-have—" She blinked rapidly against the shine of rising tears.

"To be afraid of anything," he said, helping her through it, and swung.

The crack of the strap filled the tiny room, sharp as a gunshot and the impact low enough to catch not only the lower swells of her bottom but the excruciatingly sensitive sit-spot as well.

Kitty's mouth gaped in the scream she refused to let out. Her ass and thighs shook, her will fighting back against the involuntary reaction of muscles locked in a fight for self-preservation.

Noah touched her bottom again, offering caressing comfort as he checked her. He could feel the heat of her pain rising through the layers of already swelling flesh and the pale cloth of her panties. Bright swathes of crimson extended out beyond the hug of white elastic to stain both sides of her bottom and even down onto the tops of her thighs. That color marked the extent of his target, he would go no further than that. He didn't need to.

"This isn't a punishment," he reminded, cupping first one burning ass cheek and then the other. "This is a cleansing. Take all the time you need. We'll continue when you say; it's over when you say."

Kitty sucked a hard breath. Her mouth clamped shut against the scream she would not let escape. Her teeth gritted fast to swallow it back. Through them, she started the count over. "I'm a good girl!" she snarled, and burst into tears.

He didn't need the full force of his arm to make it hurt like hell, but the sound of impact made it sound as if he had.

"I'm safe!" she shrieked, her perfect pose faltering under the tiniest hip twist. Her toes dug against the hardwood floor, scraping the wood as she fought not to squirm as the strap wrapped her ass in another fiery hold. "I'm loved!"

She gave herself no time to recover, so neither did he.

She screamed, "I don't have to be afraid of anything!"

He struck her sitspot directly and he spared her nothing.

For the first time, she broke position. Her legs snapped together, her feet snapping up to cover her fiery red bottom. She sobbed. She also started over again, and so did he. He gave her what she needed, pausing only long enough to wait for her to put her feet down or move her hands when she forgot herself. Stroke after stroke, phrase after phrase, until she lost all articulation and could only garble those key words into bedding now soaked with tears. She never said her safeword. She never got up, or tried to crawl over the footrail. And though eventually he did take her to twisting and bucking and struggling in expression of the hurt that consumed her, she never once tried to fight the strap.

He stopped when she was crying too hard even to mouth her phrases. Laying the strap on the floor, he hunkered down beside her, rubbing her back and stroking her hair. He caressed her bottom, measuring the hard spots where the swelling was the worst, but finding no blisters or split skin. He had lotion in the other room, but he was loathe to leave her long enough even to go get it. At least, not until her tears eventually dwindled into hiccups and sniffles.

He had to help her over the footrail. She made no effort to crawl into his lap, which he wouldn't have minded and, for a moment, almost regretted. But this wasn't about him. So he helped her up far enough for her to collapse upon her pillows. Her face was hot and red. The moment she touched the pillows, sobbing, she melted into them.

Brushing her dark, tussled hair back from her face, Noah checked, but her eyes were already closed. Already the sobs were breaking into gasps, and already those were easing into deeper, even breaths. She looked peaceful. A corner of his mouth lifted. She looked as if she were already sleeping.

She was quite lovely like this. All that long brown hair and soft, pale skin, her pants still tangled around her ankles and her bottom on absolute fire. He took her shoes off, then her pants so she might be comfortable in the fiery aftermath. She didn't rub her bottom once; Noah tried to resist, but he couldn't help rubbing it for her.

She mewed, the softest of protests. More a whimper really, but she didn't try to stop him. What she did do, was roll less on her side and more on her belly, giving him full access to the hurt he'd inflicted, and now tried to soothe.

He kept his touch on the summits of her cheeks. He did not dip his fingers down into the shadowy valley between her slightly parted thighs. Would he find her wet if he did, the way so many submissives became even when the pain was too much for them? His fingertips tingled to wander, but he stuck to his resolve until it became overwhelmingly clear that she was too much a temptation. The longer he fondled her, the more he ached to slip his hands beneath the elastic of her panties to feel the burning of her flesh directly against his palm, skin to skin. Flesh to flesh. Dom to sub.

He took his hand off her. She was lying on the quilt, but he untucked it and folded the wide length up over her so she would be covered. She never once opened her eyes, so he left her there to sleep.

Noah was almost out the door when he heard her mumble, "If that wasn't punishment, I don't ever want to make you mad."

The blood was pounding in his veins, the allure of her pulling him to come back to her. Maybe even to lie down beside her, roll her into his arms, comfort her tiny body with his. Only sheer force of will kept him from taking that first damning step.

"I don't punish when I'm angry," he said, for the record. "I also don't spank when it's real. And no, love, you don't want to know what my punishments are like."

Her only response was a sigh, seductively soft and filled with longing. She curled into her pillow, and Noah walked out the door while he still could.

He closed it to give her privacy, feeling nothing but the rawness of his desire to go back inside. The low, throbbing ache of his fully erect cock, thrusting stiff against the front of his jeans. He looked down at himself.

So much for his center of calm.

God. If he weren't so aroused, this would almost be embarrassing.

CHAPTER 8

*A*ustralia was nothing if not persistent. It waited a few days for the heat Noah had seared into her backside and all the tenderness of her strapping to fade, and then it tried to kill her again. This time, her imminent death took the form of the straggliest, grumpiest koala she'd ever seen.

There was a world of difference, as it turned out, between being a burdensome guest, bound to the kindness of a keeper, and being a guest with an assigned task. Noah was right. She wasn't a citizen, so she couldn't get a job in his country. But the task Noah gave her served its purpose. It felt good to do something. To be ruled by the clock and another's expectations. To be needed.

Some might have thought it sexist and degrading to be commanded to care for his kitchen, but Kitty didn't mind it, especially since Noah very quickly proved he didn't go out of his way to make messes, he treated her with respect and he made zero sexual advances against her. Zero. She found that both comforting and, in a way, disappointing.

On that first day, once she woke up from her nap, Kitty cleaned up after breakfast and scrubbed down the sink, counters and stove. She served a simple lunch of sandwiches at twelve. He was out at the time, so she put everything in the fridge and waited at the window, watching until she finally spotted him coming up from the barn around one. She had to hurry to get everything on the table before he entered the house and barely made it in time, but it felt good. Like, major accomplishment good. His simple 'thank you' made her ridiculously happy, too, though she hid all signs of it so he wouldn't see. Past experience could be a cruel teacher, and she didn't want him to say anything to ruin how she felt. No cutting criticism of what she could have done to make lunch better, what she might have forgot, and, if nothing at all was wrong with the food, then what might be wrong with her instead.

In fact, she was so afraid of what he *might* say, that she tried to hide in the kitchen so she wouldn't have to join him at the table.

"Rule Number Nine," he said from the kitchen doorway, smiling even as he tipped her a stern look. "We eat at the table together. Every meal. Every time."

It felt weird to sit with him, as if they were equals. Not only for breakfast, but again for lunch and then again when she got tea on the table at four, even though he'd told her not to. In fact, she'd sat at many an awkward table since she'd left Ethen, and so far, it hadn't gotten any easier. It was hard to shake the belief she didn't belong on a chair. It became even harder when she felt herself on the verge of doing kitten things, especially with Noah sitting right there. He liked to talk during meals, and he had a way of chatting that made her forget to watch her behavior, especially when getting up and down off her chair. She almost went to hands and knees twice at lunchtime. That was very scary, but by teatime, her concerns took a very different direction. That was when her stomach turned against her.

After feeling perfectly fine for most of the morning and afternoon, the minute she took that first sip of tea, her stomach rolled, then heaved, sending Kitty dashing to the bathroom, where she then lived for almost two hours. Leaned up against the wall by the toilet, wishing she would either hurry up and die... or that

Noah would. At least then, he'd stop fussing at her. But no, he brought her tea and crackers as fast as she threw it all up. He pulled her hair back from her face and rubbed her back through the worst of the heaving, and before it was fully over, he forcibly tucked her into bed with a bucket and made her stay there while he went into town and brought back burgers for dinner. The smell of it made her want to throw up all over again until, the clock having ticked beyond some magic point around seven, the crackers and tea finally overcame the nausea and she became ravenous.

"Feel better?" Noah asked, as she came staggering out of bed. For the first time in a long time, she ate an entire hamburger in one sitting. She even ate the chips that came with it. The only thing she didn't eat was the pregnancy test he set on the table by her plate.

"I'm not pregnant." She pushed the kit away from her and refused to touch it again. So there it sat, for several days like a silent accusation during each new bout of nausea, all of which struck in the afternoon, no matter what she did, only to magically end in the evening, leaving her ribs sore from heaving and her belly cramping with hunger... right up until Australia tried to kill her for the fourth time.

It happened at the end of her first week. It was hot for late fall, or so Noah mentioned over breakfast. But to Kitty, it had been hot pretty much every day since she'd arrived. Not that Kitty felt much discomfort in the house. Noah's air-conditioning was fantastic. The unnerving part came when she cooked and cleaned her way through both the kitchen and the day to accompanying scuttles of clawed feet on the porch outside. The koalas were coming down out of the trees to drink from the tub set out for them on the north side. It was such an unsettling sound, but so long as she didn't look out the windows, she could pretend she was hearing nothing more threatening than farm dogs or barn cats moving about. If only she'd stuck to that—that non-window-peeping resolve—then she never would have been tempted to go outside.

Except she did look. Especially when the fighting broke out. She'd never heard such squalling in her life—high-pitched baby-ish shrieks punctuated by deep, baritone belching, following by a lot of clattering and thumping as two or more beasts wrestled each other around the watering trough. It took a lot of neck craning to even catch a glimpse when they were banging into the side of the house, but the wrestling matches tended to end only when one finally knocked the other off the porch and into compliance. Victory was announced via the winner's donkey-like burping, while the loser sat in a heap in the dust, crying like a thoroughly bitten human child. It was horrible and disconcerting and, as it turned out, all for naught, because the first time she noticed a winning koala dip its muzzle into the watering trough, she realized there was no water in it. The trough was bone dry.

Filling that trough was Noah's job and she knew for a fact that he'd already done it that day. She'd seen him on his way around the house while she was making the coffee. But then, it was hot. The koalas must have drunk it all already, which she supposed wasn't entirely unbelievable. The trough was more of a metal pan. Not huge, only big enough to bathe a pug—or a koala—but not deep enough to drown one. Had Noah been up at the house, Kitty had no doubt he would have gone out and promptly filled the pan again. But he wasn't. Like the last two days before, he'd gone down to the barn to do whatever it was that occupied him there, leaving Kitty alone in the cool comfort of the house. Cleaning, and listening to the awful burping of winning koalas, and the cries of losers.

Kitty tried to ignore them, but within ten minutes, another grey beast with a beaked face crawled up onto the porch and the braying, shrieking, belching, baby-cry squalling escalated into wrestling all over again.

Hiding in the house, Kitty listened with growing guilt. She

knew what it was like to be thirsty. Being deprived of food and water was part of the punishment every time Ethen locked her in the box beneath his bed. He hadn't let her out even to go to the bathroom, preferring instead to punish her for the inevitable mess she'd had no choice but to make and then lie in. As horrible as that had been, the thirst had been worse. It had been consuming. By the end, she'd been so desperate and so barren of any moisture in her mouth, nose and throat that her lips had split open and it hurt to breathe.

Oh yes, she knew exactly what those koalas were going through. If she hadn't, she never would have gone outside.

Stepping out into the sunlit heat of the Australian outdoors was easily one of the most terrifying things she'd yet done in her life. It didn't quite rank as high as the night she'd runaway, but it did deserve an honorable mention.

The white-washed porch wrapped all the way around the house, giving her options on how best to attempt this. She crept to her right as far as the corner, but that was where the fighting marsupials were, wrestling and belching at one another, both on and off the porch, up on the railing and out in the yard.

To her left, around the back corner and all down the west side of the house, things were much calmer until she reached the far north corner. Peeking around that, she saw her end destination: the watering trough. The problem was, there were koalas all over the place. Mostly in the trees, and some sitting in the yard. One very small one was sitting not three feet from the empty trough, idly scratching its leg. Its back was to her, its attention focused on a bigger male now belching his victory over the scuffle that had ended. If she could get to the faucet, she could turn the water on now while their attentions were mostly diverted and then she could run before she got bit, burped at, or attacked.

Kitty's heart was in her throat. Her legs were shaking, but she eased around the corner, sneaking as quiet as she could until she was close enough to bend down, stretch out her arm and tickle at the faucet handle with her fingertips. The little koala didn't notice her. The big one, however, did. Its head turned, the beady black eyes locking on her. It might have been her imagination, but she could have sworn the ferocity of his donkey-braying belches intensified as he crawled towards her.

Snagging the faucet, Kitty scrambled to turn it, but it was stuck. Shit! She stretched harder, grabbing it with her whole hand and twisting with all her panic and strength. A gush of water erupted into the dry metal pan, startling the little koala, who let out a baby-cry squeal and fell over. But that gush of water was like a dinner bell to a bunch of starving inmates, and to Kitty's eye these weren't cute, cuddly koala bears crawling straight at her from literally every direction. They were just plain mean.

She would have run, but she never got the chance. As she tried to make her escape, the most straggly, beat-up, grey and brown animal with a vaguely koala-ish face crawled up onto the porch and put itself directly in her escape path.

It came right at her at a pace reserved for sloths and snails, something that should in no way have been half as terrifying as it was. But it did it with beady-eyed malice and claws that scraped the weathered floorboards in ways that sent ice shocks stabbing up her spine. It screamed—that high-pitch baby-cry. So did she, for that matter, and it promptly charged straight past her to the water spewing from the faucet, as if Kitty weren't even there.

She barely escaped with her life, but she did escape. Racing back around the house, she flung herself through the front door and slammed it shut behind her. Collapsing against it, she sagged all the way to the floor, holding her panicking heart in her chest with both hands and fighting to catch her breath without bursting into tears.

It couldn't have been more than a few seconds later, but the door suddenly bumped her back.

"Kitty?"

She crawled far enough out of the way to let Noah into his

own house. She hadn't noticed the time, but he had to have been coming up from the barn while she'd been running for her life, screaming like a crazy woman. Judging by his look of concern, he'd seen her just fine.

"Are you all right?" He came in, looking her over while she, panting and gasping and still battling back tears, dragged herself up off her hands and knees. She stood before him on badly shaking legs. "What happened?"

She couldn't even talk. She pointed back through the house toward the north, where the whisper of running water said everything it needed to about what she'd been doing. As far as she was concerned, it could run forever. She wasn't going back out there. Not ever.

Noah tipped his hat to listen, then looked at her again. Turning, he walked back out the front door. The steady tromp of his footsteps followed the veranda around to the back of the house. The friendly timbre of his voice greeted the thirsty koalas once he got there, and then the telltale squeak of the turning faucet stopped the running water.

Knees wobbling, Kitty dropped back down to the floor. On all fours, she pushed between two chairs to hide under the dining table. Her head on her hands, she stared at a knot in the floorboards, absolutely hating herself for the coward she had become. Not that she'd ever stared with fearless bravado into the straggly face of a malicious koala before, but really... had the situation warranted being this afraid?

Absolutely, her gut instinct cried.

She felt awful, and that only got worse as Noah's heavy footsteps made the journey back around the house to the front door. When he came inside, she felt the even heavier weight of his presence. The table cut her view of him from the thighs up, but nothing obstructed her sight of his lower legs taking two steps into the house, then stopping. She cowered when his feet turned toward the dining room. Giving his pants a tug, he hunkered down so he could look right at her. Flinching, Kitty avoided his stare. She buried her face in backs of her hands instead and wished she were somewhere—anywhere else in the world.

"All right," Noah said, in almost the exact same tone he'd used with the koalas. He came to the table, pulled out both chairs so she couldn't hide behind them anymore, and sat down in one facing her.

Kitty kept her face buried and dared not look at him.

"Are you all right?" he asked again, a peculiar note underlying his tone, suggesting he might not be as calm as he sounded.

Cringing, she nodded.

"Did you get bit?" Noah asked.

Sucking a breath, Kitty pushed herself to sit up and face what she had coming. She shook her head.

"Did one of them attack you?"

Sort of, but not really. Coming at her because she stood between it and the water didn't really constitute an attack, and she knew it. Kitty shook her head again.

"Look at me." His tone sounded light, and cheerful, and completely masked the very real fact that he wasn't happy with her right now.

Dragging her gaze up from her arms, Kitty met his angry stare. Her heart began to beat hard again, but not for the same reason that it had outside.

He was sitting up straight, big hands braced against his thighs. The corners of his mouth were faintly upturned, as if he were trying to smile, but it wasn't real and didn't hide the sternness in his glare. "What is Rule Number One?"

"Leave the wildlife alone," she answered.

"What did I tell you those were the very first day you arrived?"

"Wild animals." Her stomach tightened. Noah was angry with her. She was going to get punished. She looked at his hand, resting on the table. He had big hands, bigger than Ethen's, calloused and rough and used to hard physical work. She looked at his belt too.

She already knew what he could do with a strap. Her stomach dropped, a sickly sinking sensation that almost sent her running to the bathroom.

"You knew they were out there, didn't you?" he continued. "They're not quiet. I could hear them calling all the way down at the barn."

"They were out of water." Her face burned slow but hot. She felt stupid. "They were thirsty."

Noah nodded. "When I hear them squabbling like that, I know they're out. I was coming up to give them water when I saw you. My problem here is: admirable though it was for you to want to ease their discomfort, that was not your job. For all that they look cute and cuddly, they can and do bite people quite savagely."

She didn't for a second doubt that.

"Do you know what trust is?"

That hurt. Kitty stared at him.

"How about obedience?" he countered with equal ruthlessness when she didn't answer. "Because if I can't trust you to do what I ask you when I am here, how can I trust you to do it when I'm not?"

It was amazing how quickly her thoughts turned mutinous. She dropped her stare to her hands, trying to hide them. She felt stupid enough as it was, she didn't need him rubbing it in deeper.

The phone in the living room rang. When he glanced away, she crawled away from him toward the head of the table. That stopped when he snapped his fingers and pointed to a spot on the floor directly in front of him.

"If I can't trust you, you're not a roommate. You're a guest. Guests don't answer my phone."

Kitty sat where she was, hating every nuance of that scolding while he went to answer the phone. In short syllables, he responded with yeses and nos, but he was staring right at her while he did it. Towards the end of the brief conversation, he only asked one question: "What's the address? ...I'll take care of it tonight... Yep... Ta."

She couldn't remember the last time someone had made her feel this small with nothing but a stare. Not scared, per se. Not panicky, really. Just guilty and small. She hugged her shoulders for comfort, determined not to let him know how much this bothered her. She hadn't meant to break his rule. To be honest, she hadn't given any of his rules much thought. But okay, she did break one and maybe that gave him a reason to be a little upset, but hadn't she been through enough? Did he really need to make her feel worse than she already did? Because if he wanted to play that game, she thought mutinously, somebody should tell him she'd been taught these particular rules by the best of them. Compared to Ethen, Noah didn't even rank. He didn't even slam the phone when he hung it up. All he did was give her that same hard, hands on his hips glare, and if that was the worst he intended to do, well... she'd survived Ethen's beatings. She could survive Noah's fake smiling glares, too.

"Well," Noah said with mock cheerfulness. "I'll get the tea, shall I?"

The hell he would. It was her kitchen. Kitty crawled out from under the table, fully prepared to march straight past him into it and maybe even let him know how unhappy she was by rattling a few dishes louder than she needed to while she got the damn tea. Perhaps not. It had been a long time since she'd thrown a fit. She never would have dreamed of it with Ethen. She wasn't entirely sure she could bring herself to do it now. But it was a moot point. The minute she gained her feet, he snapped his fingers and pointed at her chair and she dropped with all the shaky defiance she had to sit where he told her.

"Nah," he said. "Trustworthy, obedient roommates help in the kitchen. Guests sit at the kitchen table and do nothing more strenuous than rest and relax." He walked past her, rolling up his sleeves. "Don't bother yourself, love. I'll get the tea."

Every thought Kitty had about banging cups on saucers and fit throwing went straight out of her head. As it turned out, beatings weren't the worst thing he could have done. Without raising his voice or his fist, Noah showed her how wrong she could be. In the half second it took him to strip her of her new-found responsibilities, Kitty gained a whole new respect for the awfulness of what punishments Down Under could be as Noah made her tea, and sandwiches, and cut up cold slices of cucumber and mango from the fridge and brought it all out to her as if she were Royalty and he nothing more than someone put in this house to serve her.

No one had ever served her before.

"Bon appetite," he said, setting that plate in front of her.

She didn't feel small anymore. Now she felt useless all over again.

"Rule Number Seven," he told her, when she neither touched her sandwich nor sipped her tea.

Eat every bite.

It tasted like bitterness and defeat, but she managed to choke it all down. The first half, she did angrily. By the time her plate was empty, she was struggling to swallow through a sheen of tears.

CHAPTER 9

othing was harder on a service submissive than to be stripped of her serving privileges, and Kitty was definitely a service-driven submissive. If there was any doubt left in his mind after what he'd seen that first night, then those doubts were put to rest by every flinching, teary reaction she made as she watched him clear the table after their tea. She kept trying to pick the dishes ahead of him; he had to take them away from her. After telling her no for the second time, he took away the dirty plate she immediately tried to hug to her chest and calmly, sternly, resoundingly slapped the backs of her hands.

The strapping he'd given her had been far more painful, but this was real punishment and it was effective. She broke down, sobbing at the table while he took his time washing and drying the dishes. By the time he was ready to put them away, she'd covered her head with both arms.

He lingered in the kitchen for some time afterward, mentally debating if this had been enough to get his message across. It had only been fifteen minutes, but already she looked so small and forlorn, and he didn't doubt for a second that her misery was real. Those weren't crocodile tears. What's more, her disobedience had been born from a wish to help, not out of defiance. Kitty, at her most misbehaving, did not even begin to define the word. As far as he was concerned, that ought to count in her favor as he carefully measured the punishment against the sin.

In the end he decided, like timeouts for Littles, fifteen minutes wasn't enough. A good hour, maybe two, would send the message home.

Collecting a couple books from a shelf in his bedroom, he placed them beside her on the table on his way back outside.

"So you don't get bored while you're relaxing," he said, fighting not to let her pleading stare soften his resolve. "If your butt leaves that seat for any reason other than the bathroom, I'm going to have a guest instead of a roommate all the way through to the weekend. Am I clear?"

Sniffling, she nodded, and back to the barn Noah went, with a knot in his chest and another digging in between his shoulder blades. He took a seat at the work table, rolled his neck and tried to get back into the groove of cutting strips for the kangaroo whip he was making. His hands knew the work, but his thoughts refused to focus. They kept drifting back to Kitty, in hysterics as she fled around the porch for the safety of the house. She'd broken his rule, and she'd been terrified the entire time she'd done it. Because the koalas were thirsty. And really, if a man had to have a disobedient submissive, having one that disobeyed but while doing something she thought was right, was the dubious preference.

She wasn't his submissive, he reminded himself. She was just a submissive in his house. And of course, no disobedience should come at the cost of a finger or a dozen or more stitches, because marsupial claws were made for climbing trees and were sharp as hell. Their bites were even worse.

Noah tightened his jaw. His rules were in place for a reason. He needed to know that she would follow them, and she needed to know that when it came to matters of trust and obedience, he was not only serious, but that he was in charge.

Those tears of hers, though. Oi, they got him right in the heart. He shifted on his stool, trying to shrug off the feeling. But the fact remained, if a dom failed to recognize when he needed to be a hard-ass, then he simply wasn't a dom. At best, he was a top, fit only for scening.

Still, Kitty wasn't his. No matter how comfortable the house was starting to feel with her in it, she wasn't a permanent fixture. He couldn't let himself start to believe otherwise.

And she was damaged. He couldn't let himself forget that, either. She was here to heal, which meant eventually she was going to head back home again. Back to the States where, maybe if he was lucky, he'd run into her the next time he was in Washington D.C. If she stayed there, that was.

If he ever went back.

That was a lot of ifs. He didn't like ifs. He liked an uncomplicated life. He liked peace and quiet and he'd be far better served trying to find all that in a local girl who'd be able to stick around.

Or he could convince Kitty to stay. He supposed that was a good plan too, although it wasn't likely. It wasn't even their choice, really. It was their choice pending a governmental immigration decision and, for some reason, that really irritated him.

With all the layers of whip strands cut out, he set himself to the tedious task of trimming and stretching. This was the part he both loved and hated the most. His was a big barn, but the room he'd turned into a workspace within it wasn't much bigger than his bedroom. An a/c chugged away in one of the two windows, helping to offset the heat beating down on the building from outside. A little radio on a narrow shelf above his work bench provided a beat for his motions to follow. Aerosmith provided a beat he could work to as he stretched and pulled, smoothed and stretched each and every strip he'd cut. Not a lot of thought went into this part, giving him plenty of time to think about other things. Like Kitty up in the house, sitting at the table where he'd left her, crying because he'd taken away the only thing that had let her feel useful in who knew how long.

Was he doing the right thing? Unfortunately, he'd backed himself into a corner when he'd told her he wouldn't scene with her without her asking first. But that had absolutely been the right thing to do. He wasn't her dom. He refused to rob her of what little consent she might be capable of giving at this point, and a woman desperate enough to be dominated that she would crawl through his house naked and put herself to bed hugging a strap, was not a woman he could trust to make an informed decision regarding what she actually, willingly wanted when it came to either him or his whip.

Plus, while he could make a spanking hurt like hell, it couldn't ever be a punishment to someone who viewed it as a comfort. So even if she came to him right now—on her hands and knees, his mind supplied, naked and maybe carrying that strap she so loved in her teeth—he would not spank her for her misbehavior instead. She needed to know all the way down into the marrow of her bones that he was deadly serious when it came to his rules. Whatever he did, it had to be a disciplinary measure that would in no way be confused with comfort or pleasure.

But if she did come crawling to him, his mind stubbornly whispered, letting that seductive image continue crawling through his head. If she did, what would he do?

He swiped the tiny beads of sweat building on his forehead away on the back of his sleeve. His arms were beginning to ache, his muscles burning with the repetitiveness of the motion and the strength it took to keep pulling. Fall after fall, he kept going, working the lengths and periodically checking the time. Forty minutes passed, then an hour.

An hour was long enough, he decided and took a break.

The entire walk back to the house, he watched the windows for signs of movement. He never saw any and Kitty was still sitting at the table when he stepped inside. At some point, she had got up, though. In the same chair in which he'd left her, she had her elbows braced upon her knees, her head in her hands, and there was a bucket for her morning sickness balanced on the floor between her feet. But for some spit and tears, it was empty. She was still crying, but it had dwindled to the vestiges—the gasps and sniffles, and hitches that caught at each indrawn breath she tried to take. Her face was red, so were her eyes and her nose, though it wasn't until he pulled up a chair to sit beside her that he saw how puffy and miserable she was.

Shoulders hunched, she refused to look at him.

He was so tempted to say he was sorry. Shaking his head, he rested his hand on her knee a moment, then got up to make her some tea. He doctored it with milk and honey, and fetched a few crackers to help her stomach settle. Laying it beside her on the table, he walked down the hall to the bathroom, soaked a clean washcloth in cold water, and wrung it out between his sun-bronzed hands before returning. With gentle touches, he combed her hair back from her face to press the cool wetness first to her forehead and then her cheeks. Without a word, he wiped away her tears, but after only a few caresses, her face crumpled and she dissolved into tears all over again.

Covering her mouth with both hands, she tried to block the sound, but there was no hiding how her too-thin shoulders jerked with each gasp.

He wasn't her dom. He didn't have consent to behave as if he were. He especially didn't have consent to drop that stupid washcloth and catch her in his arms instead. Pulling her up and taking her place on that chair, he drew her down to sit in his lap. He didn't have the right to press her head to his shoulder, or rock her, or kiss her hot forehead and say, "I'm sorry I had to do that.

But I need you to take me seriously, love. I need you to mind what I say so you don't get hurt."

And he sure as hell did not have the right to feel the startling shock of lust and sympathy, sadness and inexplicable pleasure that accompanied that moment when she threw her fragile arms around his neck, pulled her knees up to her chest in a broken, subconscious need to get as small as she could and burrowed into him. She butted her head against his jaw. It was shockingly catlike. He wondered if she even knew she was doing it. Probably not, since she rubbed her face to his only twice, hugging his neck while she scrubbed her tear-streaked cheeks to each side of his jaw, then burrowed into the side of his neck and simply clung to him.

"I'm sorry," she wept. "I'm sorry, I'm sorry."

"All right, now." He'd always been a big believer in aftercare. But up until this point in his life, the vast majority of his aftercare experience had been fairly generic. Generalized comfort offered to women he didn't really know and, if it affected him at all, it was usually via an erection. Holding Kitty was a whole different level to the experience. She felt good, and he'd never felt so wanted, needed, and involved. She kept hugging onto him, pulling herself into a tight ball, so he kept rocking her, kissing her forehead, and whispering into the top of her head. "Ease it down now, love. I don't want you to make yourself sick."

She wasn't his submissive, but she did her best to obey by slowing her breathing and scrubbing the tears from her face with her wrist. In a shaky voice, she muttered, "I h-hate being a g-guest."

He hid a smile in her soft hair. "Truth, love. I'd much rather have a roommate, and I really don't like having to punish you. So, if you're ready to pay attention to the rules, then I'm willing to make the kitchen once more your own."

She made no move to get up off his lap.

Although he did stop rocking, he made no move to let her go.

"Is that it?" she finally asked, her voice trembling and small. "Aren't y-you going to do… more?"

He craned in an attempt to better see her face. "Is more required in order to get my point across?"

Snuggling into his chest, Kitty shook her head, but her eyebrows were pulling into a frown that was more confusion than temper. "No," she said, but with a wary reluctance that made him think otherwise.

He studied her closely. "Kitty, love. Is more required?"

Her fingers plucked at the collar of his shirt. Her breaths were quickening again, the rise and fall of her chest turning shallow and afraid. "Wh-what would you do if it was?"

A slow thump of pure longing pulsed once in the pit of his belly, the echo of it drifting all the way down into the base of his cock. In that moment, all he could feel was the warmth and pressure of her bottom in his lap. "That depends on what you need."

Her eyebrows pulled together. She didn't shake her head, but he knew she wanted to.

"Do you need closure?" he asked, letting his fingertips play softly down her spine.

Her fingers picked and picked at one another and she didn't answer. She dropped her gaze to stare fixedly at his neck.

"Do you need to know that you're okay, or maybe that you and I are okay?"

A corner of her mouth lifted. She tried to laugh, but it was a shaky ghost of a thing and died almost the moment it was born.

"I'm okay," she said, but there was no confidence in it and he could tell by her flick of a glance before she dropped her gaze again that she neither meant it nor believed it. "Of course, I'm okay."

When she pushed slightly against him, he let her go far enough for her to sit upright. She made no move to leave his lap. Her fingers, no longer picking at her nails, wrung together tight enough to make her skin turn red.

"But... you know, for the sake of argument, if I wasn't... o-okay, I-I mean..." She swallowed hard before she could make herself finish. "What would you do?"

A dozen options immediately flowed through his brain, filling his thoughts and bringing that pulse back to the base of his cock with low-thumping vengeance.

"Ask me." He tried hard to pretend it was perfectly normal that his voice should come out sounding as husky as it did. "We can find out what happens together."

She shivered. Her thin face was haunted, twin parts reluctance and fear, but the tips of her breasts had spiked into peaks that he could see thrusting against the fabric of her t-shirt. Tiny, pinchable nubs that seemed to be reaching out to him, and which took every ounce of will that he possessed to leave entirely unmolested.

She licked her lips, the bedeviling pink tip of her tongue hiding itself away again and his own suddenly aching to give chase.

Her eyes locked with his, and in them he could read all the fears and regrets that would not be abated, ever, for as long as her experiences consisted only of Ethen and his cruelties. "Please," she whispered.

He chucked her gently under the chin, so very proud of her for finding the courage.

"You know your safeword," Noah told her. "Can I trust you to use it if you need to?"

Again, her eyebrows quirked together, as if she couldn't understand why he would even give her the option.

"This isn't a punishment, love. I've done everything I'm going to do in that regard. This, what we're doing now, is closure. It's relief, a chance for you to banish whatever guilt might remain and to know that my feelings for you haven't changed." As if he had a right to any feelings for her at all. Noah tried not to think about that. "Kitty, can I trust you to use your safeword if you need to?"

She breathed in, bracing herself. "I promise."

His pride in her blossomed even bigger. The urge to kiss her was almost overwhelming, but he locked it back and instead said, "You made a mistake, but the mistake has been corrected. What's Rule Number Eight?"

"I don't get to punish me."

"Why not?"

She tried to look away, but he caught her chin and brought her eyes right back to his.

"Why not?" he softly repeated.

"B-because that's your job?"

Noah wasn't sure if she was more afraid that she might have answered that wrong, or that she might be answering right. What he did know was the rush of pleasure that fed into him when he thought about accepting that responsibility. He patted her hip. "Yes, it is. Stand up."

She shivered again and, hands twisting with intensifying desperation, she climbed to her feet.

"That is the first thing we're going to stop." He pointed at the ferocity with which she was strangling her own fingers. She looked down at them in surprise and then quickly took a hasty step back when he stood. "What are my limits?"

Her face underwent a metamorphosis of shock. "I-I-I..."

Noah stopped her, certain she wasn't in any kind of headspace to tell him. If she'd never been allowed to have limits before, it was entirely possible she might not even know what they were. Fine. He could walk that line. "Take your clothes off. If you aren't comfortable being naked, you may keep your bra and panties on. But first, I want you to eat a little and have a sip of tea. If your stomach doesn't feel settled, sit down in your chair until it does. That's going to be our signal. If at any time you start to feel sick, sit down. If at any time you start to feel scared or want to stop, use your safeword, all right?"

She nodded and Noah left the room. He went through the kitchen and down the hall to his bedroom. His play bag was in the closet. He dropped it on the bed before unzipping it and pulling out layers of contents. His floggers were on top, each set neatly encased in a long sock to keep the falls tidy. Beneath that was his bag of sensation toys—his clamps, needles, Wartenburg wheel, and wax kit. Mentally he made a tally of what was safe to use, what was suggestive, and what might walk the line or push her past her comfort zone.

How close to that line should he take her, he wondered. What would it take to banish Ethen's touch and forever replace it in her mind with that of someone who valued her worth, both as a person and a submissive?

He pulled out a pair of cuffs. The Velcro set that attached wrists to thighs. No locks or chains required, and if panic happened, they released fast. Those went in his safe pile, along with a hair tie. In the suggestive pile, he put his baggy of nipple clamps and weights, and a small leather paddle. After a lot of internal battling, he dug to the bottom where he found his box of anal plugs and the vibrating wand, with its simple set of three variable speeds—low, medium, and according to the last submissive he'd used it on, oh-my-God. Those he put in the walk-the-line pile.

Pausing, Noah looked over his selection. Nothing in here was anything he would have considered severe. Nor was it anything he would have considered more than play. Oh sure, the paddle could be used hard enough to cause real pain. Depending on where he put the clamps, those could too. But that wasn't his intention. Right now, the only thing that mattered to him was showing Kitty how to find her way back from the darkness now that her punishment was done. This was all about giving her ease, letting her know that she truly was safe and that she had nothing to fear from him.

Because she did have nothing to fear from him, right? He looked down at himself and the high standing erection that had, over the course of the last few minutes, turned the front of his jeans into a full-on bulge. He had to adjust himself. A few minutes later, he did it again.

"You're keeping it in your pants," he told himself sternly. He'd never be mistaken for a saint, not in any religion. Hell, he couldn't count the number of women he'd enjoyed on his many vacations. Some he was pretty sure had never told him their real names. But this wasn't that kind of situation, and Kitty had enough complications in her life without adding his cock into the mix.

Just play, he told himself. Give her release. Let her feel cared for.

Perfectly, one-hundred-percent cared for, perhaps for the first time in the whole of her submissive life.

Don't get attached, mate, he told himself. She wasn't a permanent fixture here. She wasn't going to stay. *No matter what, don't get attached.*

He never in a million years would have thought he'd need to give himself this cautionary pep talk. An unrepentant matchmaker everywhere he went, and here he was telling himself not to fall in love. Not with a damaged submissive, who wasn't a citizen of his country and who would not be staying.

The only problem was, he already suspected it might be a little too late.

CHAPTER 10

*K*itty took off her shirt, folded it with OCD compact neatness and put it on the table. Then she moved it further down to the end, in case Noah should need the space. And then she tucked it out of sight on the seat of a chair behind the table, because looking at it made her feel nervous. And she was already so very nervous.

What had she done? What had she just let herself in for? Would he really stop if she asked? Ethen never had. Ethen didn't believe in safewords, or at least he didn't acknowledge them. It was his way every day, and her job was to submit. What if she just made the biggest mistake of her life?

Kitty hugged her arms, rubbing her bare flesh and telling herself that Noah wasn't Ethen. Over the last week, she'd seen that over and over again, but she was still afraid. And what she was afraid of most right now was the giant unknown of what Noah might do now that she'd asked him—practically begged him, after saying his form of punishment wasn't punishment enough, for heaven's sake; how stupid could she be?—to hurt her.

The words were out. They couldn't be recalled, and the worst part was, she wasn't entirely sure she would take them back even if she could. Awful as his punishment had been—awful in a way that didn't put so much as a bruise or long-lasting welt on her—everything inside of her was pushing for more. She was frightened right now, yes, but she had to know. She had to know the worst that Noah could and would dish out. She had to know the full and terrible extent of how much he would hurt her. If she'd learned anything from her time with Ethen, Kitty now knew the importance of knowing first-hand exactly what the dom she was with was capable of.

In the back room, she heard his footsteps moving across the bare floor. She had to hurry and finish undressing. *Take your clothes off. If you aren't comfortable being naked, you may keep your bra and panties on.* Or at least, that was what he'd said. He'd also said this wasn't a punishment. The real test, she knew, wasn't in what he said, but what he did once he came back out here.

Kitty shivered again, but still her hands dropped to the waist of her jeans. She took them off, folding them with the same ridiculous care as her shirt before tucking them out of sight on the discrete pile she'd made. She took her socks off, tucking them into her shoes and pushing those under the chair and out of the way. Then she stood there, in nothing but her hand-me-down bra and underwear, feeling stupid. She ought to take them off. Submissives should always be naked and available for their doms, always. To do anything less was to invite terrible discipline, but Noah had said... but did he mean it? Dared she test him to find out?

Her skin crawled. She didn't want to test anyone. *Take them off, take them off, take them off...* It was the mantra that ran through her head on a perpetual loop for the entire time that she stood frozen in ill-thought-out defiance. She couldn't even say she didn't know how ill-thought-out it was. Defiance was what had got her locked in the Box for two days. She'd dared once to tell Ethen no.

Stop thinking about it. Stop making the comparison. Noah wasn't

Ethen, why wasn't *that* the chant playing its merciless loop in her brain?

Chills broke out across her shoulders, running down both arms as the unmistakable tromp of Noah's boots came down the hallway. She hugged herself tighter, instantly regretting her decision to remain partially clothed. Intensely regretting requesting this of him at all, and yet just standing there, doing nothing to correct either mistake right up until Noah came back through the kitchen and into the dining room. He had a minor armload of toys, all of which burned themselves into her brain with ominous dread. Most were toys, but Ethen had once hurt her with a plastic straw, so it really didn't matter to her what he brought out. Anything could be made a punishment.

"Did you eat at least two crackers?" Noah set his armload on the table. He didn't dump them in a pile, but took the time to spread them out, allowing each implement its own space.

"Yes, Sir." She hoped he didn't ask her to eat any more. She honestly didn't think she could hold down one bite more without her stomach rejecting all out of sheer nerves.

"Did you have a sip of tea?" He looked in her cup, noting it was half empty.

"Yes, Sir." She didn't think she could handle any more of that, either.

"Good girl." Laying the last item on the table, he stepped back to give her open access. "Take a look at everything I've brought. If there is an item you do not want used during this session I want you to point it out."

Don't tell him, the ghosts of her past whispered. *If he knows, he'll be sure to use them.*

Pressing her sweaty palms to her thighs, she looked over what he'd brought. The restraints made her swallow hard. Her bottom clenched at the sight of the paddle, but it was nothing like Ethen's punishment paddle. It was small, made of leather, engraved on the back with an ornate rose and thorns. Her knees almost buckled over the butt plug, and just that fast, she was back in Ethen's play room, tied over the wooden horse, screaming and shaking as Ethen slowly worked her open on the plug he only ever used when he was in a mood to hear screams.

Don't think about it. Noah wasn't him, and the plug he'd put on the table, while not the smallest she'd ever seen, certainly wasn't huge. It was metal, though. With a very narrow neck and a pink jeweled base.

"It's fine," she whispered, her legs already beginning to shake. That butt plug meant she'd have to take her clothes all the way off. So… he truly hadn't meant to give her a choice. Sick to her stomach, she reached behind her to unhook her bra.

"Stop," Noah ordered, the steely authority of his tone snapping at her. Suddenly he seemed a little taller, a little broader in the shoulders, and whole lot stronger, particularly when he frowned like this. "I told you to present yourself in the way that made you comfortable. You followed my orders and your request is now my limit to follow. But from the moment I entered this room, our scene began. That means I am in charge now, and you will do as you are told or there will be consequences. Am I clear?"

"Yes, Sir." She didn't have the strength or the courage even to swallow. She was shaking, every inch of her trembling all the way down to her very core.

"Did I tell you to remove your clothes?"

"N-no, Sir."

"Then your clothes stay on. One more time, I want you to look at the items I've brought. I may or may not use any or all of them during the course of our scene. So I want you to be very sure that you are okay with everything on this table. If you are not okay with it, I am ordering you to point it out right now."

She looked at them again. None of them were strangers to her; most evoked anything but fond memories, but it felt so very wrong for a submissive to tell her dom what he could or could not use. She wove her fingers tight before her, clasped her hands tight and stayed silent.

"All right," he said, a glitter darkening the depths of his knowing stare. "Let's begin."

Pulling out a chair, he took the Velcro restraints off the table and sat down. "Wrists," he said, laying one across his knee and opening the other. He waited, his blue stare burrowing into her until she extended her arm.

After police-issue handcuffs, zipties, and piano wire once (which had cut her skin), having him put Velcro on her seemed a very novice thing for him to do and yet there was no denying the firmness of the grip. It hugged her wrist. It hugged her thigh even tighter when he wrapped the strap around her, putting his hand right up between her legs as he adjusted how the restraint lay as it ran through the crease between her limb and panty-clad pussy. The caress of his hand there was at once impersonal and electrifying. She almost closed her eyes, her body reacting to it with near desperate hunger.

"Hand," he said again, as if that faint scrap of his knuckle across her crotch were too common for him to take note of. For her, it raised chills all over again, only these felt different than before. They danced up through her belly and into her breasts, whereas before, they'd prickled like spider legs across her back. Both left her shivering as she offered her left hand.

With both her hands now strapped to her thighs, he stood and picked up the hair tie. Her chills became dervish dancers, moving through her faster and faster as he stepped behind her, but the comb of his fingers as he pulled her long brown hair back from her face felt almost... loverly. Ponytails were handles to a dom. There were a lot of things a submissive could be made to do with her hair grasped tight in the hands of a controlling man. And yet, in spite of herself, Kitty relaxed.

Pulling the ponytail through the last twist of the hair tie, he let his hands fall to her shoulders. For almost a full minute, he massaged her, rolling and squeezing the tension for her shoulders until she gave in to the allure, relaxing even more. The longer he kneaded, the more she forgot herself until she found herself nearly leaning back against him.

His touch changed again, the kneading ceasing as he seized hold of her ponytail, pulling her head solidly back until his breath was at her ear. His low growl sent her dancing shivers whirling all through her. "I asked you what my limits were. This is your last chance to give me some."

Her throat worked, but without sound. Her heart raced. Her captured hands clenched tight into fists, but for the first time in longer than she could remember, Kitty didn't move—not because she couldn't, but because for one crazy minute with his master-like grip in her hair and the heat of his chest searing into her back —she didn't want to.

"I don't have any," she whispered.

"Everyone has limits." His right grip tightening in her hair, holding her frozen against the dominance of his body, he reached around her and seized her breast in his left hand. He squeezed hard, but the pain barely qualified as such. It was vitalizing, zinging its shocks straight into her eager nipples. "Is this off limits?"

"No, Sir," she gasped.

Dropping his hand, he seized her pussy in the same cruel, intoxicating hold. His squeeze captured her clit, her folds, her heart, and her breath. "Is this off limits?"

Pooling warmth filled her belly, spilling in an instant all through the furrow his fingers now owned. Her knees shook, buckling in and out under her. He held her up by her pussy. If not for that grip, she'd have fallen into a heap there at his feet.

"N-no…" Her eyes closed against her will when the heat of his mouth engulfed her earlobe. She felt his teeth, the sharpness exciting all her singing nerves. Her blood pulsed, filling her head, her breasts, her sex with the same heady beat.

"Your safeword is red," he told her for the second time. "If and when I find your limits, I expect you to use it. Is that clear?"

His grip on her hair vanished, only to return with vindictive force when he swatted her ass, then grabbed.

"Yes, Sir!" she yelped. His hand was huge and hard, and the sheer sting as he squeezed that sting into her clenching flesh consumed her. Her underwear offered no padding and no protection whatsoever against hands like that.

No more than a link of chain separated her wrist cuffs from the straps around her thighs. It was enough to clink as he spun her via her ponytail and backed her until her butt bumped the edge of the table. She had only enough movement to catch it with her captured hands before he forced his knee up between her thighs.

"Spread your legs," he told her, deliberately bumping his knee up against her mons.

The table behind her became her only source of balance as she obeyed and what she had once viewed as humiliation became something both dark and new as he took his time looking her over. Her pussy hummed, a needy, greedy thing consumed by echoes of his touch.

His eyes when they returned to hers were filled with echoes of their own. Easing closer, he took firm pinching hold of both her nipples. The pressure was nothing but pleasure. Her eyes almost closed again, but his held her spellbound.

"I am..." Noah coaxed, his fingers plucked and tweaked, sultry milking motions that tugged her nipples through her bra. Already tight, they swelled, growing heavy while she fought back the urge to arch, offering them further into his hands.

She shivered. "I am a... a good girl."

He gave her breast a rewarding upward slap, the briskness making her flesh bounce and her sex clench amid the ribbons of a molten flood that drenched the gusset of her underwear.

"I am..." His fingers returned to her nipples, but the touch was a shade harsher now. The pulling was stronger, the pinching and tweaking bringing her back onto her tiptoes. She could not stop herself arching now. She couldn't stop the molten flow growing hotter as it swept through the furrow, licking up through her nether lips, her clit now pulsed in heady time with each milking motion of his stern fingers.

She mewed. "I am s-safe… oh!"

He slapped both breasts, leaving her gasping and squirming on her tiptoes before sagging back down again. Her aching nips sought his tightening hold, she all but pushed herself more firmly into his twisting grip. She pressed her lips, but there was no muffling the sheer pleasure of her moan as he pinched, harder now. Hard enough to bring notes of pain into the musical moan of pleasure that broke from deep inside her.

"I'm loved," she said, without needing prompting.

Three harsh slaps now, first to one breast and then the other, forcing a ragged cry to chase her moan.

"I don't have to be afraid of anythi-ing!" Her cry escalated sharply higher in pitch when he switched targets and laid three spanking swats every bit as hard as the others, directly upon her unprepared clit. And she could not—would not—shut her legs. She kept them wide, thighs shaking and straining while his hand gentled, fingers tracing the cotton now molded to her like a second skin. He circled in search of that nub of throbbing desire sheltered beneath the cloth.

He kept that barrier between his flesh and hers, but oh how she felt the wanton burn of his caress. He made her legs shake. Her hips rocked, grinding into each circling pass with tiny motions she hardly knew she was making. He brought her right to the brink of collapsing, her legs too weak to hold her up any more, but right as she felt the first tickling spasms that heralded orgasm—the first she'd felt in so very long—he stopped. Kitty was so crushed, she groaned her loss before she could stop herself.

The sound froze all movement, both his and hers. She stared

up at him, positive she was about to get her face slapped for daring to criticize.

"Oh really?" His eyes narrowed, but the corners of his mouth curled in devious speculation. He didn't slap her. He picked the clamps off the table instead.

"Mm!" Kitty rolled her lips tight together again, determined to stay quiet, but there was no biting back her cry as he took a harsh tweaking hold of her right nipple, plucking tight before attaching the clamp. She wished she'd taken her bra off. She regretted the barriers she'd put between them. Not that her bra spared her anything as each alligator clamp took its biting hold on her, but as he took his fingers away again, Kitty found herself missing the intimacy. It was better to be naked. It was better to be vulnerable. It was better to watch her own tender flesh swelling and darkening beneath his expert touch, than it was to suffer this intoxicating mix of hurt and hunger but see only fabric clamped between the jagged teeth.

Attaching a length of thin chain between the two clips, he pulled her back onto tiptoes by her own aching nipples. "Open your mouth," he ordered. When she obeyed, he pressed the chain between her lips. "Bite."

She didn't groan, but it was a near thing. Biting down, she kept firm hold on the chain despite her agonizing nips.

"If you let go of that for any reason other than to say your safeword, there will be consequences and I don't guarantee that you'll like any of them."

Kitty whimpered, not entirely sure she liked this one. Except her clit was throbbing in steady time with the ache in her breasts and that molten, licking sensation still tickled through her labia, proof of her body's arousal. It was thick in the air now. She could smell it.

Back his hand went, down the length of her body, pausing at her belly to circle her navel, pausing at the elastic waist of her panties to dip inside, playing with the flesh concealed from him, lingering again at her mons while he traced the plumpness of her sex before finding her clit once more. Every sensitive nerve in her was singing for him by the time he began another round of lazy circles.

"Have you any other criticisms you'd like to make regarding my activities?" Noah asked silkenly.

Her thighs began to shake all over again, which made her breasts jiggle and the bites of the twin clamps torturous. She locked her lips, holding the chain taut against her crying nipples, and didn't say a word. Whimpers didn't count. No matter how steadily they mewed out of her, it wasn't words.

He smiled. "I didn't think so."

The circles stopped and his fingers took hold of her, pinching her clit and rolling gently back and forth. Plucking at her, the way he had her nipples, while he reached across the table and selected the last clip.

Her mews turned gaspy as he lowered himself to his knees before her. "You know your safeword," he reminded. Releasing her clit, he opened his mouth, giving her ample time to realize exactly what he intended before he moved in. The heat of his breath against the gusset of her underwear sent her thoughts scattering like birds taking flight. When his mouth fastened unerringly over her clit, she all but lost her grip on the table's edge.

Her panties might as well not have been there.

God, it had been so long since a man had last done this to her. The long suckling pulls of his mouth and tongue drew her grinding down into the languid motion of his love-making. He tugged, he hummed, he rolled and pressed and bit until she was lost in it. She'd have gripped his head if only she could have got her hands free. She tried anyway, but the minute her stretching fingers grazed the short sandy hairs on the side of his head, he stopped, pulled back, and suddenly the bite of the last alligator clamp replaced his hungry mouth.

"Bad girl," he growled, licking the taste of her from his lips. Which was impossible. Her underwear had been a barrier between them. He couldn't possibly be tasting her the way the stormy blue of his eyes suggested.

"Mm!" Kitty bent almost double, her body's ache for orgasm no longer a tickle, but a roar. Her nipples were in agony. Her clit, unaccustomed to the harshness of the clamp, threatened quickly to follow, but neither pain was enough to banish her need. It amplified it. She wanted more. More twists and pinches. More suckling pulls of his mouth. More bites of more clamps in whatever places he saw fit to affix them. And above and beyond all of that, she wanted him. The heat and the hardness of him touching her, skin to bare, burning skin.

He stood up, so close to her that his body dragged her in places. His hands caught her hips, his chest bumped the clamps on her breasts and set her near to sobbing. Or maybe that was her fault. The inadvertent touch made her jerk back, pulling the chain until the unbearable pain lancing through her nipples stopped everything. And still her clit pulsed and her panties flooded. Wanton, pulsating flows of lust that drenched her everywhere his mouth had been.

His was the smile of a man who knew exactly what he was doing. Catching the base of her ponytail, he turned her around and, with a not-so-gentle shove, bent her over the table. Her bound hands did not allow her to arrest her fall. She landed on her belly, her breasts and pussy both crying and throbbing even louder, overriding the discomfort, feeding off of the clatter of each clamp striking the table. Why had she kept her damned underwear on?

Her body knew this position and reacted with instant obedience, her legs spreading wide, her hips arching back, offering herself—pussy, ass, what he wanted, however he wanted it, if only she didn't have the damned underwear in the way.

She would not have cared if he'd taken it down right then.

More than anything, she ached for the brush of his fingers, slipping into the elastic waistband before baring her. The clip on her clit would have prevented it dropping too far. It was hooked to her, with little metal teeth she could feel in excruciating detail.

As it turned out, he didn't need to remove it and it wasn't the elastic of her waistband that he hooked his fingers into. It was the elastic to either side of her crotch, right before he dragged them to one side, baring her ass cheeks, the glistening folds of her puss, and the dusky rim of her anus.

"Mm!" Kitty locked her lips around the chain, afraid she might accidentally let go. If she did, all this would stop. He'd said there would be consequences that she wouldn't like, and she believed him. And, oh, how she did not want this to stop. Not yet. Not even when she saw him reach for a bottle of clear lubricating gel.

She snapped her eyes shut, because seeing made her remember and she didn't want any part of Ethen invading what was happening now. She wanted to feel, for once—just once—without also being afraid. A dollop of cold dropped into the crack between her ass cheeks, sliding down toward her anus before a swipe of his fingers helped it along.

"You know how to stop this," he said, applying that lubrication all around her rim. "There will be no punishment or consequences if you do." One finger invaded, sinking into her with delicious slowness. "I won't be angry, and if you don't want to stop everything, then we'll leave out the parts that make you uncomfortable."

Kitty spread her legs wider, pushing back her hips and impaling herself by centimeters on his finger.

"There's a good girl," was his chuckling reply. One finger became two, and then simple penetration became thrusts. There was no pain. Not even a little. He didn't call her ugly names or take her dry so it would hurt as much as he could make it. He made it feel good, the way she remembered it feeling way back in the beginning when she first set foot in Black Light and a dom there offered to teach her all the things that up until that moment she'd only dreamed of. She could barely remember his face and his name not at all. When she tried, Ethen's came to mind.

Burying her face into the table, Kitty banished him. She focused on the steady in and out of Noah's fingers in her ass, and now his thumb, slipping down between the slick folds of her pussy to find entrance there too. He pumped her both ways, but only for a moment more. Then he patted her on the bottom and took his hand away. She mewed her disappointment, but his touch had already returned. Not his finger now, the blunted nose of the metal plug circled the rim of her ass, giving her ample time to guess what was coming next.

Another slow invasion, colder than his fingers with only a pinch of discomfort as the widest section pushed through her involuntary clench. Then it was in, seated deep and cool and weighted. She could really feel it—it had been so, so long.

Gripping the jeweled base, Noah twisted the plug inside her. He rocked it, pumped it, tangled his hand in her ponytail and pulled her head so far back that the chain between her mouth and nipples tightened, making the clamps bite harder.

"This is not a punishment," Noah said, turning her mew of half-hearted protest into a startled, lusty grunt when he yanked the plug out of her, only to slam it back home again.

Kitty nearly came up off the table, but his grip on her hair, the size and weight of him behind her, and the slow, steady thrusts as he fucked her from behind, it all worked together to hold her pinned.

Eyes no longer closed, she stared at the wall straight ahead, seeing nothing, but feeling everything. From the pinch and pull as she was taken with her damn underwear still mostly on, to her near tear-inducing disappointment that it should be this metal thing inside of her instead of his rock-hard cock piston ramming in and out as he reinforced, "Bad submissives don't get treated like this, only good girls. You're a good girl, Kitty. You've been a good girl and you're giving me a lot of pleasure. So I'm going to return that favor."

One last deep pump, and the plug settled all the way into her singing body. She missed him the minute he let her go. Conversely, she didn't miss him quite so much a half second later when she felt the flat head of the leather paddle caress a warning circle across her round ass. He took his time arranging her underwear, tucking the sides into the crack of her buttocks, pulling it up floss tight, until the fabric was cutting up through the folds of her needy pussy and all three clamps felt as if they were biting right through her.

"It's been a while for me," Noah said, and she could hear the smile in his voice even though his grip in her hair meant she could not twist back far enough to see it. "Come to think of it, I haven't had the use of a woman's body since Black Light. So, thank you for your submission, love. I'm really going to enjoy this."

If he gave her a warmup first, it didn't feel like it. From first smack to last, every swat of his paddle bit straight through her flesh and into her rapidly unraveling soul. The sting was unbearable and yet she welcomed it. It grew teeth more jagged than the clamps, and yet she refused to cry out. She bit the chain until it hurt, but she would not let go. Not because she did not want to cut his enjoyment short, but because she needed this too.

She *needed* the sting, the smart, the increasingly excruciating hurt that only grew more vindictive the faster and harder he spanked her. Because he wasn't letting up; he wasn't stopping. He didn't pause to rub and he didn't spread out his swats to find other places to bite. He focused all of that paddle's attentions on the absolute swells of her bottom cheeks, above her thighs, in the only two places guaranteed to make sitting impossible later on. And she needed it to be like this.

Because she was an idiot.

Because she'd let herself live with a monster who'd used her, degraded her, stole everything she'd ever valued—her house, her car, all the money she made and even her job—away from her. Worse than that, she'd let him steal her dignity and her self-respect, leaving her this... this shell of a person she barely recognized and didn't at all like. And for what? Because by the time she recognized him for the monster he was, his abuse had become familiar? Because it had become excusable?

Exactly when she broke down, Kitty didn't know. But by the time he finally lay the paddle aside to rest the heat of his naked hand on her fiery ass, not rubbing to soothe, but squeezing each cheek to amplify the hurt, she was bawling too hard to control it.

"There's a good girl." He paused between squeezes to swat her again, this time measuring out pain with the flat of his bare hand. "Let it all out, love. Time to let that poison go."

She cried when he put her panties back to right, and again when he took off the alligator clips. She cried even harder as the blood came rushing back into all those tender places, but not because it hurt—although it did, and dreadfully. She cried because it had been so long since anyone had cared enough to give her this, and because this—this thing between her and Noah, well... it wasn't real. Who knew how long it would be before she'd have it again.

She had to hold onto this feeling—the fire and the hurt, the sadness and relief—to everything, including the strength she found in Noah's arms as he pulled her up off the table and into his embrace. When her knees wouldn't hold her, he sat, providing her with the comfort of his lap, holding her for what felt like hours.

She had to remember this, because it wasn't real and it wouldn't last. And she was terrified she might actually be pregnant.

She had nothing. She hated herself. Who would ever want a woman who came with baggage like this? Nobody, except more people like Ethen. Maybe she didn't deserve any better.

His hand roving up and down her back, Noah pressed a kiss to her forehead. "I..." he said

Kitty closed her eyes. "I'm a good girl," she echoed, dutifully but dead inside. She would have thought she was all cried out, but the tears started all over again.

Patience personified, he rocked her as he asked, "What else?"

"I'm safe."

"And?"

"I'm loved." Her breath hitched so badly, she could barely understand the words she was saying. "I-I don't have to be afraid of anything."

"Do you believe it?" Noah asked when she was done.

Tempted as she was to lie, Kitty shook her head.

His hand never once stopped its comforting caress. "That's all right, love. We've got time. One day, we'll get there. I promise."

When he turned his head to kiss her on the forehead, if she closed her eyes, she could almost believe he meant all the unspoken things that kisses like that ought to mean when a man held a woman in his arms.

CHAPTER 11

$\mathcal{K}$itty was physically, mentally, and quite possibly spiritually exhausted, and so Noah prescribed a nap as a part of his aftercare and tucked her into bed. He left a cup of tea and cookies on her nightstand, told her she didn't have to sleep, but she did have to lie there with her eyes closed for at least twenty minutes. Then he packed himself a lunch, made up a thermos of coffee, loaded his croc traps into the back of his pickup, hooked up his boat, and headed to work.

The call he'd received was for a nuisance animal with a habit for basking in the middle of daycare playgrounds. His first stop was at the school, where he walked the fence line, locating two places where the animal might be getting in. Pliers, rebar, some extra twists of wire and quick-mix cement fixed that problem. Unloading his boat into the sluice that ran behind the daycare was his second step. Within half an hour, he had found several slides and flattened vegetation near the water's edge. Setting his traps, he went back to his truck to break out the coffee and wait. While he waited, he occupied himself thinking.

It had felt good holding Kitty on his lap, rocking and

comforting away her tears. Had he fixed anything for her? No, he wasn't that arrogant or naïve enough to think so. But holding her had felt… unexpectedly fulfilling. Kissing her had been rousing as hell, and it had only been sheer will that had restricted those kisses to nothing more intimate than her forehead. He needed to stop calling her love. Generic as that pet name was and, granted, he had used it on dozens if not hundreds of women from the elderly to the lovely, all the way down to sweet little infants, the word was taking on connotations it had never held before. Not with anyone. He didn't know why he was surprised. Wounded things had always roused his protective side, and he'd never met anyone more wounded than Kitty.

Still, he shifted behind the steering wheel, firmly ordering his lower half to knock it the hell off. There were more reasons than he had the fingers to count them for why he should make it a point to never again put himself through the sexual hell of doing to Kitty what he had done today. It might be the coffee he was drinking, but it was her smell he was savoring in his nose and on his tongue. That thin barrier of underwear might have prevented him from putting his mouth directly on her, but it had been saturated with her arousal. God, the taste of her. The heady aroma. The mewling need that had pricked at his iron-will with every muffled cry she had tried to stifle as he'd licked and nipped at her with his lips and teeth.

The sun went down slowly, but only half as slowly as he relived going down on Kitty. Not that finger fucking her hadn't been just as fine. Later tonight, he'd probably fall asleep rock hard because he couldn't shake the memory of it—the tightness of her ass locking down on his thrusting fingers, the pulse of her heartbeat through the slickness of her walls. Her grunts and moans and the arching of her hips as she pushed back on the anal plug he'd used on her so fucking jealously. That should have been him. Under any other circumstance, it would have been.

He had to stop thinking about it. It was done, he'd given her what she'd needed and he'd kept his damn pants zipped. That was Herculean, that's what that was. He ought to be proud of himself. Someday maybe he would be... if and when the erection ever went away.

"Get your mind off it, mate," Noah told his lap. "This isn't helping."

Plus, he had work to do. And that right there was dangerous enough, even without distractions.

The sun had only been down an hour when he got out to check the traps. He knew better than that, too. Under any other circumstance, he'd have put the seat back in his truck, lowered his hat over his eyes and gone to sleep until about midnight or so. Or hell, even gone home, depending on how local the job was. But waiting in his truck when he had someone like Kitty waiting for him at home just did not seem like any way for a bloke to spend the night.

Fate must have had a thing for hard-up men in sticky non-relationships, because against all odds, he found a salty in the second trap he'd set. It was only a little fellow, not even two-meters in length. Since the problem with the fence was fixed, he tagged it, re-baited his traps and went home. First thing in the morning, he'd return to check for something bigger and, if he had to, deal with the rest of it then.

Noah found the house dark when he got home. The only light on, he noticed, was Kitty's lamp in her bedroom. Not because she'd gone to bed, he realized, but because she hadn't got out of it after he'd left. He sat behind the wheel almost a full minute after parking the car, not really sure he wanted to know if that was because she'd gone to sleep despite her protests (and maybe still was asleep) or because he hadn't thought to leave instructions that allowed for her to get up again.

He knew some submissives who needed that level of control. Up until now, though, Kitty had been pretty independent with her days. Deeply hoping he hadn't left her to deal with bad ghosts alone, Noah went inside.

Everything was so quiet he had halfway convinced himself that she'd fallen asleep before he reached her door, but that was proven wrong the minute he glanced beyond her threshold. Kitty was sitting up in bed, fully dressed under the quilt and hugging her legs. Chin resting on her knees, only her eyes moved when she saw him.

"I didn't mean for you to stay in bed all night," Noah ventured. "You could have got up any time."

She didn't answer, but picked up something he hadn't noticed lying on the quilt between her feet and held it up. The pregnancy test. She'd taken it.

He didn't need to ask what the result was. The sag in her shoulders said it all.

"I hope you like roommates," she muttered. "I figure in about six months, you're going to have two of them."

He honestly couldn't tell if she was trying to make a joke or not, but it fell flat. She knew it too. Almost as soon as she'd made it, her face crumpled into a groaning cringe.

"What the hell is wrong with me?" she asked before covering her face with both hands.

Noah came to sit at the headboard beside her. When he put his arm around her shoulders, she curled against him. "Is there any chance at all that it isn't his?"

"Does it matter?"

Not to him it didn't. He was more worried about her, at this point.

"He never shared me that way," Kitty finally said. "I did fluffing sometimes, but Pony was the one he liked to pass around to his friends. Usually only if they had something he wanted more than he wanted her."

She was quiet. Noah was too. What could be said to comfort

something that awful? Somehow 'you're well shut of him' didn't seem quite right, although it did feel true.

"I can't stay here," she said softly, almost under her breath.

Noah, however, heard it loud as summer thunder. He was off the bed before he realized he was going to move. "What do you mean?" he demanded. "Why not? If you're afraid he's going to come after you out here, I'd love to see the fucker try. I—"

She looked at him, and in that dead-eye stare Noah suddenly heard everything she wasn't saying out loud.

"You're thinking about going back to him," he said flatly.

"You don't think he has a right to know he's going to be a father?" she countered. She hugged her knees again, a defensive reaction that made him instantly check himself. His body was squaring off against her. He tried to stop that, to find his center of calm. She was a grown woman, after all. She was entitled to her opinions, her feelings, and even to make her own mistakes, if that was what she—oh, hell no, mate, to fuck-all with that and who cared about calm? No way was he going to stand by while she got on a plane, flew halfway across the world where he couldn't possibly protect her, and back into the cruel keeping of that son of a bitch!

Except he couldn't say *any* of that and to make sure of it, Noah covered his mouth with his hand until the urge had passed. "When exactly do you reckon he's earned that right? You name me one time, just once, when that man has done something that's been good for you. One thing that hasn't broken you down or left a scar, physical or not."

She didn't. He liked to think it was because she couldn't, but that didn't mean he was right. Or even appropriate. If she wanted to go, what right did he have to stop her? None, and for a hair-split second, in the very pit of his gut where he had never in his life ever felt such a chillingly-pierce sensation before, Noah knew exactly what it was going to feel like when she walked out of his house.

He pointed at her. "No," he said. He struggled for calm, but both his voice and his finger, hell, all of him, was shaking. "No," he said again. There were a thousand other words jumbling through his head, vying one another to come spilling out between them. He needed calm and rational, a reason that would help her think straight and change her bloody mind—*I really like you, love, please don't go*—not one of them knocked free in time to follow 'no.'

So, he left it at that and he walked away, fast, before he did something Ethen-ish. Something he would regret. His bedroom wasn't far enough, so he left the house. The porch wasn't far enough either, neither was the barn, although his workshop was where he ended up, facing the wood-plank wall where his half-made whip was dangling. Open hands braced against the weathered boards, the chaos of his thoughts churned themselves into a fevered maelstrom, all of it centered around *She's leaving you, mate, she's going back to him.* The guy who hurt her in ways Noah could hardly imagine, and frankly didn't want to.

What did that say about him? What had he done to all of a sudden make Ethen the better option? As if, Noah scolded himself, he could even consider himself an option. He wasn't. He was a friend of a friend who was doing a favor for—God damn it! He didn't want to be *that*, he *wanted* to be an option! What more, he wanted to be the option Kitty chose!

But, honestly, why would she, that nagging voice in his head kept whispering. Why would she want to stay when they barely knew one another? At what point had he declared himself, or let her know he was interested? So he could what, that other voice in his head argued back, make her even more anxious about the dark intentions of the stranger she was staying with? No, he'd been right to be careful with her. He'd been right not to do anything that might be construed as him taking advantage of a battered woman. But now, look where that caution had left him?

At what point had they ever sat down and talked about themselves, their childhoods, their hobbies or thoughts or dreams for the future? Or, her baby's future, for that matter? Try though he might, the only real conversation Noah could recall apart from his setting the rules, her breaking of them, the punishment he'd given and the relief that had followed—apart from all that, so far their only conversation had been about the weather. Looked at that way, was it any wonder if she was considering moving on?

And now there was the baby to consider. At least she'd accepted her pregnancy, putting it out in the open where they could deal with it. Except, none of these were his complications to deal with, were they? No, it was all on Kitty. She was an American, faced with having a baby in a country where she didn't hold citizenship, couldn't get employment, an apartment, or any kind of legal or financial aid. He'd bend over backwards to help her, she had to know that, but at the same time that didn't make things automatically better? Australia was not an easy country to migrate into, although he supposed marrying her would solve a lot of problems...

...not to mention opening up a slew of different ones.

Noah wasn't crazy. He knew he liked her, but he wasn't sure he was ready for marriage. And he sure as hell wasn't ready to marry someone he'd then spend the rest of his life struggling to convince he didn't marry solely for citizenship or because she was knocked up.

What he did know was, whether they'd had a decent conversation yet or not, he wasn't ready to let Kitty go. This was more than her being broken or him doing a favor for a friend. This felt different from anything he'd ever experienced with any woman he'd yet known. Every shred of gut-feeling he had was screaming that this went deeper than it had a right to go for a time period as short as theirs had been, and he knew—*knew*—to the depths of his marrow if he didn't do something to change her mind, he would not only lose her, but he would regret it to the end of his days.

Noah hit the wall, the heel of his hard palm shuddered it.

Frustrated, he hit it again, four times in rapid, banging succession, shaking the whole damn barn, the whip hanging from its hook, and himself. His palm stung, but the hurt was good. It was grounding. He closed his eyes, breathing deep and struggling for control. He didn't often lose his calm like this and he certainly wasn't proud of it, but he swallowed back the rising chaos of feelings he wasn't prepared to deal with just yet, and focused.

When at last he opened his eyes again, he had the start of a plan firmly in mind. No way was he going to stand by while she groveled her way back into Ethen's good graces. Considering what that sadistic bastard had already done, he didn't want to know what Ethen was capable of doing to a baby. That right there was going to be Noah's number one reason on his list why she should stay. He'd work out the other reasons on the walk back up to the house, because if Kitty was still awake, then they needed to have a serious talk. He had to make her see reason. Failing that, he had to make her tell him why she had to go, at least then he'd know exactly what the problem was.

Firm as he was in his decision, Noah only got as far as shoving off the wall and turning around. That was when he saw Kitty. She hadn't gone to bed; she'd followed him out to the barn. Standing in the open doorway, her face was a mask he didn't know how to read. Probably because he'd hit the wall and scared her, who knew how close to Ethen he must have looked when he'd done it. But try though he did to find hints of it, it wasn't fear that he kept glimpsing as she crept a few steps closer. Hands wringing, the mounds of her small breasts rising and falling a little too fast as she breathed, she came to stand bare inches before him. So close that the tips of her breasts nearly grazed his chest on every shaky inhale and her hands, clasped so tight in front of her, almost brushed his stomach. Just a gnat's wing of empty air remained between him and her non-existent touches. His body didn't care; he burned already in both places, his blood beginning to pulse and roar as he breathed in her shallow exhales and bathed in the body heat he imagined was building in the ribbon's space of distance she'd left between them.

It would have been such an easy thing to reach for her, catch the back of her head and pull her mouth straight up to his. Forget calm, lists and rational reasons, he'd let his kiss do his arguing for him. Except he already knew he'd never be able to stop at one. Or a dozen, for that matter. Or the crushing grip he'd fold her in when his restraint finally snapped and he couldn't help but grab her by the ass, before pinning her with the wall at her back and nothing but his hard body flush up against her front.

Trembling, she reached for his hand. The size difference between them was startling: his fingers were huge, calloused and squarish compared to hers. His palm as she turned it upward was red from where he'd punched the wooden planks. Her hands were so much smaller, soft and pale, with fingers as soft as butterfly wings when she caressed the tender redness.

She did not look at him, but bent and kissed the mark of impact, then turned her face to press her cheek into his palm.

Her face was already in his hand, so it was a tiny matter to turn her mouth to meet his. Her breath caught, moist lips parting on a sigh as his claimed them. Compared to the storm inside him, it was a gentle kiss. Little more than a taste, really. Kitty deserved better than to be fucked in a barn.

Noah tried to pull back, already licking the flavor of her from his lips. Her fingers touched his cheek. He saw the tip of her own tongue dart out, savoring him in turn and she opened her eyes. The midnight depths of her gaze had deepened with stormy desire.

He rolled his shoulders. Time to stop. But she inched closer, lifting her chin, and the next he knew, her mouth was beneath his again. Noah shook through the battle for gentleness as the softness of her lips opened to him. Wet and willing, yielding to the flick of his tongue, tapping for entrance. She gave it; there was no pulling away from that either and for the second time that night, Noah lost a measure of control.

She caught his shoulders as they fell together against his work table; catching a fistful of her hair, he unleashed himself in kiss after hungry kiss.

She mewed; forget measure, he just plain lost control.

He clawed his shirt off, his mouth leaving hers only long enough to whip it over his head and cast it away. Hers had buttons; both their shaking hands torn down the line of them until he finally ripped the remaining two off in his haste to bare her. He barely heard the pattering rain as they scattered across the barn floor at their feet. In the next instant, he had her bra unfastened and her breasts were in his hands.

Hello, my darlings. His palms welcomed the jut of her budding nipples, her flesh molded to his kneading touch, and her head fell back, casting her sigh to the ceiling when the heat of his mouth claimed the first. He nipped, suckled, matching the motions of his lovemaking with that of his fingers as he teased both nipples at once. She arched into his pulling tugs. Her small hands kept trying to touch his hair, as if to weave her fingers through the short, sandy strands and guide his head to stay where she needed to feel him most. Each time, she caught herself and her hands returned to grip his shoulders. Accepting whatever pleasure he chose to give without demanding anything.

That became his instant goal. He was going to make her forget not just herself, but the selfish ass who had taught her that. He wanted her to demand.

He wanted her to demand *him.*

Catching her throat in his hand, the heady beating of her heart teasing his fingertips, he ordered, "Pants. Get them off."

She was kicking out of her shoes almost before he finished the command. For all that he could see, she was damn near fearless as she shimmied out of her remaining clothes. She let her loose jeans fall and the white cotton underwear that had stood between them earlier that day, followed, crumpling into a heap around her ankles. She stepped out of both and with her heel, nudged them under the table and out of the way.

"Now mine," he directed. He cupped her jaw, his thumb caressing one cheek, his long fingers so brown against the pale of her skin. Her swallow bumped his palm, and he could still feel the beating of her heart, which quickened as she unbuckled his belt. "Give that to me."

He watched carefully, but still there was no fear, not even as she pulled the supple leather from his pant loops, folding it in half and handing it to him.

He lay it upon the work table near her hip. "Continue."

She unfastened him, her fingers slipping between his jeans and skin, gliding in under the elastic of his underwear. Her hands roved hot over the skin of his buttocks as she pushed all layers of clothing that still remained between them down his long legs. She licked her lips again, but she did not look down. His cock ached for her to look at it; his nerves fired with every awareness of her as her hands came back to rest on his ass. That was where she stopped moving, and that was okay. He couldn't wait to touch her ass either.

Bending slightly, he caught her cheeks in both hands, squeezing once and prizing her legs apart as he lifted her in a single, strong heft and deposited her on his work table. She gasped when her butt made contact, but the minute pain—if such it could even be called—was already vanishing from her eyes and she pulled him closer.

She was at the right height now, eye to eye with him, hip to hip. A nudge of his hands parted her knees, letting the rest of him push between as he shifted his grip to her waist. He massaged, pulling her right up to the edge of the table. And him.

Instinctively, she leaned back, bracing her weight on her arms.

"You know your safeword," he said, but she was already shaking her head.

"I don't want to use it. Not right now."

A corner of his mouth lifted. Moving his hands to the insides of her thighs, he pushed them open wider. "That's your choice. I just want you to know you have one."

That she fully expected him to move in closer, angle his cock to the heated furrow of her sex and drive himself into her body was written in the way she tried so seductively to wrap her legs around him. She bit her bottom lip, taking her weight on her arms in an effort to make entering her that much easier. Her entire body jolted though, her eyes widening and her mouth rounding, when he bent to hook her thigh over his shoulder and dove mouth-first between her legs.

There were no more barriers, no cloth to dilute the taste of her, no fabric to conceal the sheer thrill with which his tongue lashed between her folds, drinking in the milk of her arousal as he sought the straining nub of her clit. She gasped and grabbed his shoulder, her nails digging into him, but he'd already found her. His arms tightened, locking her in place no matter how she writhed. She was in his mouth, between his lips, captured greedily between his teeth while he flicked and rolled and licked her with his tongue.

"Sir! Oh!" Her head fell back. Something else fell too, clattering off the table and onto the floor, but he couldn't have cared less what tools got knocked aside. She flailed for something, anything to hold onto. But time and again, her hands came back to him, gripping, pulling, once even clawing as her hips bucked up into the lashing fury of his tongue. "I-I'm s-sorry—"

She tried to stop, but her body had no interest in apologies. Her hips ground to the motions of his mouth, and he rewarded those mini demands with a three-fingered thrust, as deep into her pussy as his palm would allow. Her fingers locked in his short hair. Her silken walls clamped onto him, quivering as he found that smooth spot no bigger than a dime inside her. The one that with a flick of his finger made the whole of her pussy spasm and her hips jerk.

Noah filled his work room with her ragged moans and the wet slapping of his palm against her pussy as he fucked her with his hand and his mouth. She shouted and he sucked at her pussy lips, scrubbing the tiny pebble of her swollen clit with all the roughness of his tongue and the stubble on his chin. There was a time for gentleness, but every buck and shout she gave in to told him this wasn't it.

She almost fell off the table; his arms tightened, locking her safely into place. Her straining movements turned wild. The milking spasms of her pussy quickened as her breath caught and held, caught and held, and suddenly every line and muscle of her fragile body seized. Her fingers in his hair became claws, but he only laughed at the pain when she pulled. Her high-pitched mewling cries turned shuddery as her thighs quaked, her sheath spasmed, and a flow of sultry pleasure flooded his mouth. Noah laughed again, loving every minute of it and he didn't stop flicking, stroking, or licking until he'd wrung from her every last convulsion.

If not for his arms around her waist, she'd have wilted down flat on her back on the table, but as he straightened, savoring her taste on his lips, he made her stay upright with him.

"I'm s-sorry," she whispered, dazed. She blinked, not quite focused on him. That was a victory too. One he could have gazed on every day for the rest of his life and never tired of seeing. "I'm s-s-sorry."

"You've nothing to be sorry for." He looped his belt around her throat, letting the length of the leather tail dangle along her spine, an impromptu collar and the leash by which he now owned her.

"I-I'm sorry," she whispered again.

"Don't be sorry with me." He wrapped his hand in her hair, pulling her head back, forcing her dazed gaze to lock on him once more. His thumb hooked between his belt and her neck. He gripped the buckle, preventing the belt from either tightening or loosening on its own. She was his now, she could look nowhere but right into his eyes as he brought his cock to the slick mouth of all her luxurious heat.

Her lips parted. She shivered an indrawn breath as he dragged the crown of his cock up through her folds. Up, then down. Parting her open to him.

"What do you have to say to me, love?" Noah coaxed as sultry as the flesh of her body, trembling there at the end of his dick.

Her whole body shivered. Her light brown nipples were hard as pebbles, scraping his chest as she breathed. "I am a good girl."

He dipped his cock into her, a slow invasion that sank only far enough for her heated flesh to engulf him. "And?"

"I am safe." She moaned, her brow buckling into a mask of the most exquisite pleasure as he sank into her as deep as her body would allow. There was no space left between them, no more ribbons between their bellies, no air apart from the breaths they shared.

Noah gave her collar a shake, and she obediently opened her eyes and locked on him again. "And?"

"And I'm loved," she whispered to him.

"Yes, you are." He withdrew only to thrust again, long, slow, and deep, forcing her to relive every nuance of his invasion and the grind at the end as his pubis pressed once more to hers. Her thighs locked around his hips. "In a minute, you'll be very well loved, because I'm going to fuck you until I come. I want you to come with me; you'll do it on my command."

Her pussy flexed around him like a fist, warm, soft, and milking.

"Put your fingers on your clit," he ordered. "I want you back on edge, right now."

She wasn't multi-orgasmic. She winced through those first few strokes, her wince telling him her body found more pain than pleasure in having to rouse again, but she did it.

"Good girl," he sighed, feeding her submissive needs as tiny twitches in the walls of her sex began twitching again. It was so much better with that pulling, squeezing, sucking motion moving all around his cock instead of his fingers. He watched her face, her heavy-lidded eyes as she gave in to the allure of her own fingers, rubbing slow circles around her swollen clit. He watched the circles getting smaller, tighter, more frenetic until he could see the shivers moving through her belly as well as dancing along his cock as he thrust.

His pace quickened. His breathing fell into cadence with hers and his blood roared, pounding through his veins, in his temples and his cock. The tightening of his balls drove the rhythm of his hips until he found himself pulling her closer so he could pound her harder. He shook the work table. He shook her, his grip on her impromptu collar keeping her face right in front of his. Her siren's stare pulled him in to drown alongside her. Her tiny broken breaths fed him with all the air he needed, and she never disobeyed him once. Her fingers, smashed between their wet slapping bellies, rubbed so fast now they were barely wriggling.

She mewed, near panic flooding her features as her pussy clamped down hard around him.

"No." He yanked her head back, keeping her centered on him. He was sweating. She was sweating; God, she was beautiful, gasping her squeak-high mews of orgasmic distress. "Not yet... not yet..."

Not that he wasn't there. Every shuddering pull of her body milked at his cock. Her arms clung to his shoulders, her ankles were locked and digging into his ass, pulling him back into her. As if she could not stand to let him get away.

He didn't want to get away either. He always came surging back, harder. As hard as he could, his strength unchecked, because every thrust and shove burrowed him deeper into the welcoming well of her body. It was his new home. It was where he belonged. They weren't even two separate people anymore, but one heartbeat, one fiery pulse, one unit pushing and pulling and straining toward the same shuddering goal, and it went so very much deeper than the orgasm twisting his balls so high and tight he thought he might explode.

He could have held her like this forever. He could have fucked her, made love to her, been inside of her, deep and hard and surging like this, for forever.

His flesh had other ideas.

"Come," he growled, the spasms of orgasm ripping through him even as he felt the first tickling spasms of her own dancing all along the length of his shaft. He slammed home, pressing as deep as he could reach, the undulations of her body as she writhed in the grip of her own climax the most beautiful thing he'd seen in years.

Eventually, those undulations ceased, but still he held her fiercely close until Kitty fell limp and still. Draped and panting against him, her arms and legs both dangled.

He didn't move either. At first, he couldn't, not until he got his breath back, not to mention strength enough to lift his arms and unbuckle his belt from around her neck. It fell on the table and he let his hand glide down the slick heat of her back. He checked to make sure there were no chafe marks, but the worst he found was around her lips. Swollen by kisses, he could see the tiny marks her teeth had made while she'd been trying so hard not to come.

He stopped himself from leaning in for one last kiss. He had no self-control when it came to stealing tastes of her from those flushed and swollen lips.

"Be careful." His softening cock fell out of her when he lifting her off the table, letting her slide down him until her feet found the floor. They were both unsteady.

He gathered his clothes, she gathered hers, and somewhere in the aftermath, the pleasurable silence in which they re-dressed turned to just plain silence. By the time he realized it was growing awkward, it had been between them for so long he wasn't sure how to break out of its weighted grip.

"I won't kill my baby." Down on her hands and knees, probably so she wouldn't have to look at him, Kitty searched the cracks in the floorboards for her two missing buttons. "I don't care who the father is. That's not its fault."

Hands pausing on the fastenings of his jeans, Noah's chest tightened. "I would never ask you to make that decision." As much as it grated on him to hear Ethen referred to as her baby's father, he stopped short of volunteering himself for that particular job. So really, what right did he have to complain?

Now, he was irritated. He stuffed his shirt back into his pants and began feeding his belt back through his pants loops. Of course, he wasn't going to volunteer. He wasn't the sort who made promises he couldn't keep, and marriage wasn't any old promise, it was a commitment. Not only to her, but to the child she was carrying just under her heart. Commitments that big should never be made on the spur of an emotional moment, or while her sweat was still drying on his skin and his cock still felt the phantom twitches of being inside her. He needed to wait, and think.

Unfortunately, Kitty wasn't waiting. "The longer I stay here, the more I start looking like an illegal immigrant instead of someone on vacation. I can't risk having my baby in a country where I am not a citizen."

So... she had been thinking clearly after all.

And there it was again, springing right up into the back of his throat again, that ill-thought out urge to say: *Well, let's get married then.*

Noah choked it back. What he heard himself say instead was, "Give me one month."

Having found the last button, Kitty raised her head and looked at him at last. "Why?"

"Because I like you." A man couldn't be more honest than that. "Maybe it won't be enough. Or maybe it'll be the start of something more, I don't know. But I do know I want the chance to find out. One month, love, thirty days." It was surprisingly hard for him, but he made himself add, "We'll treat it like a scene at Black Light, and you can say red at any time. I promise, I'll stop and drive you straight to the airport."

And he always kept his promises. No matter how much it hurt, he would keep this one, too.

CHAPTER 12

"*N*o, really," Noah said, laughing as he cut his breakfast eggs apart. "It's Zechariah. Noah Zechariah Carver. Real New Testament stuff. My parents were big believers. Deliberately drove my grandfather bonkers when they joined a different church from him."

The morning sun was up. Coffee was hot on the table and she'd made breakfast—eggs and toast, with disgusting green stuff for him and plain butter for her with strawberry preserves on the side to tempt her appetite. It had worked, some. So far, she'd managed to put away two eggs, half a sausage patty, and most of a piece of toast, thanks to the jam.

"That was too easy a question." Noah knocked on the table. "Come on, now, love. Let's really get to know one another. Ask me something else."

"Something else," Kitty said, with a smile and a sigh, even though she hated games like this. She wasn't any good at coming up with questions. It felt subversive, somehow, and when questions led to other questions, it only made her more uncomfortable. But how else were two people supposed to learn about the other if not by asking questions, as Noah had quite sensibly argued at the start of this game. She cast about the table, as if she might find a random question lying among the breakfast dishes. "Okay," she finally said, glancing into the living room. "I've got one. You told me you don't like spanking, so what made you choose the whip?"

Caught between a smile and surprise, Noah blinked twice. "What makes you think I don't like spanking?"

"Because you said so."

He arched both eyebrows. "Oh no, no, love. I love all forms of impact, including spanking. You lay yourself down across my knee, young lady. I'll show you a man what loves his work. What I told you was I don't spank for punishment."

"Fine." Ignoring the way her belly quivered at the thought of being taken across his knee and held, tucked right up close to his body, she said, "I'll change my question: Why don't you spank for punishment?"

"Because it's not effective."

"It's not about effective."

Noah arched both eyebrows. "Oh no? What's it about then, love? You tell me."

A touch of warmth flushed her face. She wished she had a way to avoid the question, but that would have violated the newest rule, Rule Number Ten: Quid Pro Quo. Put on the spot, Kitty picked at her toast and shrugged. "I don't know…"

Noah refused to accept that. "Nah, you don't, me girl. You're not getting off that easy. Question ball's in my court now. Why spank if it's not effective? And I don't care how small you shred your toast. I'll bring you a spoon if I have to and add a good-sized dollop of Vegemite to hold it all together, but you will eat it."

Glancing at him from out beneath her lashes, she gauged him entirely too believable for her mouth and stomach to want to risk. She dropped her toast so she wouldn't be tempted to keep picking at it.

"You aren't answering the question," he sang, which made it easier for her to laugh even as rattled as she was.

"Because it's how you know someone really likes you," she finally blurted, then covered her face with both hands, moaning. "Please don't read me the riot act about how abused people come to expect abuse, blah blah blah. I already regret saying it."

"Why?" he asked, still smiling but not in a way that made her feel mocked. She didn't know how he did that, but she appreciated not feeling laughed at.

"It's hard enough to explain our lifestyle to someone not in it without them looking at you like you're crazy. But then try being me, explaining to someone who is in the lifestyle, how it's not what a dom says or does that means anything in a relationship. It's how he hits that matters."

Noah studied her, unmoving, his smile seeming more fixed in place than genuine. "Is that how you knew Ethen loved you?"

"It's how I knew he didn't," Kitty confessed. "Because spanking is gentle and intimate, and it takes time and effort on the dom's part. If he doesn't care, he won't bother; he'll do other things. But if he loves you, he'll take the time to do it every time."

Noah nodded. "I don't spank for punishment because too many submissives enjoy it. When you reward bad behavior, pretty soon bad behavior is all you get. But—" He held up a staying finger, the corner of his mouth curling. "—how about this: I will never spank for punishment, but I will always spank for closure. Do you think those actions might reassure a subbie how much she's still loved?"

Her bottom was tingling; her face felt hot. Afraid he'd read her too closely, Kitty tried to look away, but her guilty gaze kept creeping back, stealing greedy glimpses of him—his hands, his arms, his face. She could hardly control her breathing and she dared not speak at all, for fear her voice might crack. Hiding behind a shaky smile, she nodded.

Holding up his coffee cup as if it were wine, Noah said, "To always feeling loved and never sitting comfortably again."

Kitty couldn't help it, she laughed. She also picked up her mug and they both drank.

Setting his cup back on the table, Noah gestured to her plate. "You've had enough to fortify a small bird. I'd like to see you finish the sausage and at least half your second slice of bread. You've someone else to think of now. I need you to start eating like it."

Hoping he never knew how much she liked it when he got bossy like this, Kitty used her fork to scrape together her shredded toast.

"My turn to ask a question," Noah said, as she polished off her last bite. "What's Kitty short for? Vicky? Victoria? Katherine?"

And so, they leapt from one awkward round of questions straight into another.

Pausing, Kitty took a moment to swallow, giving herself as much time as possible before answering. It didn't change the truth, and though she was tempted, she couldn't bring herself to lie. "It's, um... It's not my real name."

"What is your name, then?"

She poked and re-poked the sausage.

"It's dead," he joked. His smile hadn't dimmed, but his gaze sharpened. It was on her again, once more reading her in that frightening way that saw way more than she wanted him to. "Come on. I'm not going to laugh at you. What's your real name?"

She rolled her lips, then cleared her throat, steeling herself for the harder questions that were sure to follow. "Portia."

"Very pretty. What's your last name, Portia?"

"Raine."

"Middle name?"

"Louise."

"Portia Louise Raine." Noah let it roll off his tongue. "Very nice. I like it."

In the pause that followed, she knew she should say

something, so she thanked him. But, she could already hear it coming.

"So." He sopped his egg with his toast, his gaze firmly on her. "Why Kitty?"

And there it was. She almost hung her head.

"Is that something he chose, or did you get a say?"

"No, no." She tried to wave it off, laugh it off. Anything to avoid the question. "It wasn't like that. It…"

"Quid pro quo," Noah reminded. "Rule Number Ten, either of us can call a Q&A, but while it's in force, any question asked must be openly and honestly answered. We both agreed to that and there's still ten full minutes left in this session."

She didn't quite groan, but she did sigh. Under the table, her leg jiggled.

"It was a mutual thing," she said, hoping that might be an end to it.

It wasn't.

"How so?"

He was going to laugh at her. She dropped her fork on her plate and clasped her hands tight in her lap. God, she didn't want him to laugh at her.

"How so?" he gently repeated.

She wished she could smile as easily as he did. Then he might think she was joking, or that it didn't matter as deeply as it honestly did, or maybe he'd see that it did matter, but let her gloss over it so they could go on to a different question.

"Do you need to bend over your bed while I fetch the strap?" he asked gently, as if he hadn't just threatened to spank her.

"It was what I did," she finally choked out.

"When?"

"The very first time he saw me playing." She stared back at him, waiting for that twist of a smile of his to broaden into a grin, or a chuckle, or even an outright laugh. He didn't, he only waited. "At Black Light," she made herself specify, and when he still didn't laugh, "I used to be a kitten. Before I even knew what it was, I was doing it. But once I discovered Black Light, it was almost all I did."

His brow quirked. "Used to be? You're not anymore?"

She didn't realize she was holding her breath until her chest began to hurt. She shook her head, but it came out more like a shrug and she couldn't even convince herself that she was being completely open or honest about any part of this.

Now it was his turn to shift, swiveling to face her directly. "Sausage," he reminded her, giving himself time to think.

She ate, with time slowly ticking its way down to the end of this game, just not fast enough.

"Granted, here we are coming perilously close to 'there's more than one way to do things and always someone willing to say you're doing it wrong.'" Noah paused, holding up both hands. "Far be it for me to pass that judgment on anyone, much less you, love, but how does that happen? I mean, I've met my share of kittens in the lifestyle. Not only kittens, puppies, foxes, bears…" He thought about it. "Littles, too, for that matter. I don't think I've ever met a reformed one. Wait." He held up his hands again. "Let me backtrack. I've met some who tried the kink to see if they liked it, only to decide they didn't. I've even met a few who played at it because it gave their partner a thrill. But I don't believe I've ever met someone who actually *identified* as being a kitten and then just…" His facial expression did his shrugging for him. "…stopped."

"That's what I meant," she hedged. "I tried it and…"

But, the lie refused to come out, and it was while she was still struggling with it that Noah began connecting the dots. "That's what you were doing when I saw you crawling through the house. And that day you got in trouble, when you hid under the kitchen table. You triggered, didn't you? You were being a kitten?"

Embarrassed as she was, she wanted to lie, but she couldn't make herself do it. Her mouth opened, but nothing came out. And through it all, Noah sat there, with that tic of a smile pulling at the corners of his mouth again.

"Did you have kitty ears?"

Pink ones. Soft as real fur. Ethen had them somewhere. He'd taken them from her the night he'd presented her with her harness and that stiff, leather mask that eventually she had come to hate. Kitty nodded.

"Tail?"

"It was a set." She missed them.

"The kind you string on your belt, or the kind you insert?"

She squirmed again. "Both. Eventually."

"You started with the one," he guessed, "and progressed to the other. Was that your choice or... someone else's?"

"I didn't have a partner at first," she confessed. "It was just me." He still wasn't laughing and that helped her find the courage to add, "I had the paws too."

"And you played like that, all by yourself, but not anymore?"

It wasn't safe anymore. It hadn't been for a long time.

"Why not?"

"You know why not." She pushed her breakfast plate away. "How much time do we have left?"

"Enough for you to answer, and no. I don't know why. I could make assumptions, but chances are good I'll make the wrong ones. What's the point in doing this if I'm only going to assume the wrong thing?"

"He wouldn't—" Perilously close to snapping, Kitty stopped herself. She rolled her lips and tried not to sound annoyed when she finished, "He wouldn't let me."

"See, that's the part I don't understand," Noah said, refusing to let it go. "Don't I remember Ethen had you in a kitten outfit? And you just said he named you Kitty, and he continued to call you that because you were a kitten."

"That was his kitten." She caught herself, rolling her lips tight again because that really had come out abrupt and angry enough to be considered snapping. Good submissives didn't snap at their doms. Not without getting their faces slapped. Ethen would have been out of his chair already, but Noah sat watching her and waiting.

"I take it there's a difference then," he asked, "between his kind of kitty and yours?"

Jesus, these were the longest ten minutes of her life. She dragged a calming breath. "His Kitty is only for show. She's quiet, and still, and looks pretty. She doesn't get to play unless he allows it."

He tapped the edge of his forgotten breakfast plate with his finger. "I take it, that doesn't happen very often."

Kitty shook her head. "It's not dignified. Mostly he uses it to humiliate and punish."

She expected Noah to keep pushing for details, but he didn't. Instead, he said, "Time's up." Getting up from the table, he ruffled her hair. "Finish your toast."

It was probably her imagination that turned that casual caress as his hand slid off her head into a parting rub behind the ears. Kitty rolled her shoulders while he walked away. Trying to ignore how her skin prickled with wanting, she finished the last few bites on her plate.

SOMEWHERE IN THE LOFT ABOVE HIS WORK SHOP, HE HAD A PLASTIC tub of pelts. Years ago, someone had given them to him in exchange for a matching set of boots, belt and a hat, all made out of crocodile hide. He'd done the work himself; it had taken weeks and he was supposed to have received cash for it. Unfortunately, when he presented his part of the agreement, a brand-new baby and a broke-down truck meant there was no cash for the other man to pay him. The hides hadn't even come close to equaling what Noah estimated his stuff was worth, but after watching the embarrassment with which the younger man struggled to fulfill his end of the deal, Noah had graciously accepted the hides. He'd also spent the rest of that afternoon, under that old truck's hood to get the beast running again, and the minute he'd got home, the hides had gone into the loft.

Noah hadn't thought of them in years. Now, as he tore through a storehouse worth of stacked up boxes, old tax records, and half a century's worth of outdated kitchenware and bric-a-brac, not to mention his grandmother's massive collection of crafting supplies, he prayed he hadn't thrown them out.

He never threw anything out, God damn it. So why couldn't he find them?

Slinging aside a box of quilting scraps, Noah stood up. Hands on his hips, he swept an annoyed eye over the clutter of plastic totes, wooden crates, and old suitcases stacked knee and hip high in places all around him. A flash of white cardboard with the letters H-I-D in black-felt marker, stashed behind a roll of old carpet and his mother's old dress mannequin, jumped out at him. Wading and shoving his way to it, he pulled the mannequin back to reveal two more letters: E-S.

"Ha!" he crowed. Unfolding the top flaps, he dug through the layers of individually-wrapped plastic bags. It was almost entirely red-fox hides, an invasive species early colonial settlers had released into the Australian wild for the sake of sport hunting. Unfortunately, the foxes not only thrived, but more than a hundred years later, they were the reason more than ten native species had gone extinct.

Noah had absolutely no love for foxes. The furs were soft though, and at the very bottom, he found several that had been dyed. The one at the very bottom was jet black with a stark white tip on the very end of the tail.

That was his baby. Noah pulled the hide from its bag and tipped it into the light shining through the loft's only window. Dust danced on the beams as he examined the edges and fur for imperfections, but it was the tail that made his decision. This would work. This would absolutely work. Not that he'd ever made a kitten costume in his life, but then, he'd never had a kitten before, either. So...

"Here's to trying new things." Smiling, Noah stuffed the hide back into its protective plastic, put the box back where he found it, and headed back down the ladder to his work space.

He spent more time online looking up how to do it, and then digging back through his grandmother's crafting supplies for enough wire mesh, than it did for him to make the ears. But when he was done, he was satisfied not even Hollywood could have crafted a better pair. Using pictures of a bobcat as his model, he put them on a wire headband meant to be completely hidden by her hair. He was especially proud of the wisps of tufting hair. Not only did they add realism to the overall effect, but the time it took to trim and glue, trim and glue, was well worth it. Those ears were strikingly feminine.

The kitten gloves were little more than fingerless mittens, with soft pads added to the undersides to make them look more like kitten paws. He doubted they'd last very long. No matter how often she used them or how careful she was, what he ended up making weren't hardy enough for crawling around on floors. Within months, they'd be scruffy and bedraggled, if not outright falling apart, but that would give him the time and practice he'd need to make something sturdier. Out of faux fur, preferably. That way, she could wash them without fear they'd fall apart.

He only had to convince her to stick around that long...

Banishing that thought, Noah turned his attention to the last puzzle in his masterpiece: the tail. Since he needed to do nothing to make it a, well, tail, this last piece in his kitten's costume required both the least amount of work and the most. How did he want Kitty to wear it? Attached to the back of her belt so she could sashay through the house, swinging her little bottom and feeling the soft brush of fur caressing her ass and the backs of her knees? Or, should he attach a butt plug and have her wear it properly, with its invading presence inside her as a constant reminder that she was owned?

He could well imagine her holding this tail in her hands, rolling her lips as she nerved herself up to wear it, knowing the whole time she eased the plug part inside her that he'd not only made it for her, but that he'd chosen which anal plug to use, the material, the size, everything. He wondered if she'd blush. Probably. He wondered if she'd muffled another of her tiny, breathless mews as the widest part finally worked its full way in. Almost certainly.

Forget the belt. He even knew which anal plug he wanted to use—metal for easy cleaning, long and weighted so she'd never forget what pressed inside her, a wide base so she'd always experience that bit of a pinch, just for him, and a narrow neck, so she could romp, play and even pounce without fear it might come out before it should.

Before he said it could.

If he was even still around.

Stop thinking about it.

Start to finish, it took him more than six hours of fixing, fussing, cutting, sewing, gluing and adjusting, and in the back of his mind, he couldn't help thinking every minute he spent working on them, he might well be wasting for nothing.

No, not for nothing. For Kitty, the best reason he could think of.

All he had to do now was figure out how to give them to her.

CHAPTER 13

*D*inner was pork chops and potatoes. Or at least, it looked like it might be pork chops. It was hard to tell. Like all the other packages stacked neatly in his freezer, it had been hand-wrapped in white freezer-paper and it wasn't marked. Mentally, every dinner she made for him started off as Mystery Meat and vegetables. Tonight's mystery meat looked like pork, so that was what she called it, although a slight gamey texture and flavor suggested she might be wrong. Kitty didn't ask for clarification. If it wasn't pig, she didn't want to know, and in that way she worked very hard to keep the conversation pleasantly benign.

They talked about work: How she used to be a teacher before Ethen got her fired; what he did every time the phone rang, summoning him out sometimes even in the middle of the night.

"I was going to guess drug dealer," she said when he told her, which made him choke on his coffee, he laughed so hard.

"Do you want to come with me?" he countered, once he could breathe again.

"No, thanks." Kitty wasn't much of a boat person. To be honest, she'd never been on a boat, but she knew she couldn't swim and she wasn't particularly keen to watch him go fishing for gigantic reptiles. But she did listen while he described how he caught them, bound their jaws so they couldn't bite, and she absolutely believed it when he assured her that he'd been doing this for a very long time and knew how to keep her safe. Still, no way was she going to put herself in that kind of situation. Australia had been trying to kill her since she got here. She wasn't about to get in a small boat with a prehistorical carnivore that had clawed its way to the top of the food chain back when dinosaurs roamed the earth.

"I promise." Noah tried again, "I won't shoot them unless I have to. To be honest, most of the ones I have to remove end up going to the croc farms, but I don't even like to remove them. Ninety percent of my job is catching, tagging and identifying potential troublemakers that might need relocating, and showing people how to live safely alongside them. People like to live near water. Waking up with a salty in your swimming pool or sunning in the driveway is a good reminder that crocs like it too."

"Is that the call you got the other day?"

"Nah, love. Last call was for a little bloke who lived a little too close to a daycare playground."

"Did you shoot him?"

"For warming himself in the sandbox?" Noah tsked. "I fixed the hole in the fence. Then I tagged him and let him go again. I only shoot the ones the authorities label a menace. It's not good policy killing them. Crocs have a place in the world, and the world's a better place for it."

"Says the man with a closet full of alligator boots."

"Croc boots," Noah corrected, his smile saying he didn't take her criticism seriously. "Plus, I didn't make all of those. Some were given to me in trade."

"Trade for what?" she asked, her curiosity reluctantly pricked.

"When I have to relocate an animal, it goes either deeper into the wild or to a farm, where it then becomes a fashion accessory or part of the breeding stock. Shooting them is a last resort. I only do that when the authorities give the leave because they have no other choice. Shooting them's not good policy."

Kitty didn't care about policy, good or not. She cared about being stuck in a boat with a carnivorous reptile that was bigger than she was. Having already made four attempts on her life, she wasn't about to give Australia another chance.

After dinner, she cleaned up the kitchen while Noah enjoyed his evening tea at the table and finished reading the morning's paper. Or at least, that was what she thought he was doing right up until the little red dot flashed into appearance on the cupboard door about head level in front of her.

Kitty jumped, nearly dropping the plate she'd been drying, but it was there and gone again faster than she could blink. In the dead silence of the house that followed, she stood, stunned, the dish in her hand forgotten. She'd almost convinced herself she hadn't really seen it at all when, clear as a little red dot could be, it popped into existence again, smack on the flat brown cupboard door in front of her, tiny and quivering, and one hundred percent identifiable.

Laser pointer, her brain supplied at the same exact moment that Kitty triggered. She dropped the plate and pounced, her hands slapping one on top of the other over the vanished dot. The dish clattering to the counter top, before sliding off onto the floor. She grabbed after it, fumbled and it fell. It was a miracle it didn't shatter. Instead, the plate made the most God-awful racket and Kitty jumped all over again.

"I'm sorry!" She dropped to her knees, scrambling after it. "I'm sorry, I'm sorry!"

"It's just a plate," Noah said from the table. That tiny, quivering dot appeared on the floor almost directly in front of her, freezing Kitty where she knelt. She hugged the dish reflexively and looked up. No longer pretending to be interested in his newspaper, Noah sat with a pen-sized laser pointer not quite concealed in his hand.

A corner of his mouth curled. He wiggled the pointer to make the dot dance off the end of her knee, teasing her with its close proximity, and the long-subdued kitten inside her triggered hard all over again.

She all but flung the plate in her haste to pounce, but missed. The dot zipped to her right, and then zipped again, out of the kitchen and into the hallway with her chasing on all fours after it. Barely aware of Noah following behind her, she scrambled and pounced, jumping from floor to wall in wild pursuit of the uncatchable. Flicking from wall to wall, that dot bounced her like a pinball all the way down the hallway and through her open bedroom door.

Caught up in the silliness, Kitty forgot herself. She actually laughed. For the first time in a long time, honestly, freely laughed, as she leapt to clap her hands over the laser dot, catching it against the edge of her mattress. Except she knew she hadn't. In some distant recess of her mind, she knew he'd only taken his thumb off the button, and still, Kitty couldn't resist the impulse to peel her fingers back for a quick peek beneath her palms. Tiny and quivering, there it was, captured in the cup of her hands against the blankets.

It had been a very long time.

She wanted to cry, but it came out like laughter again. Right up until she spotted the kitten costume lying in four neat piles across her bed.

"I reckon maybe it's not as 'used to' as you thought," Noah said from the doorway.

Kitty said nothing, she just stared at the tail—soft and fluffy, jet black with a stark white tip. It was nicer than her pink set. The fur, when she touched it, lacked that synthetic feel. Trimmed in black tufts, she petted the knee pads, her fingers beginning to shake as she crawled up on all fours to sit on her bed. She pulled the paws into her lap, touched them to her cheek. The ears made her eyes tear, black and white, like the tail, but gently rounded like a real cat's. Reverently, she stroked the tufts. Nestled underneath, where she hadn't noticed it until she picked the ears up, was a pink leather collar, studded all the way around with silver bells.

She looked to Noah in wonder, hardly able to keep the tears back. "Y-you've had a kitten before."

His smile softened. He shook his head. "Nah."

The bells on the collar jingled as she traced them. He'd made these things for her. He'd *made* them. Dropping everything, she hugged her hands to her chest. They were too precious to touch.

"You can wear as much or as little as you like," Noah said, retreating from the room. "Or even not at all."

He walked out, not quite closing the bedroom door behind him to give her privacy.

Did he mean now? Did he mean only in this room, or any time? Or, did he mean—

He'd meant, she suddenly realized, exactly what he'd said. Just like he always did. He meant that with him she would always be safe. That she would always have a choice and the freedom to be herself. He meant she would never have to live in dread that every word he said had an ulterior meaning or motive hidden behind it.

Pulling her new tail into her lap, Kitty pet the softness. The silliness of only a few seconds before was gone. In its place, was a strange mixture of awkwardness, hyper-awareness, and budding excitement. She picked up the ears and clutched them too. Dare she put them on? Dare she strip down to what had once been her most comfortable and, in front of Noah, try for a little while to truly be herself? Where someone else could see it?

If not here and now, then when?

That thought stuck into her needle-sharp and piercing. God, she was so tired of being afraid. And this? This side of herself that she had once been so proud of, it was another part of herself she'd let Ethen steal away. She thought about the red dot and Noah, waiting in the living room for her to emerge. Maybe with his laser pointer still in his hand. Maybe once more reading his paper, relaxing for the night.

If she didn't put this on for him now, Kitty realized, she wasn't ever going to. If she let herself lose her nerve, that would make it all the easier for her find the mental excuses she needed never again to find it. And then her kitten self really would be lost. All because of Ethen.

Kitty stripped. She didn't have to, but she had always been nude whenever she let her kitten out, even before Ethen made it mandatory. Clothes were binding; Kitten was free, unencumbered and natural in both her body and her reactions. Kitty needed to find that again.

She slipped into her kneepads, the collar with the jingling bells that tinkled so beautiful when she moved, and then her paws. Pulling her long dark hair back into a ponytail to keep it out of her face, she slipped the wire headband on and, this first time, didn't bother trying to hide it. Without a mirror to check herself, she did her best to adjust her ears so she wore them straight. But, the tail...

Her heart in her throat, she picked up her tail in her mouth and, on hands and knees, nudged her bedroom door open and crawled to the living room. Noah waited on the sofa, a soccer game playing softly on the TV. His attention wasn't on it though. The moment she came around the end of the couch, his eyes were on her. Her heart was still in her throat, but it didn't stay there long. When his smile softened, every uncertainty inside her seemed to melt back into the shadows. A rolling warmth flooded through her. She loved his smile. It was gentle and accepting. He wasn't asking her to be anything other than who she was.

"Kitty, kitty," he sang, making kissing noises as he tapped his fingers to his knee.

She went, dropping her head as she neared and losing herself in the scintillating allure of simply being. She rubbed against him, breathing in the wonderful masculinity of his scent as she let his knee caress its way down her body. His fingers followed suit, but he didn't force it, and because he didn't, it all came flooding back to her. She blinked against the tears as she crawled back to him, climbing straight up his legs to straddle his lap.

Because Kitty was bold like that. She never had to wonder if she'd be hurt or rejected.

His hands settled warm on her hips. She let hers rest on his shoulders while she stared into his eyes. Every place he touched her tingled. It was at once the most natural of things, and the most erotic, and Kitty never used to like sex play when she was in her kitten mode. This was supposed to be free time. But apart from touching her, Noah made no move to take it further.

"Is this for me?" he asked, reaching for her tail.

Kitty let him take it from her mouth, then bent to touch her forehead to his. Kittens didn't cry, she wouldn't either. But she did offer a fragile thrumming purr before hopping back off the couch and presenting herself to him. She dropped her head to her hands, keeping her bottom well up.

He patted her rump once, then stood up. "I'll be right back."

Kittens didn't like to be alone. She followed him, hesitantly at first, but quickening her step when he didn't censure her. He led the way back down the hall to his bedroom. She paused at the door. Rule Number Four meant she couldn't go in. She mewed, half expecting him to close the door, but he didn't. He kept it open so she could watch while he dug lubricating gel out of his top dresser drawer.

When he started toward her again, she presented once more right there in the doorway. He stepped around her and kept going, blowing smoochy noises to draw her back to the living room. She scampered after him, diverting only long enough to give brief but furious chase to the red dot that suddenly reappeared on the area rug, pouncing and pouncing again until it vanished. By then, Noah was once more sitting at his end of the couch and her attention immediately realigned itself. She came to him without needing to be called. Turning, she presented one last time.

"Good girl," he said as she heard the plastic top of the gel tube snap open. "Deep breath… and hold it."

There was no discomfort at all, just a brief moment of both liquid and metal cold, and then the plug was inside her. Kitty closed her eyes. Soft fur nestled up against her buttocks and the caress of the long tail brushed the backs of her legs.

She was whole again. For the first time in over a year, she was free. Free to cover her face and cry without fear that her tears would be used against her. Free to crawl up on the couch to straddle Noah's lap again, and press her forehead to his and feel nothing but peace and security as his hand settled on the back of her head, gently rubbing and stroking and accepting her.

He didn't one time tell her not to cry. He didn't say anything at all, he simply held her while she curled up against his chest and wished she could go back and do things differently. She wished she'd walked away from Ethen the very first day they'd met. She wished she hadn't been so damned eager to have a dom—any dom —in her life that she took the first option to present itself. She wished she'd waited for someone like Noah.

She wished she'd waited for Noah.

Curling up tight against him, she buried her face in the side of his neck. If only she were a little braver, she wanted so much to thank him. Or even to tell him she liked him too, but he was right. Thirty days wasn't going to be enough time, and just because two people liked one another, that didn't change the facts. She couldn't stay where she didn't belong, in a country where she wasn't legal and couldn't hold a job. She couldn't hide here for the rest of her life, with a man who, one subtle day at a time, was stealing away all the broken pieces of her heart. She certainly couldn't have a baby here—how would that even work immigration-wise? How long could she say she was on vacation before someone called her an illegal immigrant and could they, would they, arrest her for it?

Take her baby from her once it was born? She didn't know, but it scared her.

She *couldn't* stay here. At some point, Kitty realized, she had to stop running. She had to clean up her life, get a job, find her independence and be responsible again, and she simply couldn't do any of that from here.

Kitty *had* to go home.

Preferably before it hurt too much to leave.

CHAPTER 14

*N*oah got called out to work at four in the morning. The only reason Kitty knew that was because she was sleeping in bed right alongside him when the phone rang.

Well... sleeping was probably not the right word. She'd done very little sleeping, despite his efforts to exhaust her in the most pleasant of possible ways. Most of the night had been spent wide-eyed and staring at the ceiling, trying to think of how she might make staying here work. Sometime around two a.m., she got up and for almost an hour sat on the toilet with the light off, reading up on Australian immigration laws. Except that with every passage she read, inside she knew she was only taking running away to a whole new level. Two weeks ago, Noah hadn't even known who she was. What, did she think he was going to marry her? With someone else's baby in her stomach? Things like that only happened in Hollywood movies.

She went back to bed and lay there, wide awake and scared. At some point, Noah rolled over, hooked an arm around her waist and drew her in to spoon with him. His chin rested on top of her head where his slow, even breaths proceeded to rustle her hair, and the heat of his hard body cradled hers. Afraid she might wake him, she couldn't help but touch his forearm. Just to touch him and burn into her memory how very good this moment felt, for all the long nights ahead of her when she no longer had it.

Then his phone rang and Kitty, who'd been awake for hours, snapped her eyes shut and pretended to be asleep so he wouldn't know. He took the phone into the bathroom with him, so as not to wake her, but she still heard half of what he said, enough here and there to figure out he was being summoned to work. When he came out of the bathroom, he paused at her bedside to brush her hair back from her face. He didn't wake her though, and she didn't let on that he didn't have to.

It would be better this way.

Before he left, he scrawled a quick note and left it on her bedside table. She waited until she heard the front door close and then the truck chugged off into the night. Sitting up only after he was gone, by the flashlight of her cellphone she read the note: *Gone to work. Croc under police dispatcher's car. Gonna relocate it. No need to make brekkie. I'll be taking you out when I get back. Ta.*

She huddled against the headboard for a long time afterward, holding her phone, trying to figure out the time difference and even who to call. As if she had more than two options. It was a fourteen-hour difference, which made it afternoon in Washington D.C. Hadlee would be at work. A phone call from her was probably the last thing her friend would expect and perhaps even have time for. What was Kitty going to say, anyway: 'Hey, can I borrow enough for airfare?'

The second she was off the phone with Hadlee, Garreth would be on the phone with Noah and before she could pack what few things she had to take with her, back his truck would come, barreling down the driveway. She'd have some explaining to do then, and, God, the last thing she wanted was to have to have to tell Noah everything she was thinking right now. Not that she wasn't right; she knew she was. So, with knots twisting in her stomach, Kitty finally gave in to option number two.

Ethen O'Dowell answered his personal cellphone on the forth ring. "Hello?"

It was such a normal, utterly anti-climatic thing to say. She'd been so braced to have his first words to her be snarling and cruel. It took her almost five panicky heartbeats before she remembered that she'd left her cellphone with him when she'd run. This was a new phone, one given to her by Hadlee and Garreth. He didn't know this number. He was probably wondering who the hell was calling him on the phone he reserved only for his Menagerie.

"Hello?" he said again, a touch impatiently.

She had to say something. If she didn't, he would hang up, but her breathing wasn't right. She could feel her chest moving up and down, but her lungs hurt as if she weren't getting any air and when she opened her mouth, nothing came out.

Somehow, Ethen must have heard her panic. He'd always had a knack for hearing it, and knowing she was in trouble. "Well," he said, impatience giving way to thin notes of triumph. "Just when I thought I might never hear from you again."

A bitter bilious taste seeped into her mouth. "I need to come home."

"Yes, you do." She could almost hear his smile.

"We have to talk." She felt sick.

"All right," he agreed. "Where are you?"

"I'm in—"

"Oh, wait," he interrupted with a low laugh. "I'm sorry, I just realized I don't care."

The connection went dead, snapping every tangling knot in Kitty's stomach and sending them slicing through her as if they were knives.

She stared at her cellphone in shock. Never once in her wildest imaginings had she thought he would cut her off. As if he didn't care; as if he'd *never* cared.

Pure panic, cold as ice, filled up the void where the broken knots had been. She dialed Ethen's number again.

He answered immediately, his icy tone chilling her all over again with its lack of caring. "Do you need me to come and rescue you?"

"Yes," she choked, but he hung up on her again.

Kitty was out of bed and pacing, her fingers shaking so badly she had to try twice before she could redial. "Please!" she cried, when she heard the click of him answering.

"Please, what?" Ethen snapped back, no longer smug. No longer triumphant. His voice was cold, every bit as cold as she was right now.

"P-please help m-me," she stammered. Tears obscured everything, but she covered her eyes with her hand anyway. So she wouldn't have to see. Hating herself.

"Why should I?"

She fought not to cry, and lost. "Because I don't have anyone else."

"Why," he slowly repeated, "should I?"

She knew it wasn't because he hadn't heard her the first time. He simply wanted to hear her voice break while she admitted how pathetic she was. "I don't have anyone else."

She could hear his smile even in the silence that followed.

"Where are you?" he finally asked.

Expecting him to hang up again, she told him.

"What a naughty girl you are. You're going to have to work extra hard if you want my forgiveness. Even so, I don't think you're going to get it for a very long time." She heard the faint rustle as he shifted his phone, pinning it between his shoulder and his ear. "Give me your address."

Kitty had to find a piece of mail, but eventually she obeyed.

"I'm going to hang up now," he told her. "I don't know how long it's going to take me to fix this mess of yours, but I expect you to be there when I call back and I expect you to do exactly what I tell you to when I do. I'm going to see you very soon, Kitty-girl. If you're half as smart as you think you are, I suggest you use all the quiet time between now and then to plan out your apologies."

Kitty sank all the way to the floor, her phone in her hand for a long time after he hung up. She already knew, no matter what she said or did, it would make no difference. If she went back to him, Ethen was going to hurt her because he got off on it. Hands creeping up to caress the slight rounding of her stomach, Kitty drew a deep, but shaky breath. Well, she guessed it was a good thing she wasn't going back to Ethen.

He'd taken everything from her—home, money, her job, everything right down to the tiniest shred of self-confidence and any kind of security. He was the reason she had nothing. Didn't that alone make it okay to use him now? She could pretend to be obedient, couldn't she? Just long enough for him to buy her a plane ticket. She could pretend long enough to get whatever was left of her things out of his house and then...

And then she would call Hadlee and Garreth to come and get her, so she could start building her life back up again. The right way, this time. Without running away or hiding from anyone.

Once she was home, she'd call Noah. She'd tell him what she'd done and why. She'd say she was sorry. She'd probably cry.

She was already crying, because it already hurt. Which only strengthened her resolve that she was doing the right thing. If she waited another thirty days, like she'd promised, there was no way she'd ever be able to make herself go.

On the way back to town, Noah stopped at the gas station parked across the street from the only strip mall within twenty kilometers of Cooktown. It had six shops, five of which catered to the tourists who made this little section of Australia a congested hell for eight months out of the year. Of course, they also made life in this tourist town financially possible for the other four, so no one complained too much.

Among those six shops was Bronson's Pets, where free puppy kisses were advertised on the store front window in great blue and white-trimmed letters. From across the street, Noah read that advertisement while he pumped gas into his truck. No one would ever accuse him of being a hard-ass again, that was for sure. As soon as his tank was full, he drove across the street to see what they had in the way of cat toys.

Twenty minutes and twenty dollars later, he emerged from the shadows of that store with a full supply of catnip mice, bells inside of little plastic balls, and even a metal food bowl with goldfish playing around the outer rim. His next stop was the grocery store and then he was on his way home, with a bag of cracker goldfish bouncing along on the seat beside him. For treats, he thought, as he turned down the long driveway back to his front door. He couldn't wait to see what she thought of them.

His next thought was how Kitty must still be sleeping, because when he walked into the house, everything was quiet. All the lights were off, but the sun was high enough and the living room bright enough that he could see all the way down the hallway, past his open bedroom door, to the mound of disheveled blankets that made up Kitty's side of the bed. It was empty now, and Kitty wasn't anywhere that he could see or hear.

"I'm home," he called, coming down the hallway. He paused at the bathroom door to knock, but no one was inside. A damp towel on the rack told him she'd taken a shower, but it had been long enough ago for the tub to have dried. A slow knot began to pull from the pit of his stomach up into his chest.

He tapped at her closed bedroom door next. "Kitty?"

When there was no answer, he cracked it ajar on the off chance that she might be changing. But no, this room was empty too, and then he saw her bed.

She'd made it up, but in a very specific way. The sheets were stripped and the patchwork quilt folded neatly across the foot of the bed, as any polite guest would leave a bed once they had no more need of it. The closet door was open. Her clothes were gone. Her bag no longer hung on a hook in the back. Kitty had left.

Noah stood in the middle of his guest room, too bewildered even to be hurt. That would come later as he charged back down the hall, through the kitchen, the dining room, the living room, and back to the kitchen again. His was a small house, it simply wasn't big enough to hide anyone, not even long enough for him to fool himself into thinking maybe he'd missed her the first time through.

No, she really was gone. He didn't want to heed what common sense was telling him. In the end, he didn't have to. At the head of the table where he usually sat, he spotted a slip of white paper. She'd left him a note. In fact, she'd used the same note he'd written her, the one in which he'd promised to be back, to write her farewell. Short and to the point, it read simply: *I've gone home.*

Sprinkled along the bottom were little blotches where her tears had fallen. Noah ran his thumb over them, but those were dried now too.

He was supposed to have thirty days. What had happened? And how much of a head start did she have on him?

He started off walking, but ended up running and made it back to his truck with that stupid letter still in one hand and his cell in the other. He tried Kitty's cellphone, but his call went straight to voicemail. Swearing under his breath, Noah switched to a different contact number. He took the ruts in his driveway much faster than his truck was used to.

"What the hell, blokey!" he snapped once Garreth picked up on his end of the line.

"What?" was the response he got between chews.

Noah checked his watch. It was the supper hour in America, but he didn't apologize for the interruption. "You heard me. I thought we were mates?"

Garreth swallowed what was in his mouth. "What's happened?"

"That's what I want to know," Noah shot back. "Are you telling me she didn't call you?"

"No, she didn't call me! This is the first call I've had all night. What's going on?"

In the background, a distant female voice called, "Who is it, honey?"

"Noah," Garreth replied, and then back into the phone asked, "Where's Kitty?"

"Shit," Noah said, half under his breath. Shifting into higher gear, he sped back to the main road even faster than before. "Whoever hears from her first calls the other, yeah?"

"Right," Garreth said grimly. They both hung up and the rest of the ride into town was made in absolute silence.

If he were an American without money, friends or means, where would he go, Noah tried to think. What would he do?

She'd gone home, or so her note had said. And yet, why would she write that without calling the one person who could help her get there? He searched the road for signs of anyone walking. She didn't have a car, so she had to be out here somewhere. Unless she'd turned to hitch-hiking. He swore again, hoping desperately that she wouldn't be that stupid, but Cooktown was too small even for a bus system. Except the tour buses, but those only ran during the height of the tourist season and usually only back and forth from the hotel to the beach.

Unless she took a cab, a little voice in his head suggested. Cooktown did have one of those. Literally, one.

Pulling a U-turn in the middle of the road, he very nearly side-swiped another vehicle and drove straight to Old Man Jennison's home, which doubled as the base of operations for his single-cab business.

Frail and bent-backed, seventy if she was a day, his wife, Maybelle, answered the kitchen door when he pounded. The thickness of her glasses amplified her owl-eyed shock at seeing him. "Mr. Carver?"

Pushing past, he searched the cluttered three-room home. "Kitty!"

There was no answer and no sign of either her or Jennison. His beat-up Studebaker of a cab wasn't parked within sight of the house, not via any of the windows Noah checked.

"What on earth?" Maybelle declared, chasing after him in confusion. "You need to calm down right now, young man. This isn't seemly!"

"Is she with him?" Noah demanded.

She tried to give him a stern frown, but he pushed past her again, storming back through her equally small house to the living room where a work station made up of phones, books, maps, calculator and a visa machine cluttered the top of a narrow desk.

Drawing herself up to her tallest diminutive height, she knuckled her hands onto bony hips. "Sometimes you have to let them go if it isn't meant to be."

Sure enough, the last call logged in the notebook he found lying open on top of the pile had Kitty's name and his address written on it. He checked the time against his watch. Shit, that had been almost two hours ago. "Where's Jennison taking her?"

Maybelle's frown deepened, but not without a glimmer of sympathy. "Cairns Airport."

"He got his cello on him?"

She folded her arms across her chest. "Even if the fare hadn't already been paid in full, in advance, the answer would still be no. She's a grown woman."

Paid in full? The notebook had a money amount, but nothing that showed a payment taken. "How was it paid?"

Pushing him aside, Maybelle dug through the stacks to show him a slip of a paper and credit card receipt. "The card cleared," she said, thrusting it at him. "I can get a hold of him, but I can already tell you right now, he's not going to bring her back against her will. That would be kidnapping."

Noah barely heard her. Taking the receipt, he read the name again. Not Garreth, which he'd been expecting, or Hadlee, which would have been understandable. He'd still paddle Kitty's bottom to within an inch of all sitting ability, but he'd have understood. But no, the name on the receipt was Ethen O'Dowell, complete with verification information and a home address.

Kitty hadn't called Hadlee for help. She'd called Ethen.

"Jesus," he breathed.

Maybelle barely got out of his way before he bowled past her. They had a two-hour head start on him, but Cairns was a four-hour drive. He broke every speed limit along the way, but it didn't make any difference. Kitty's plane was taxi-ing down the runway by the time security tackled him at the gate.

"She left me," he said, watching in disbelief as the plane lifted off the ground.

"Yeah, well," the arresting officer said, snapping him into handcuffs, "I reckon if you were this much of a nut with her, she can't be blamed, can she? After you, mate." Catching him by the collar, the officer pulled him away from the windows. "Start walking. *Through* the turnstyles this time, instead of hopping over 'em, eh?"

CHAPTER 15

The flight back to the States took four hours longer than leaving it had, with three plane transfers instead of two and a layover in excess of seven hours. She didn't know if Ethen had done that on purpose or if he'd simply got her on the first flight out and that had been her luck of the draw. It was the sort of thing he would have done, but for her own mental sake, Kitty chose to believe it was the latter. Beggars couldn't be choosers, and all that. It wasn't like she'd had a lot of options.

She didn't sleep a wink the entire trip. She laid the seat back on each plane she boarded, but when she closed her eyes, all she ever saw was another long and awful ride in Ethen's car. Once he picked her up at the airport. If he picked her up.

Of course, once she got back to the States, she wasn't quite as stuck as she'd been overseas. She had Hadlee once she got to D.C. Hadlee would drop everything to come and get her. But she'd probably bring Garreth with her. Kitty knew she had some hard explaining to do. Frankly, with every plane transfer that brought her closer to home, all the reasons she'd been nursing for leaving Noah in the first place seemed to weaken. She wasn't sure she knew anymore how to explain to herself what she was doing or why. How could anyone else understand? Especially not Hadlee, who although she'd run away first, had gone straight into the arms of a man who loved her, and had for months.

She didn't have to flee the country.

She didn't lose everything first.

She didn't... For fuck's sake! Scrubbing her hands through her hair, Kitty turned off her miserable thoughts. She was tired of running down her own litany of woes. Everyone had problems. No one had a perfect life. She'd got herself into this and, one way or another, she'd get herself out. She didn't know how yet, but the solution would not involve becoming dependent on strangers to straighten it out for her.

Or making Noah responsible for the baby growing inside her.

The layover was more exhausting than it was restful. She stretched out along a row of empty seats and tried again to sleep, but her stomach wouldn't settle and she had no money even for crackers. By the time she reached the States, she'd been holding onto an airsick bag for half a day. The black circles were back under her eyes. The rest of her looked green, but at least she hadn't vomited. She saved those awful heaving attempts for that ugly moment when she staggered out of the interior of the Reagan National airport and into the lobby where Ethen was waiting amongst the crowd. Her stomach rolled at the thinness of his smile. His eyes said 'just wait until I get you alone' and she barely made it to the nearest garbage can before her guts rebelled.

Ethen turned away, every stiff line of his body unhappy with the scene she'd made. As if she weren't already in enough trouble; as if he didn't already have a list of things to make her pay for.

As if she could help it, she thought bitterly, spitting the bile from her mouth and accepting the napkin some sweet old lady offered her, as she patted her back and stroked her hair and murmured, "It's all right, dear. That turbulence is awful, isn't it? Well, you're on the ground now, so things are bound to be better soon, won't they?"

Arms braced on the trashcan rim, she hung her head until she was sure her stomach was done.

"Disgusting," was all Ethen said once she reached his side. "Remind me again why I wanted you back."

Some months ago, a comment like that would have filled her with guilt and fear. Funny how long flights and too little sleep could change things. Right now, it only pricked her temper.

"I'm pregnant," she told, making almost no effort at all to hide her annoyance. "And yeah, it's yours."

She stared at him, almost daring him to question that. His smile even thinner than before, Ethen looked away first. Neither of them spoke again. When he turned away, she followed him, out of the airport, through to the second floor of the terminal parking garage and away from the bustling crowd. Her irritation, more at herself now than at him, seemed only to grow with every step. Her inability to hide that irritation was growing too, keeping an even pace, and that annoyed her more. She was usually pretty good at hiding her feelings. What was wrong with her now?

She was back in D.C., said the practical voice in her head.

When they reached his car, Ethen opened the rear driver's side door for her and waited for her to take her place. Neither Puppy-girl nor Pony-girl were present. She was going to be in the car with him for the duration of this ride, alone.

"I'll make some phone calls," he said, looking everywhere but at her. "I'll have it sorted out by Friday. In the meantime, I hope you've given some thought to how you want to fix the real situation."

Warning tickled at the back of Kitty's neck as she followed his gaze up the nearest support column to the security camera tucked into the shadows, and then half a row further away, to the group of men and women in business suits, laughing and talking on their way to their own vehicle. He was checking to see how many people were around.

"I'm waiting," he said and she snapped back to find him watching her again. His eyes hooded; his face, masked and cold.

He wouldn't hurt her while there was a chance of witnesses. That, however, changed the moment she got into his car.

What was she doing? She was back in D.C. now and could call Hadlee at any point. She didn't have to pander to Ethen's dominance anymore; she didn't have to pretend. To be perfectly honest, she couldn't think of a single thing of hers that he still had that she wanted badly enough to risk getting into his car. And yet, that moment of defiance she had plotted out in her head for when she at last could lock eyes with Ethen and tell him to his face what a piece of shit 'dom' he was, that she'd been using him for a change, and that he had nothing she wanted anymore—that defiance was far, far easier to imagine than it was to initiate now that she was standing in front of him.

"Get in," he ordered.

Kitty climbed into the backseat, pulling her foot in quickly in case he decided to make that first pre-emptive strike a hobbling one.

Smirking, Ethen shut her door.

I'm a good girl. Kitty closed her eyes, rubbing her damp palms against her jeans. *I'm safe.* Except she wasn't. *I'm loved.* Not in this car. *I don't have to be afraid of anything.* Opening her eyes again, she watched Ethen get in behind the steering wheel. The car came to life at the push of a button. He smiled at her in the rearview mirror, but his eyes offered neither mirth nor friendship.

"I should think you would thank me for coming all the way out here in the middle of the night to collect you."

"Thank you." Her tone was as flat as his stare. She couldn't believe she was sitting here; she felt like such an idiot.

"A few months out of my care and you've already forgotten how a proper apology should go. I can see you'll need some re-educating."

The *déjà vu* was strong. The last time she'd been in this car, catching glances from him in that mirror, she'd been scared shitless and he'd been angry. Ethen was doing his part, but something had changed in Kitty. Her chest was every bit as tight as back then, but not with fear this time. Well, not a lot anyway, but what fear there was wasn't overwhelming. Instead of feeding into her panic, all she could feel was the dull throb of anger building up under the back of her skull.

"That's all right," Ethen promised as he backed out of the stall and headed for the nearest exit ramp. "I have nothing else to do with my time. We can go all night, if that's what it takes."

Was she really going to let him drive her back out to the isolation of his country house where he'd beat and raped her so brutally? And how fucked up in the head did she have to be to actually *excuse* him for that? She'd huddled on the kitchen floor, naked, with nothing but a litter box, barely able to walk even a few feet to steal her own cellphone off the kitchen counter, and *she'd excused him.*

What *the hell* was she doing?

Kitty glared at the back of his head, tightly clenched fingers squeezing tighter and tighter, until she could feel the pain radiating out of her whitening knuckles. The urge to strangle him with his own seatbelt was at once the most terrifying and exhilarating plan she'd ever hatched, and it was all she could see when she looked at him.

"Don't," he softly warned, his own eyes darkening in the rearview mirror. "Don't you dare look at me like that. Not after all I've done for you."

Drop your gaze. Look at your hands, your feet, anything but him. That old fear was right there, as fresh and vibrant as ever, and yet what came pouring out of her mouth was an equally soft and accusing, "You mean like stealing my money and leaving me with nothing?"

Ethen laughed, a low chuckle as cold as the promise his stare was making. "I don't have to steal. Everything you own is mine, remember? As per the agreement *you* signed when *you* accepted my contract of ownership."

"That's bullshit and you know it!" she spat. "You got me fired! You beat the shit out of me!"

They were almost at the line at the exit gate, but he slammed the brakes and threw the car into park. Hooking his arm over the back of the seat, he twisted far enough around to stab a finger back at her. "You will speak to me with respect—"

Kitty snapped. She grabbed his finger, yanking his arm down behind the seat and punched. He both ducked and flinched, and her knuckles connected with the back of his head. It was the wrong place to hit a person. Pain exploded through her fingers, all the way up through her hand and into her wrist, but it was at once the worst and the best feeling of her life.

Swearing, he yanked his captured arm back out of her grip, but she hit him again. And again, despite the pain. His own temper snapped, but his seatbelt held him hostage and Kitty was already out of hers, slapping and slugging around the back of his headrest, scratching and screaming as months of pent up rage she hadn't even known she was drowning in came vomiting out of her. If she could have got at him around that blasted headrest, she'd have sunk her teeth into the side of his neck, she was so angry. It was that vicious and terrifying desire more than the pain in her hand that finally stopped her attack.

That and his wallet, which she took out of his inner coat pocket, swiping all the cash he had. She hit him with that too, twice, while he was still fumbling to get out of his seatbelt.

She took his cellphone too, which she beat to death against the dash of his car, right before she kicked her door open and fell out of the back of his car.

Flinging his seatbelt off, Ethen started to follow her, but she wasn't running. The minute she got her feet under her, she grabbed for his door. Anger gave way to shock. He slapped the locks down before she wrenched it open.

"Come on!" When yanking the handle didn't work, she switched to kicking his door. She slammed two glorious dents in his perfect, tidy, shiny black car. "Come on!"

She lost her balance when the car took off, nearly falling on her butt.

"Go on and run!" she bellowed after him. "I know where you live, coward!"

She was a little surprised he would run. But then, this was an airport, with plenty of cameras and cops. If he looked back, she didn't see it through his tinted windows. Ethen got to the exit gate right as the last car in line went through it, but he still had to stop.

"I'm coming after child support!" she shouted.

He barely stopped long enough to tap his credit card to the chip reader, and then he was through. Tires squealing, he took the corner without hitting his brakes.

"You just landed yourself the world's craziest baby-mama!" she roared from the middle of the exit ramp, haloed in the headlights of half a dozen cars that were keeping a wary distance behind her.

God, that felt good.

Panting, weaving on her feet, Kitty came slowly back to herself in time to see the first car tentatively drive around her. Her head was pounding. Barely aware of the odd looks she was getting from those inside, she was a little surprised airport security wasn't speeding their way to arrest her.

She looked down, a wad of his money still clutched in one hand, astounded by her own capacity for violence. Her other hand was bleeding, thin rivers of crimson that dribbled down her shaky fingers from where she'd split her knuckles and cut herself smashing his phone.

The faint crunch of tires on pavement pulled up behind her. Kitty startled when a man with entirely the wrong accent asked, "Are you okay? Do you need me to call someone?"

He was the driver of a yellow cab. The light was off, and it was empty.

Flying high on euphoria, but coming down fast, Kitty's hand shook when she offered him her money. She had no idea how much was even there. She saw twenties and tens and several ones, but she was buzzing too much to count. "C-can I get a ride?"

The look he gave her said he didn't mind helping, but that letting her into the back of his cab wasn't his first option. But he also looked at the money in her hand and, unlike her, was fully capable of tallying the sum. "Where are we going?"

She gave him Garreth's home address, but even as she wrapped her wounded hand in the napkins the driver gave her and crawled into the back of his cab, she realized her mistake. Australia was fourteen hours ahead of D.C. time. "Is it still Friday?"

Switching on the fare light, the cabby glanced back at her. "All day long."

Fridays Garreth would be at Black Light. He worked there most weekends, but Fridays were different. On the first and third of every month, he was a dungeon monitor and resident EMT. On the second and fourth Fridays, however, he and Hadlee got to play. They wouldn't be home, not until late. Which meant Kitty had a choice: she could either sit outside Garreth's apartment until whatever o'clock they came home, or she could go to Black Light and surprise them. Maybe sit in the bar, have a sip of something to calm her rattled nerves, and then figure out what her next step should be.

"Are you sure?" the cabby asked when she changed addresses.

No, she wasn't sure of anything, but she fed enough money through the slot in the protection barrier to satisfy him, and off they went. At least she was home.

Honestly, she thought it would feel better than this.

CHAPTER 16

*N*oah's arresting officer was a man by the name of Billy Cuthrie, and he was a complete git. But, the airport's security supervisor was not. He was, in fact, a romantic fellow at heart. He not only let Noah go with a warning, but he looked up Kitty's flight and even found Noah an alternative.

"You're in luck," he said. "It'll cost a helluva lot more, takes two extra flight changes and the first plane won't leave for another two hours, but it's half the layover time if you go to France first, then Canada, and then Washington. You'll actually land within half an hour of her."

If he hadn't been to China recently and still had his passport in his truck, he couldn't have done it. If he didn't have a cousin willing to drop everything and run to his bank in Cooktown, transferring over enough money from his account into Noah's, he wouldn't have been able to do it either. Fortunately, Noah had both, although the loan did cost him a leather jacket and the use of his boat.

"If you get drunk and crash it, you're a dead man," Noah promised him.

MAREN SMITH

"Bring me home a swanky American girl," his cousin brightly returned. "I like red heads."

And back around the world Noah went, not for the purposes of rest and vacation, but for the first time in his life because he was chasing a woman. He didn't even know why.

By the time his plane touched down in Washington D.C., the shock of Kitty's actions had worn off. Now Noah was pissed, partly with himself because he really couldn't afford to do this, and partly with her, because money and affordability aside, he couldn't bring himself not to follow her. All he'd wanted was one month, and she'd agreed to that. So, what the hell? Why would she leave? He was determined to find out and to keep his temper firmly under control until he did, and then when it was over and done and he'd given her a piece of his mind, then he'd probably just go home.

Yeah, who was he kidding? He'd never wanted to paddle a woman so hard in all his life. The whole trek from the plane to the car rental counter, it was all he could think about. He didn't have anything with him, but that was okay. He had his belt, he had his hand, and if push came to shove, he was pretty sure he could find a switch to cut even in the States' capital.

As if it would come to that. He'd never struck a woman in anger and he wasn't going to start now. He also never spanked for punishment, but in Kitty's case, he was sorely tempted to make this the exception. She deserved it for running back to Ethen alone!

He just couldn't understand it. And yeah, he wasn't thinking straight right now, and yeah, the way his palm kept itching made him wary about trusting his instincts, but if he did nothing else, he wasn't leaving until Kitty was away from that abusive son of a bitch.

"How long will you need the car?" the lady at the counter asked as she entered the information from his International Driving Permit into her computer.

Noah held up one finger. He honestly didn't know how long it would take. An hour to track down Ethen's house, five, maybe ten minutes to storm the place and throw Kitty back in the car, another hour to drive to Garreth's where she'd be safe. He rolled his shoulders. From everyone but him, that is.

"One day rental," she said, more to herself as she finished registering him. "Let's see what we've got..."

"You got one with GPS?" That would make finding Ethen's house and then Garreth's afterward much easier. Once he got Kitty in the car, he was going to have enough to do scolding —*paddling*—and talking sense into her—*shake her until her eyeteeth rattled; Ethen? Seriously? What the hell, love?*—he didn't need the added aggravation of also having to street-map his way around a foreign city.

"We can do that," the lady behind the counter said brightly, and soon Noah was heading for the highway in a relatively new business special with excellent gas mileage and an onboard GPS, stammering out directions to Ethen's house in a spot-on imitation of Porky Pig.

The farther out of town he went, the more Kitty's initial reaction to his house began to make sense. Ethen's home was every bit as remote as Noah's, and though he'd not been out this way the last time he was in D.C., Garreth had told him about that midnight run when he'd gone to rescue Hadlee. He'd told him about Kitty's rescue too. As Noah drove, certain gut-churning details kept popping into his head.

There was no mistaking the abandoned gas station when he passed it. Not with the bones of old gas pumps protruding from the concrete, its lot grown over by weeds, and that graffiti-tagged phonebooth in the corner. Wadded trash littered the bottom, and for the next several kilometers all Noah could think about was a broken, battered Kitty walking this country road in the black of an icy night, without clothes, without shoes, only to end up huddled in the bottom of that phonebooth with nothing but a layer of garbage to keep her warm. For four kilometers he thought about it, his grip strangling the steering wheel, his jaw locked so tight it made his teeth ache.

For all that it was dark as pitch out here, he found Ethen's wooded driveway. It wasn't half as long and winding as Noah's back home, but it was unpaved and as full of weather ruts, none of which stopped him from speeding down it a good ten kilometers faster than he should. It must have rained earlier in the day. The ground was muddy and he slid when he braked, mud splattering the side of the house and only missing ramming the porch by a fender-width.

A tall blonde woman peeked out the kitchen window when Noah slammed out of the car. She was naked, not that he cared. Up until that moment, he thought he was doing rather well at keeping his temper in check, but as they stared at one another, his rapidly darkening mood must have shown itself. Her mouth moved in a whispered curse he didn't need to hear to recognize.

Oh shit didn't half cover it.

The woman bolted for the front door, getting there ahead of Noah barely in time to lock it. She leapt back wildly though when he reared back and kicked it in. Wood splintered and glass in two of the six old-fashioned frames shattered as the door slammed into the opposing the wall.

The blonde slapped both hands over her mouth, but otherwise didn't make a sound.

"Where is she?" Noah growled, and from the more brightly lit living room, where all he could see was the form of a woman hunched inside a dog kennel, came a man's, "What the hell was that?"

Noah *had* thought he was keeping his temper under control. Right up until Ethen ventured out of the living room and the two men saw one another. After that, all Noah saw was red.

"Who are you?" Ethen said, a half second before recognition lit and his eyes widened. "Pony-girl, call the police."

But Noah had already closed the half dozen steps between them. His balled fist knocked Ethen sprawling backwards to the accompanying screams of two horrified women.

Grabbing his nose, Ethen rolled on his back.

Stepping over him, Noah had the padlock on the dog kennel in his hand before he realized the woman staring wide-eyed back at him through the wire door was not Kitty. She had gag cuts at the corners of her mouth and fading impact bruises across her shoulders, hips and ass. She looked terrified.

She looked terrified of him.

"Where's Kitty?" he asked her.

Shaking her head, the woman shrank as far from him as the back of her kennel would allow.

Sniffling through the blood and involuntary tears, Ethen half-laughed as he eased himself to sit up. "She's not here."

"Don't lie to me," Noah warned. "I know you bought her a cab and plane ticket, so don't even try to—"

"She's not here." Laughing, Ethen pulled a white handkerchief from his pocket and wadded it over his bloody nose. "You people." Making no effort to get up, he glared at Noah as if he both hated and was amused by him. "Yes, I paid for her to come home, and she assaulted me. Just like you assaulted me. And, just like I intend to do to her, I am going to sue you over it."

"You're going to sue me?" Noah echoed, unimpressed.

Ethen smirked.

"Good on you, mate," Noah said, only too happy to return the smile. "Let's make it worth the price, yeah?"

Ethen grabbed his arms when Noah grabbed him, dragging the taller man to his knees by his hair.

"Crawl," Noah ordered, damn near scrubbing his nose to the floor. If it wasn't broken before, it was before they were halfway through the kitchen. "Crawl like you made her crawl."

The blonde got out of his way. Hands clutched to her chest, she followed from a safe distance as Noah dragged her dom through the house to the back bedroom. He found the cage built into the framework of Ethen's bed, exactly as Hadlee had once described it. She'd said it was the cage he liked to put Kitty into, the one that had left her terrified of confining places. It was the reason Noah always left the bathroom light on at night. It was one of many reasons why Kitty shook when she thought he was going to punish her.

Flinging Ethen up against the cage, he unbuckled his belt and ripped it from around his waist. "Get in."

Ethen scrambled, but Noah still managed to whip him twice across the back and legs before he was too far under the bed to read. Slamming the door, Noah threw the sliding-bolt and padlocked it with the one he found hanging on the door. No doubt waiting for Kitty's return.

"I hope you like prison," Ethen spat, cowering in the shadowy back of his own cage. "You have no idea who you're fucking with!"

"The best civil lawyer in his field, or so I've been told." His belt still in his hand and the urge to keep using it tickling at the back of his neck, Noah hunkered down to better see Ethen through the wire of the door. "Go ahead, extradite me. It might take awhile, since I don't reckon you'll have much sway once you get done explaining this—" He tapped the wire of the cage. "—or that battered girl in your living room to your cop buddies. You may be King Shit out here, but I don't live here and you don't scare me. So, go on; jump, since you're feeling so froggy. I'll take you down with me, mate, but I promise that'll feel like a slow leisurely fuck in the garden compared to what I'll do if you ever bother my Kitty or her friend again."

Ethen's eyes narrowed, but already his confidence was dimming to a mere ghost of what it had been.

"That's a promise," Noah warned. He turned away, half expecting to find Pony-girl with a phone in her hand and, at the very least, emergency services on the other line. But although they had walked right past a line of cellphones on the kitchen counter, the tall blonde had made no effort to grab one. She hovered in the bedroom doorway, posture perfect, her nervousness revealed only in the fidgeting of her fingers and the swallow of her throat when he came toward her. She looked from him to her master and back again, every inch of her a woman who had been told what to do every minute of every day for so long that she didn't know what to do now.

When he neared the door, she backed away. "Go to your room," he ordered.

She obeyed.

"Stupid fucking—" Ethen said, only half under his breath.

Noah closed the door on him, following a few paces behind Pony-girl until she was in her room. There wasn't a bed, just a leather sex-swing hanging from the ceiling and some hay on the floor. An assortment of crops and whips lined the hooks on the wall, alongside a giant black horse-cock of a strap-on. "You may not come out until the police get here."

He had no idea if she'd obey that or not, but he didn't lock her bedroom door when he closed it on her. Dialing 9-1-1, he put the phone on the counter and left.

"OH MY GOD!" HADLEE SAID, SHOCK AND HAPPY SURPRISE LIGHTING her face as she came shoving through the door that separated the main play area from the locker room's security desk where Kitty had been waiting now for almost twenty minutes. Getting past Luís had been a nerve-wracking ordeal because Kitty had nothing with which to prove her membership. Ethen had always taken care of that. For a while, she had been so convinced that Luís would turn her away, but in the end, a quick phone call had got her through the first checkpoint, through the tunnel that ran under the alley and straight to Danny, who was content although in no great hurry to investigate further. "What are you doing here?"

"Trying to get in," Kitty said, pretending she couldn't see the look Danny shot her as he waited silently, cellphone pressed to his ear. The old her would have felt guilty for causing him trouble. All the new her felt right now was tired, but still she tried to smile as she accepted Hadlee's welcoming embrace.

"You look so much better," her friend said. "You've put on weight—oh, but not in a bad way," she hastened to assure. "It looks good. You needed it."

If she had put on weight it couldn't have been more than a few pounds and was due entirely to Rule Number Seven. Something she hadn't paid much attention to since she'd left Noah's house. She did feel guilty about that, though she tried not to think about it. She also changed the subject. "So... apparently, I was banned?"

"Oh, uh..." Hadlee winced a glance to Garreth who was standing quietly beside her, arms folded across his chest, a very domly and disapproving frown on his face. "Yeah, about that..."

"Ethen got banned," Garreth corrected. "Because of the cellphone incident on Roulette night." He traded looks with Danny, who was finally off hold and softly relaying information to whomever he'd called—probably Jaxson or Chase, Black Light's co-owners and the only two people with the power to confirm or rescind a banned membership. "I don't think the Menagerie was included in that order, but we'll get it straightened out."

As if, now that Garreth was on the case, the problem was practically resolved, Hadlee changed the conversation back again. "When did you get back?"

"Almost two hours ago," Kitty said, but inside all she could think was how nice it must be to have that kind of confidence in the man in your life. That no matter the problem, he could just... fix things and magically make everything all better.

Noah had that kind of magic.

Yeah, well, Noah wasn't here, she told herself. From here on, she was going to have to learn to do things on her own.

"Did you not like it there?" Hadlee gently pried. "Did you and Noah not get along?"

"It was time to come home." Kitty did her best to offer what she hoped was a believable smile. The way Hadlee's was fading, she suspected she might not be as good at hiding things as she used to.

Garreth wasn't smiling at all. A tic of leaping muscle played along his clenching jawline as he drew himself stiffly upright. "Does Noah know where you are yet? Because he didn't have a clue when he called us last night."

A tiny fist of guilt took squeezing hold inside her chest. "He called you?"

"Yes, he did," Garreth said sternly, still not smiling, arms still folded. "One might even say he was worried about you."

"I left him a note."

"A note?" Hadlee echoed, shoulders sagging, eyes widening. "What did he do?"

"Nothing!" Kitty recoiled, the fist squeezing even tighter because that was the conclusion they'd jumped to. "He didn't do anything wrong at all. In fact, he did everything right!"

"Then why would you run away?" Garreth demanded, the lash of his disapproval knocking her back a step.

"The whole point was to stop running away!" Kitty protested, once she'd recovered her shock. "Everybody's so busy trying to clean up my mess, and I appreciate the help, I really do, but at some point, don't you think I should be trying to clean it up too?"

Hadlee caught her arm, glancing back toward the secret passage where the distant noise of someone else crossing under the alley could faintly be heard. "Let's not talk about this here," she said, and turned pleading eyes to Danny, who was no longer on the phone.

"Are we good?" Garreth asked.

"She can enter tonight so long as she understands her membership is being put under review. Also"—Danny held out his hand—"cellphone, please." His was a thin, impersonal smile. "Sorry, but if it's not in my hand, you don't go in."

Digging through the duffel bag that held her few belongings, Kitty passed him her cellphone. It vibrated when she first touched it, signaling she'd missed a call. Multiple calls, she saw when she glanced at the screen. That she hadn't heard it ring didn't surprise her, she'd muted it the day she boarded her first plane, the one that had taken her to Noah. Afraid of accruing traveling fees she didn't have the money to pay, she'd kept it off... until yesterday's ill-fated decision to call Ethen. She checked the return number, half expecting Ethen's to pop up on the screen, but it wasn't. It was a mess of numbers instead, an international call. Noah.

"I texted it to him before I ever put you on a plane," Garreth said, solving the mystery. "I texted it again after we found out where you were going. I was hoping he'd be able to talk some sense into you." He got the locker room door for her, and he did it with the utmost disapproval. "Store your things. We'll go to the bar."

She didn't want to have this conversation with him any more than she wanted to have it with Noah. Leaving her luggage in her assigned locker, she followed her friends out to Black Light's play area. The lights were low, even around the bar where the infamous black lights lit the array of liquor bottles and drinks as they were served, amplifying the club atmosphere. Submissive men and women dressed in little or, as was the case of one slender red-head, nothing at all as they wove through an audience of voyeurs and players in pre- or post-scene negotiations. Garreth chose the table, a quiet place in the back, while all the sights, sounds, and smells of the once familiar club dungeon swept over her.

For once, her first gut reaction to the smell of leather and massage oil didn't seep into her like an old haunt. Kitty slid into a seat with her back to the wall, but it felt more like slipping into a warm bath, with the low erotic thump of the music keeping time with the beating of her heart and the fleshy smacks of impact play happening in coincidental tandem both on the St. Andrew's cross and in the medical play area clear across the room. Another woman was being double-fisted as she hung upside down from the ceiling hoist, her body trussed in black and red predicament bondage ropes and, God help her, a submissive kitten on hands and knees crawled on a leash behind her owner. Kitty caught a glimpse of her as she was led through the curtains of an aftercare alcove, her sapphire blue fox tail swishing across the backs of her naked thighs.

In that instant, Kitty forgot where she was. No longer was she sitting in Black Light with Hadlee on one side of her, mouthing to Garreth to be nice, and Garreth on her other, fighting to take deep breaths so he could 'give her space' as if she were still so... fragile. The way she'd been fragile right after she'd left Ethen. Not like she'd been in Australia, with Noah who'd forced her to ask for the strapping she'd received when she'd bent over the foot of her own bed. Who hadn't hesitated over punishing her when she'd broken his rules. Who'd spent all day making her a tail, paws and ears, for no other reason than because she'd said she'd been a kitten once.

The low thump of the music crawled up through Kitty's chair and into her flesh as she remembered the feel of his arms, the heat of his chest, the press of his fingers as he lubricated her ass and stretched her open. Her stomach quivered, the way it had quivered when she'd been presenting herself to him, asking without words for the privilege of his own hand pushing her new tail into her.

The thump of the music became the low, heady thump of her own blossoming arousal, even as notes of sadness wound their way through her. She'd made the right decision, she told herself. For all the reasons she'd already told herself, both before she'd left

Australia and again, over and over throughout the long flight that had brought her home again. To sitting here, with Garreth and Hadlee. To them, she was still fragile, but that wasn't how she felt. She wasn't the same Kitty that she had been the night she ran away from Ethen.

Across the floor, coming through the shadows, she recognized Jaxson's grim face. Chase wasn't with him, but his pretty and pregnant submissive, Emma, was. She trailed along behind him, a huge smile on her face and one hand resting on the swell of her belly.

"Wow," Kitty marveled.

"Big as a house," Emma exaggerated with a smile and shrug. "I know. Twins. Fortunately, being in a poly relationship means there will always be someone available to change a diaper and I can stay in bed."

Having only reached the table, Jaxson stopped and gave his wife a Look. Beaming back at him, she bounced once on her heels and then changed directions.

"I'll go get some water," she said and headed to the bar.

Oh, how things did change in the short time since she'd been gone. Kitty didn't remember Emma sporting so much as a baby-bump at the Roulette party. But then, the only thing she'd been paying attention to that night had been Ethen's rapidly souring mood.

She was going to have a baby bump like that pretty soon, and then she wouldn't be able to hide it anymore.

On the heels of that thought came another, every bit as startling: She missed Noah.

She missed the gentle brush of his hand on the small of her back and the touch of his lips on her forehead. She missed the way he'd wrapped his arm around her waist, pulling her back into the cradle of his body as he'd slept. She missed the way he accepted her—her sad pathetic side, her kitten side. Her everything side.

"I've made the biggest mistake of my life, haven't I?" she

suddenly said, more to herself than to either Garreth or Hadlee. But now it was out there, verbalized for everyone, including Jaxson and Emma who'd returned from the bar.

"I apologize for the way you were greeted at the door," Jaxson said, but in a tone that seemed better reserved for scolding. "Considering what happened the last time you were here—"

"What *Ethen* did the last time she was here," Hadlee interrupted, but stopped when Garreth touched her knee. It was the kind of touch Kitty recognized as both comforting and silencing.

"His club, his rules," Garreth told her. "Let him talk."

"I know what you went through," Jaxson told her, but then his attention locked back on Kitty. "I didn't know about any of it, however, until well after the fact. So, since I don't know exactly what role you may or may not have played in the violations that occurred that night, I have decided I would rather break my own rules and err on the side of caution. I am going to allow for the possibility that you had nothing to do with your master's violation of our digital recording policy."

"Good, because she didn't!" Hadlee blurted. "He's not her master anymore either."

Kitty's heart and pussy both danced, fluttering spasms that were equal parts sexual delight and wistfulness when Garreth caught the back of Hadlee's neck. He leaned over the arms of both their chairs, bringing his mouth very close to her ear. What he'd said was for his submissive alone, and it made Hadlee both frown and blush.

"I mean it," Garreth re-enforced, once he sat back again. "Not one more interruption."

Kitty envied the severity of the warning frown he shot Hadlee. Her friend pressed her lips together, but though she wilted under the sternness, it wasn't anything like the way she used to look with Ethen. Because Ethen had never loved her, and for all that Garreth wasn't happy with Hadlee's interfering behavior, no one could doubt for a second that he did. He'd been hopelessly in love with her back when Kitty lived with them and she'd seen that love expressed in a hundred tiny ways every single day. She could see it right now, even in Garreth's disapproval. Maybe even especially in it.

Noah had looked at her like that, Kitty suddenly realized, and a pang of startled wonder thumped hard inside her chest.

"Did you hear me?"

Wide-eyed, Kitty snapped her gaze back on the unsmiling club owner.

"You're the second person I broke my rules for tonight. I sincerely hope you don't give me a reason to regret that decision."

"Second person?" Blinking twice, now it was Garreth's turn to interrupt. "Who was the first?"

"Him," Jaxson said dryly. The pit of Kitty's belly twisted into an instant knot as he very pointedly turned and nodded toward the locker rooms. "Let's just say, he was persuasive as hell."

Hadlee turned all the way around in her chair to follow the direction of Jaxson's nod. Kitty didn't need to. All she had to do was turn her head and there Noah was, standing in front of the locker-room door, his face void of smiles, his blue eyes scouring the faces of everyone in the bar until he found her.

Her legs weakened and yet, Kitty stood up. Her chest was so tight, she couldn't hardly feel the suddenly lurch of her own panicking heart, and yet a flood of welcome heat washed over her, swelling her breasts, tightening her nipples in the wake of the shivers that followed. Her belly ran both molten and frozen. More frozen than warm the moment his gaze locked on her, fixing, sharpening. Hardening.

He was so angry with her.

What was he doing here?

He'd come after her. He'd come all this way... after her.

And he was so angry.

And for the first time since she could remember, Kitty was on the verge of tears, but not because she was scared. Not of Noah. Never of Noah. No matter how angry he was, she already knew, he might hurt her but it wouldn't be in the bad ways.

He wouldn't treat her as if she were fragile, either.

In the very back of her mind it occurred to her, angry as he was right now, that *might* not be such a good thing.

CHAPTER 17

e calm. That was Noah's only thought and it began a repeating loop through his head from the moment he spotted Kitty sitting in a quiet corner of the crowded bar. *Be calm, rational, and soft-spoken.* He started toward her, weaving his way past waitstaff and Black Light members. *Give her a chance to explain herself if she wants to try.* Then he was going to tell her what a shitty thing it was to leave like that, without a word or giving him a chance to help. For Ethen, of all fucking people.

He was halfway across the room now and his steps were picking up steam.

Kitty stood up from her table. So did Garreth and his little submissive, Hadlee, who positively whitened when she saw him. He recognized Jaxson, one of Black Light's owners, who he'd called from the parking lot because he couldn't think of anyone else.

"You could send her out to me," Noah had said, already knowing the answer.

"Not a chance," Jaxson had replied. *"But if you promise to behave yourself, I might be inclined to allow you in."*

"I just want to talk to her. Once I know she's all right, then I can go

home." Standing outside the psychic shop, that truly had been Noah's only intention.

He didn't realize he'd been lying until now—with little more than three... two... one meter separating them—the desire to talk was disappearing as fast as the distance between them.

Garreth tried to step between them. He held up a cautioning hand, a glitter in his dark eyes suggesting he knew the maelstrom cutting through Noah had to be far closer to explosive than it was to calm. "Let's sit down over here." He tried to intercept Noah and lead him to a different table. "I'll get us a drink—"

Side-stepping him, Noah brushed past Jaxson's outstretched arm too, skirting right past Hadlee, who jumped up to block him.

"Wait," she said, but over the last twenty-four hours Noah had pinballed his way from confused abandonment to concern, through all five bloody stages of fucking grief, and right now, he was well and beyond the ability to wait.

Watching him come, Kitty didn't back away. She stepped out instead, away from the table, away from Hadlee who moved to shield her. At the very last moment, right as Noah reached her, she lifted her chin. He didn't even know he was reaching for her until he saw his own hand clasp her throat and all hell erupted.

Hadlee screamed. People at the tables nearest to them jumped from their seats, scattered backwards. Garreth shouted his name and both he and Jaxson grabbed his arms, but from Kitty there never was a sound. Not from the moment he seized her, first by the throat and then by her ponytail. Yanking her from the wall, he took her all the way to the floor.

It was the gentlest takedown he'd ever performed and he wasn't even angry when he did it. From the moment he touched her, that maelstrom of temper that had propelled him vanished. He more guided than threw her down, but down she went and his grip on her ponytail kept her pinned there, with one knee drawn up and her weight balanced more on her hip than her belly. Her forehead touched the floor so close to his foot that all she had to do was turn her head to press the softest kiss to the side of his shoe.

"Don't," he warned, only half laughing, but it didn't stop her from whispering to him, that trembling plea that needled straight through every common-sense reason he could think of not to listen and stabbed into the dominant heart of him.

"Please..."

'Be careful what you ask for' didn't even begin to cover his gut-reaction to that single, whispered word. *Please*, just like they were back at home and she was asking for his dominance. Were he not being restrained, he might have given it. His grip on her hair tightened. So did his grip on her throat. He caressed his thumb along the curve of her throat until he found the heady rhythm of her pulse. Heightened, but not frightened.

Not like Hadlee, whose frantic attempts to duck past Garreth were only growing more panicked. "Please, what are you doing? You have to stop! Don't you know what she's been through?"

Jaxson and Garreth were different. Experienced doms both, they crowded to either side of him, their grips on his arm tense and ready to intervene if he gave them a reason, but Noah wasn't anywhere close to losing control.

As soon as Hadlee came close enough, Garreth tried to catch her, but she dodged him.

"Stop," Garreth told her, but her eyes were huge and she wasn't listening. She couldn't see what Noah could feel—Kitty beneath his hands, as soft and submissive as a woman could be. She was purring, of all things. God, he loved this woman. She had no idea the trouble she was in, or maybe she did and just didn't care. Either way, she'd closed her eyes, trusting him completely. If he let go of her neck, he had no doubt she'd have crawled up onto all kitten fours and rubbed herself against him.

Letting go of her hair, Noah slapped her ass sharply twice, bringing her back to the here and now. The kitten could come out later, once he got her home again, and head down, ass up, with her tail inserted and flipped up onto her back. He could already see her little hands kneading the pillow as she bit it, smothering her cries as he set a punishing rhythm—yeah, sure it would be punishing. His cock stirred, sending low pulses of arousal throbbing all the way through him.

"You have to stop him," Hadlee begged, tears spilling down her cheeks.

"No," Garreth said over his shoulder. "You have to stop. Sit down."

"B-but..."

"Sit. Down." His tone would brook no argument.

Neither did Noah's, although his command was not for Hadlee. He lowered himself over Kitty. He didn't care if they were in the bar, on the floor, surrounded by gawkers with every alert club DM hovering on the periphery while they waited to see what Jaxson would do. Jaxson, who only adjusted his grip on Noah's arm, watching carefully as Noah dragged Kitty up by her hair until the shell of her ear brushed his lips. "I have never in my life gone halfway around the world for anyone. You pissed me off. You scared the hell out of me. You," Noah said, with no small significance, "went to Ethen for help when you should have come to me. Why didn't you come to me, Kitty?"

She opened her eyes, no longer purring but still not scared. "I was tired of being a burden."

Hot sparks of temper came very close to rekindling. After everything he'd just been through, she had the nerve to say that to him? He flexed his fingers on her throat, opened his mouth, and then closed it again without a word before turning to the club owner, still gripping his arm.

"I need a private room," he growled.

"Not a chance," Jaxson replied.

Oh, for... Noah ground his teeth, but he managed to refrain from saying something that might get him thrown out or arrested, and once he was sure he could be civil, tried again. "How about my arm, mate? Can I have that?"

Glancing at Kitty on the floor, the club owner released Noah's arm and stepped back.

Noah turned his smile on Garreth next. "Blokey?"

"No, you can't!" Hadlee wailed.

Letting go of Noah's arm, Garreth grabbed his submissive and pushed her back until the crowd in the bar swallowed them both. The last Noah heard from either of them was Garreth's low voice demanding, "Do you trust me?"

"I don't trust him!"

"He's not going to hurt her."

"He's hurting her now!"

"No, he's not. He's handling this. Let him handle it."

Let him handle it. No more powerful words existed in a dominant's repertoire. He was going to handle it, all right. Letting go of Kitty's hair and neck, he seized her by the waist instead. He yanked her up even as he dropped to his knee, pinning her hips in tight against his side, and then he paddled the hell out of her. He spared neither his hand nor her backside. A dom who never spanked for punishment, he didn't bother with a warmup. He simply spanked her, with all the strength of his arm and in a way she was sure to feel right through the seat of her jeans.

Because, of all the things he thought of when he thought of her, 'burden' didn't make the list. It wasn't a burden he was chasing in his truck, first to Cooktown and then all the way to Cairns International. It wasn't a burden he couldn't wait to take home with him again, and hold all night long, if only she would let him. And that was the problem with spanking, frankly, because no matter how hard or fast his hand clapped over every bucking, squirming inch of her ass, no matter how fast he took her from squeaks and gasps to desperately muffled cries of growing distress, no matter how fast even that he broke through Ethen's 'hold still' training to the point she actually snapped a hand back, palm up in defense of a bottom that had to be smarting at least as much as his hand—no matter how much he spanked her, it didn't get any of the important things said.

Like:

"You're not a bloody burden, damn it," he said through his teeth, grabbing her wayward arm and pinning it in the iron grip of his other hand. While he was paused anyway, he fumbled under her stomach until he got the fastenings of her pants open. Two quick yanks bared her bright pink bottom completely, and thank God for it, because her jeans were killing his hand.

Kitty sucked a yelping breath when he started up again, the sound crisper now, the steady assault of his hand flattened the summits of each cheek, deepening the flush to a hot cherry red as the conversation continued with: "You are free to leave at any time, but you have the decency and respect for me to tell me so!"

"Please! I'm sorry!" she broke down wailing.

"You went to Ethen?" Noah paused to shake out his smarting hand. "You'd best hang on for this one, love, because this right here is going to be the beauty of the lot. You will never—"

Someone tapped his shoulder and Noah glanced up to find Jaxson offering him a small wooden paddle, the size and shape of a hairbrush, with a long handle contoured to better fit the palm.

"From the dom in the side booth," Jaxson said. "On the off chance you'd like to borrow it."

"Oh." Taking the paddle, Noah followed the club owner's nod to a shadow figure, who offered a commiserating wave from across the bar. "Tell him thanks, mate."

Hugging her hips, Noah let Kitty have it. He ignored her kicks, cries, and escalating shrieks, he ignored everything except the use of the safeword she never once gave him and the condition of her bottom, which he took as close to overripe strawberry as he dared. It was only when she went limp and he decided she couldn't bear anymore, that he finally stopped. Dropping the hairbrush, he dragged her up until she had no choice but to look at him. She was a mess—her dark hair in the tangled process of escaping its hair tie, her face wet and almost as red as her bottom. No one had ever looked half as beautiful as his naughty kitten, staring up at him through a sheen of tears and remorse, with her pants around her knees and her sore bottom hugged in rueful hands.

"Well," he said softly. "Do you feel loved, sweetheart?"

Her shoulders jerked and her face crumpled all over again. Kitty launched herself at him, hugging his neck and burrowing into his answering embrace. "I'm sorry, I'm sorry!"

He'd crossed a lot of 'nevers' off his list since he'd met Kitty. Sitting down in the middle of a bar to cuddle a sobbing woman on his lap was one of the most natural ones. He rocked her, caressing her hair and kissing her forehead until the storm had passed.

"Did you think I cared?" he whispered once she was reduced to ragged sniffles and hiccups. Sliding his hand from her hip to her belly, he let his palm rest upon her baby bump. "Or worse, Kitty love, did you think I wouldn't care?"

She lay against him, weary and hoarse from crying, both shaking her head and shrugging. "I was just really tired of making messes for everyone else to clean up."

He caressed both her and the baby both. "This isn't a mess to me. It's not a burden. Had I considered it one, I never would have asked you to stay with me."

"You didn't know about the baby when I first came."

"I'm not talking about when you first came. I'm talking about when I told you I wanted you."

She started to pull away, but he switched his grip from her stomach to her chin. Eye-to-eye and nose-to-nose, he didn't let her escape so much as an inch.

"I'm not rich," he said, giving her chin a gentle shake. "I don't need much to make me happy—my home, my land, two good hands to make a living with, and someone worth coming home to. I've lived on my own for a very long time, but I had no idea how quiet the house was until I came home to find it empty. I want you with me, Kitty, but I don't want to force you if that's not what you want too."

When he let go of her chin, she burrowed back into his chest, hiding her face from him again. As if he couldn't read her body every bit as clearly as her eyes. Her hands on the side of his neck were petting, caressing, unable to hold still in near desperate need to keep touching him.

"I didn't want to leave," she finally confessed. "But I couldn't see how to stay. And then, once I was here, all I wanted was to go back." She sniffled, her body tensing all over again. "Aren't you afraid?"

"Of what?"

"That it'll be hard? That it won't work?" She swiped a new-falling tear from her cheek. "That you'll be cleaning up my messes for the rest of your life?"

Craning his neck, he silenced her fears with a tender kiss upon her forehead. "Only thing that scares me, love, is the thought of going home alone. Compared to that, I'm damned near fearless."

"I'm not," she whispered. "Most of the time, I'm afraid of everything."

"That's okay," Noah said softly into her hair. "You won't always be."

"You don't know that."

"Sure I do. I heard what you did to Ethen. We'll be renaming you Muhammad Ali when we get home." Noah buried a smile in her hair when he both heard and felt her laugh. It was watery, but she wasn't crying anymore and that was a good start. "You've got a lot of courage inside of you. But don't you worry, those days when you don't feel it quite so keen, I can be fearless enough for the both of us."

Pulling back from his shoulder, Kitty raised her eyes to his. When she smiled, he kissed her.

EPILOGUE

*K*itty stood at the door leading back through the tunnel to the psychic shop. She had her luggage strap slung over her shoulder, her cellphone in her pocket, and Hadlee clinging to her right hand with both of her own. Together, they waited for their men who were still in the locker room, talking to Jaxson and Chase. Poor Hadlee looked shell-shocked. She stared at the door, her eyes huge and slightly watery. Her chin was up though, and if those were tears Kitty suspected were trying to form along her lashes, she blinked constantly, refusing to let them fall.

"Are you all right?" Kitty asked, giving her hands a squeeze.

"My bottom hurts," Hadlee replied.

No mystery there. Because of her constant attempts to interfere, Garreth had taken her into one of the semi-private spaces to 'talk.' The curtains had done a great job blocking out all sight of the scene that followed, but it hadn't done much for the sound.

For the first time, Hadlee looked up at her. "Are you all right?"

Kitty almost laughed. Half nodding, half shrugging instead, she said, "My bottom hurts."

The women exchanged bemused glances, then chuckles.

"Yeah, okay," Hadlee admitted first. "I deserved it."

"So did I."

"Frankly, I won't be at all surprised if that wasn't just a taste of what I've got coming when we get home."

Noah didn't spank when it was real, but Kitty would not be surprised if there weren't some other form of punishment waiting for her in Australia. She didn't know what form that would take and yet, though she waited for them to come washing over her, those old familiar, dread-filled waves, they never did. Instead, what she felt was a kind of eager giddiness to get moving. Home. For all she'd thought that's what she had been doing from the start, the revelation that 'home' was wherever Noah was still struck as a bit of a surprise.

That watery sheen in Hadlee's eyes grew. "Are you happy?" she finally asked.

"Are you?" Kitty just as softly countered. She held her friend's searching gaze until the first tears at last slipped free and, with a hiccupy gasp, Hadlee flung her arms around Kitty's shoulders. The two women embraced.

"There's always Skype," she declared, and then it didn't feel so much like goodbye.

Kitty didn't answer. She didn't know how.

The ferocity of the hug diminished and they stepped back, both still uncertain what more to say when the locker room door swung open and Noah and Garreth came through. Noah was in the lead, his long-legged stride quick, his blue eyes bright. "What a bloke! A good mate to have, I tell you."

"How much did Jaxson give you?"

"The full refund," Noah exclaimed. "Everything Ethen paid for Kitty's membership, from the point of the ban to the end of the year." Grinning as he passed them, he paused long enough to cup Kitty's cheek. "We can pay our airfare. Come on, love." Passing his grin to Hadlee, he ruffled her hair and then took off again, his voice echoing back through the passage as he headed up and out. "We've got less than an hour, I reckon, before any plane I'm on won't be getting off the ground."

Startled, Kitty's eyes widened. Hadlee and Garreth exchanged the same look of alarm, and all three quickly hurried to follow him.

"What the hell did you do?" Garreth accused.

"I hit him," Noah answered to the accompanying bang of both hands popping open the door at the opposite end of the tunnel. He cast them back a wink and out he went.

The look Hadlee and Garreth exchanged was even more alarmed.

"He hit *Ethen?*" Hadlee gasped. "My God, is he crazy?"

Garreth rushed to catch up. "You did what?" Kitty heard him demand as he too disappeared through the far door.

"He is," Hadlee said, answering her own question. "He's crazy. He was *smiling* about it!" Her wide eyes snapped up to Kitty's. "Oh my God, you're smiling too and you *know* what Ethen can do!"

And that was a funny thing, too. She knew exactly what Ethen was capable of and yes, she was smiling. Inside, she was flying. She'd never been so happy or so free. Noah had hit Ethen, because he wasn't afraid. Not of the man or of the consequences that surely would follow. For some reason, instead of scared all Kitty was… was proud.

She stood marveling, both at him and herself, until the door popped open again and Noah stuck his head back through far enough to beckon her. "Cabby's waiting. Put a hoof on it, yeah?"

"How can he be so cheerful about it?" Hadlee whispered, all but appalled. But only because she didn't know him, not like Kitty did. The cheer was part of his charm.

So was the wink when she went to him and he said, "Just wait until I get you home, love. You've never been in more trouble in your life."

And still she couldn't stop smiling, nor did she hesitate before taking the hand he offered her. Because this was Noah and perhaps she had never been in more trouble, but she'd also never been more safe.

And she loved him for it.

She loved him.

It was fifteen thousand miles to Australia and home. Who knew, maybe somewhere along the way she'd find the courage to curl into his side, rest her head upon his shoulder... and tell him so.

The End

ABOUT THE AUTHOR

Fortunate enough to live with my Daddy Dom, I am a Little, coffee whore, pain slut, administrator at two of my local BDSM dungeons, resident of the wilds of freakin' Kansas (still don't know how I ended up here) and submissive to the love of my life. An International and USA Bestselling Author, I have penned more than 150 novels, novellas and short stories, and am the author of the Masters of the Castle series.

I also write under the names of Denise Hall, Darla Phelps, and Penny Alley.

CONNECT WITH HER

Visit Maren Smith's blog here:
http://badgirlscorner.blog

ALSO BY MAREN SMITH

Black Light Releases:

Shameless (Black Light: Roulette Redux, Book 7)

The Red Petticoat Saloon Series:

Jade's Dragon

Warming Emerald

Masters of the Castle Series:

Book 1, Holding Hannah

Book 2, Kaylee's Keeper

Book 3, Saving Sara

Book 4, Sweet Sinclair

Book 5, Chasing Chelsea

Book 6, Owning O

Book 7, Maddy Mine

Book 8, Seducing Sandy

Witness Protection Program Box Set

Corbin's Bend:

Last Dance for Cadence (Season 1, Book 8)

Have Paddle, Will Travel (Season 2, Book 7)

A Few Other Titles:

B-Flick

Build-A-Daddy

The Great Prank

BLACK COLLAR PRESS

Did you enjoy your visit to Black Light? Have you read the other books in the series?

Black Collar Press is a small publishing house started by authors Livia Grant and Jennifer Bene in late 2016. The purpose was simple - to create a place where the erotic, kinky, and exciting worlds they love to explore could thrive and be joined by other like-minded authors.

If this is something that interests you, please go to the Black Collar Press website and read through the FAQs. If your questions are not answered there, please contact us directly at: blackcollarpress@gmail.com.

WHERE TO FIND BLACK COLLAR PRESS:

- Website: http://www.blackcollarpress.com/
- Facebook: https://www.facebook.com/blackcollarpress/
- Twitter: https://twitter.com/BlackCollarPres

Made in the USA
Columbia, SC
01 March 2020

88566255R00138